ORPHAN TRAIN

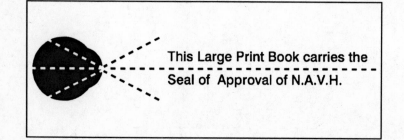

This Large Print Book carries the
Seal of Approval of N.A.V.H.

ORPHAN TRAIN

CHRISTINA BAKER KLINE

KENNEBEC LARGE PRINT
A part of Gale, Cengage Learning

GALE
CENGAGE Learning·

Detroit • New York • San Francisco • New Haven, Conn • Waterville, Maine • London

GALE
CENGAGE Learning

LIBRARY OF CONGRESS CATALOGING-IN-PUBLICATION DATA

Kline, Christina Baker, 1964–
    Orphan train / by Christina Baker Kline. — Large print edition.
      pages ; cm. — (Kennebec Large Print superior collection)
      ISBN 978-1-4104-6052-3 (softcover) — ISBN 1-4104-6052-5 (softcover) 1.
    Women—Fiction. 2. Orphan trains—Fiction. 3. Female friendship—Fiction. 4.
    Large type books. I. Title.
    PS3561.L478O77 2013
    813'.54—dc23   2013016079

Published in 2013 by arrangement with William Morrow, an imprint of HarperCollins Publishers.

Printed in the United States of America
2 3 4 5 6   17 16 15 14 13

To Christina Looper Baker, who handed me the thread, and Carole Robertson Kline, who gave me the cloth

In portaging from one river to another, Wa-banakis had to carry their canoes and all other possessions. Everyone knew the value of traveling light and understood that it required leaving some things behind. Nothing encumbered movement more than fear, which was often the most difficult burden to surrender.

— BUNNY MCBRIDE, *Women of the Dawn*

PROLOGUE

I believe in ghosts. They're the ones who haunt us, the ones who have left us behind. Many times in my life I have felt them around me, observing, witnessing, when no one in the living world knew or cared what happened.

I am ninety-one years old, and almost everyone who was once in my life is now a ghost.

Sometimes these spirits have been more real to me than people, more real than God. They fill silence with their weight, dense and warm, like bread dough rising under cloth. My gram, with her kind eyes and talcum-dusted skin. My da, sober, laughing. My mam, singing a tune. The bitterness and alcohol and depression are stripped away from these phantom incarnations, and they console and protect me in death as they never did in life.

I've come to think that's what heaven is

— a place in the memory of others where our best selves live on.

Maybe I am lucky — that at the age of nine I was given the ghosts of my parents' best selves, and at twenty-three the ghost of my true love's best self. And my sister, Maisie, ever present, an angel on my shoulder. Eighteen months to my nine years, thirteen years to my twenty. Now she is eighty-four to my ninety-one, and with me still.

No substitute for the living, perhaps, but I wasn't given a choice. I could take solace in their presence or I could fall down in a heap, lamenting what I'd lost.

The ghosts whispered to me, telling me to go on.

SPRUCE HARBOR, MAINE, 2011

Through her bedroom wall Molly can hear her foster parents talking about her in the living room, just beyond her door. "This is not what we signed up for," Dina is saying. "If I'd known she had this many problems, I never would've agreed to it."

"I know, I know." Ralph's voice is weary. He's the one, Molly knows, who wanted to be a foster parent. Long ago, in his youth, when he'd been a "troubled teen," as he told her without elaboration, a social worker at his school had signed him up for the Big Brother program, and he'd always felt that his big brother — his mentor, he calls him — kept him on track. But Dina was suspicious of Molly from the start. It didn't help that before Molly they'd had a boy who tried to set the elementary school on fire.

"I have enough stress at work," Dina says, her voice rising. "I don't need to come home to this shit."

Dina works as a dispatcher at the Spruce Harbor police station, and as far as Molly can see there isn't much to stress over — a few drunk drivers, the occasional black eye, petty thefts, accidents. If you're going to be a dispatcher anywhere in the world, Spruce Harbor is probably the least stressful place imaginable. But Dina is high-strung by nature. The smallest things get to her. It's as if she assumes everything will go right, and when it doesn't — which, of course, is pretty often — she is surprised and affronted.

Molly is the opposite. So many things have gone wrong for her in her seventeen years that she's come to expect it. When something does go right, she hardly knows what to think.

Which was just what had happened with Jack. When Molly transferred to Mount Desert Island High School last year, in tenth grade, most of the kids seemed to go out of their way to avoid her. They had their friends, their cliques, and she didn't fit into any of them. It was true that she hadn't made it easy; she knows from experience that tough and weird is preferable to pathetic and vulnerable, and she wears her Goth persona like armor. Jack was the only one who'd tried to break through.

It was mid-October, in social studies class. When it came time to team up for a project, Molly was, as usual, the odd one out. Jack asked her to join him and his partner, Jody, who was clearly less than thrilled. For the entire fifty-minute class, Molly was a cat with its back up. Why was he being so nice? What did he want from her? Was he one of those guys who got a kick out of messing with the weird girl? Whatever his motive, she wasn't about to give an inch. She stood back with her arms crossed, shoulders hunched, dark stiff hair in her eyes. She shrugged and grunted when Jack asked her questions, though she followed along well enough and did her share of the work. "That girl is freakin' strange," Molly heard Jody mutter as they were leaving class after the bell rang. "She creeps me out." When Molly turned and caught Jack's eye, he surprised her with a smile. "I think she's kind of awesome," he said, holding Molly's gaze. For the first time since she'd come to this school, she couldn't help herself; she smiled back.

Over the next few months, Molly got bits and pieces of Jack's story. His father was a Dominican migrant worker who met his mother picking blueberries in Cherryfield, got her pregnant, moved back to the D.R.

to shack up with a local girl, and never looked back. His mother, who never married, works for a rich old lady in a shorefront mansion. By all rights Jack should be on the social fringes too, but he isn't. He has some major things going for him: flashy moves on the soccer field, a dazzling smile, great big cow eyes, and ridiculous lashes. And even though he refuses to take himself seriously, Molly can tell he's way smarter than he admits, probably even smarter than he knows.

Molly couldn't care less about Jack's prowess on the soccer field, but smart she respects. (The cow eyes are a bonus.) Her own curiosity is the one thing that has kept her from going off the rails. Being Goth wipes away any expectation of conventionality, so Molly finds she's free to be weird in lots of ways at once. She reads all the time — in the halls, in the cafeteria — mostly novels with angsty protagonists: *The Virgin Suicides, Catcher in the Rye, The Bell Jar.* She copies vocabulary words down in a notebook because she likes the way they sound: *Harridan. Pusillanimous. Talisman. Dowager. Enervating. Sycophantic . . .*

As a newcomer Molly had liked the distance her persona created, the wariness and mistrust she saw in the eyes of her peers.

14

But though she's loath to admit it, lately that persona has begun to feel restrictive. It takes ages to get the look right every morning, and rituals once freighted with meaning — dyeing her hair jet-black accented with purple or white streaks, rimming her eyes with kohl, applying foundation several shades lighter than her skin tone, adjusting and fastening various pieces of uncomfortable clothing — now make her impatient. She feels like a circus clown who wakes up one morning and no longer wants to glue on the red rubber nose. Most people don't have to exert so much effort to stay in character. Why should she? She fantasizes that the next place she goes — because there's always a next place, another foster home, a new school — she'll start over with a new, easier-to-maintain look. Grunge? Sex kitten?

The probability that this will be sooner rather than later grows more likely with every passing minute. Dina has wanted to get rid of Molly for a while, and now she's got a valid excuse. Ralph staked his credibility on Molly's behavior; he worked hard to persuade Dina that a sweet kid was hiding under that fierce hair and makeup. Well, Ralph's credibility is out the window now.

Molly gets down on her hands and knees

and lifts the eyelet bed skirt. She pulls out two brightly colored duffel bags, the ones Ralph bought for her on clearance at the L.L.Bean outlet in Ellsworth (the red one monogrammed "Braden" and the orange Hawaiian-flowered one "Ashley" — rejected for color, style, or just the dorkiness of those names in white thread, Molly doesn't know). As she's opening the top drawer of her dresser, a percussive thumping under her comforter turns into a tinny version of Daddy Yankee's "Impacto." "So you'll know it's me and answer the damn phone," Jack said when he bought her the ringtone.

"Hola, mi amigo," she says when she finally finds it.

"Hey, what's up, *chica?*"

"Oh, you know. Dina's not so happy right now."

"Yeah?"

"Yeah. It's pretty bad."

"How bad?"

"Well, I think I'm out of here." She feels her breath catch in her throat. It surprises her, given how many times she's been through a version of this.

"Nah," he says. "I don't think so."

"Yeah," she says, pulling out a wad of socks and underwear and dumping them in the Braden bag. "I can hear them out there

16

talking about it."

"But you need to do those community service hours."

"It's not going to happen." She picks up her charm necklace, tangled in a heap on the top of the dresser, and rubs the gold chain between her fingers, trying to loosen the knot. "Dina says nobody will take me. I'm untrustworthy." The tangle loosens under her thumb and she pulls the strands apart. "It's okay. I hear juvie isn't so bad. It's only a few months anyway."

"But — you didn't steal that book."

Cradling the flat phone to her ear, she puts on the necklace, fumbling with the clasp, and looks in the mirror above her dresser. Black makeup is smeared under her eyes like a football player.

"Right, Molly?"

The thing is — she did steal it. Or tried. It's her favorite novel, *Jane Eyre,* and she wanted to own it, to have it in her possession. Sherman's Bookstore in Bar Harbor didn't have it in stock, and she was too shy to ask the clerk to order it. Dina wouldn't give her a credit card number to buy it online. She had never wanted anything so badly. (Well . . . not for a while.) So there she was, in the library on her knees in the narrow fiction stacks, with three copies of the novel, two paperbacks and one hard-cover, on the shelf in front of her. She'd already taken the hardcover out of the library twice, gone up to the front desk and signed it out with her library card. She pulled all three books off the shelf, weighed them in her hand. She put the hardcover back, slid it in beside *The Da Vinci Code*. The newer paperback, too, she returned to the shelf.

The copy she slipped under the waistband of her jeans was old and dog-eared, the pages yellowed, with passages underlined in pencil. The cheap binding, with its dry glue, was beginning to detach from the pages. If they'd put it in the annual library sale, it would have gone for ten cents at most. Nobody, Molly figured, would miss it. Two other, newer copies were available. But the library had recently installed magnetic antitheft strips, and several months earlier four volunteers, ladies of a certain age who devoted themselves passionately to all things Spruce Harbor Library, had spent several weeks installing them on the inside covers of all eleven thousand books. So when Molly left the building that day through what she hadn't even realized was a theft-detection gate, a loud, insistent beeping brought the head librarian, Susan LeBlanc, swooping over like a homing pigeon.

Molly confessed immediately — or rather tried to say that she'd meant to sign it out. But Susan LeBlanc was having none of it. "For goodness' sake, don't insult me with a lie," she said. "I've been watching you. I *thought* you were up to something." And what a shame that her assumptions had proven correct! She'd have liked to be surprised in a good way, just this once.

"Aw, shit. Really?" Jack sighs.

Looking in the mirror, Molly runs her finger across the charms on the chain around her neck. She doesn't wear it much anymore, but every time something happens and she knows she'll be on the move again, she puts it on. She bought the chain at a discount store, Marden's, in Ellsworth, and strung it with these three charms — a blue-and-green cloisonné fish, a pewter raven, and a tiny brown bear — that her father gave her on her eighth birthday. He was killed in a one-car rollover several weeks later, speeding down I-95 on an icy night, after which her mother, all of twenty-three, started a downward spiral she never recovered from. By Molly's next birthday she was living with a new family, and her mother was in jail. The charms are all she has left of what used to be her life.

19

Jack is a nice guy. But she's been waiting for this. Eventually, like everyone else — social workers, teachers, foster parents — he'll get fed up, feel betrayed, realize Molly's more trouble than she's worth. Much as she wants to care for him, and as good as she is at letting him believe that she does, she has never really let herself. It isn't that she's faking it, exactly, but part of her is always holding back. She has learned that she can control her emotions by thinking of her chest cavity as an enormous box with a chain lock. She opens the box and stuffs in any stray unmanageable feelings, any wayward sadness or regret, and clamps it shut.

Ralph, too, has tried to see the goodness in her. He is predisposed to it; he sees it when it isn't even there. And though part of Molly is grateful for his faith in her, she doesn't fully trust it. It's almost better with Dina, who doesn't try to hide her suspicions. It's easier to assume that people have it out for you than to be disappointed when they don't come through.

"*Jane Eyre?*" Jack says.

"What does it matter?"

"I would've bought it for you."

"Yeah, well." Even after getting into trouble like this and probably getting sent away, she knows she'd never have asked Jack

20

to buy the book. If there is one thing she hates most about being in the foster care system, it's this dependence on people you barely know, your vulnerability to their whims. She has learned not to expect anything from anybody. Her birthdays are often forgotten; she is an afterthought at holidays. She has to make do with what she gets, and what she gets is rarely what she asked for.

"You're so fucking stubborn!" Jack says, as if divining her thoughts. "Look at the trouble you get yourself into."

There's a hard knock on Molly's door. She holds the phone to her chest and watches the doorknob turn. That's another thing — no lock, no privacy.

Dina pokes her head into the room, her pink-lipsticked mouth a thin line. "We need to have a conversation."

"All right. Let me get off the phone."

"Who are you talking to?"

Molly hesitates. Does she have to answer? Oh, what the hell. "Jack."

Dina scowls. "Hurry up. We don't have all night."

"I'll be right there." Molly waits, staring blankly at Dina until her head disappears around the door frame, and puts the phone back to her ear. "Time for the firing squad."

21

"No, no, listen," Jack says. "I have an idea. It's a little . . . crazy."

"What," she says sullenly. "I have to go."

"I talked to my mother —"

"Jack, are you serious? You told her? She already hates me."

"Whoa, hear me out. First of all, she doesn't hate you. And second, she spoke to the lady she works for, and it looks like maybe you can do your hours there."

"What?"

"Yeah."

"But — how?"

"Well, you know my mom is the world's worst housekeeper."

Molly loves the way he says this — matter-of-factly, without judgment, as if he were reporting that his mother is left-handed.

"So the lady wants to clean out her attic — old papers and boxes and all this shit, my mom's worst nightmare. And I came up with the idea to have you do it. I bet you could kill the fifty hours there, easy."

"Wait a minute — you want me to clean an old lady's attic?"

"Yeah. Right up your alley, don't you think? Come on, I know how anal you are. Don't try to deny it. All your stuff lined up on the shelf. All your papers in files. And aren't your books alphabetical?"

"You noticed that?"

"I know you better than you think."

Molly does have to admit, as peculiar as it is, she likes putting things in order. She's actually kind of a neat freak. Moving around as much as she has, she learned to take care of her few possessions. But she's not sure about this idea. Stuck alone in a musty attic day after day, going through some lady's trash?

Still — given the alternative . . .

"She wants to meet you," Jack says.

"Who?"

"Vivian Daly. The old lady. She wants you to come for —"

"An interview. I have to interview with her, you're saying."

"It's just part of the deal," he says. "Are you up for that?"

"Do I have a choice?"

"Sure. You can go to jail."

"Molly!" Dina barks, rapping on the door. "Out here right now!"

"All right!" she calls, and then, to Jack, "All right."

"All right what?"

"I'll do it. I'll go and meet her. *Interview* with her."

"Great," he says. "Oh, and — you might want to wear a skirt or something, just —

y'know. And maybe take out a few earrings."

"What about the nose ring?"

"I love the nose ring," he says. "But . . ."

"I get it."

"Just for this first meeting."

"It's all right. Listen — thanks."

"Don't thank me for being selfish," he says. "I just want you around a little longer."

When Molly opens the bedroom door to Dina's and Ralph's tense and apprehensive faces, she smiles. "You don't have to worry. I've got a way to do my hours." Dina shoots a look at Ralph, an expression Molly recognizes from reading years of host parents' cues. "But I understand if you want me to leave. I'll find something else."

"We don't want you to leave," Ralph says, at the same time that Dina says, "We need to talk about it." They stare at each other.

"Whatever," Molly says. "If it doesn't work out, it's okay."

And in that moment, with bravado borrowed from Jack, it is okay. If it doesn't work out, it doesn't work out. Molly learned long ago that a lot of the heartbreak and betrayal that other people fear their entire lives, she has already faced. Father dead. Mother off the deep end. Shuttled around and rejected time and time again. And still she breathes and sleeps and grows taller. She wakes up

24

every morning and puts on clothes. So when she says it's okay, what she means is that she knows she can survive just about anything. And now, for the first time since she can remember, she has someone looking out for her. (What's his problem, anyway?)

SPRUCE HARBOR, MAINE, 2011

Molly takes a deep breath. The house is bigger than she imagined — a white Victorian monolith with curlicues and black shutters. Peering out the windshield, she can see that it's in meticulous shape — no evidence of peeling or rot, which means it must have been recently painted. No doubt the old lady employs people who work on it constantly, a queen's army of worker bees.

It's a warm April morning. The ground is spongy with melted snow and rain, but today is one of those rare, almost balmy days that hint at the glorious summer ahead. The sky is luminously blue, with large woolly clouds. Clumps of crocuses seem to have sprouted everywhere.

"Okay," Jack's saying, "here's the deal. She's a nice lady, but kind of uptight. You know — not exactly a barrel of laughs." He puts his car in park and squeezes Molly's shoulder. "Just nod and smile and you'll be fine."

"How old is she again?" Molly mumbles. She's annoyed with herself for feeling nervous. Who cares? It's just some ancient pack rat who needs help getting rid of her shit. She hopes it isn't disgusting and smelly, like the houses of those hoarders on TV.

"I don't know — old. By the way, you look nice," Jack adds.

Molly scowls. She's wearing a pink Lands' End blouse that Dina loaned her for the occasion. "I barely recognize you," Dina said drily when Molly emerged from her bedroom in it. "You look so . . . ladylike."

At Jack's request Molly has taken out the nose ring and left only two studs in each ear. She spent more time than usual on her makeup, too — blending the foundation to a shade more pale than ghostly, going lighter on the kohl. She even bought a pink lipstick at the drugstore — Maybelline Wet Shine Lip Color in "Mauvelous," a name that cracks her up. She stripped off her many thrift-store rings and is wearing the charm necklace from her dad instead of the usual chunky array of crucifixes and silver skulls. Her hair's still black, with the white stripe on either side of her face, and her fingernails

27

are black, too — but it's clear she's made an effort to look, as Dina remarked, "closer to a normal human being."

After Jack's Hail Mary pass — or "Hail Molly," as he called it — Dina grudgingly agreed to give her another chance. "Cleaning an old lady's attic?" she snorted. "Yeah, right. I give it a week."

Molly hardly expected a big vote of confidence from Dina, but she has some doubts herself. Is she really going to devote fifty hours of her life to a crotchety dowager in a drafty attic, going through boxes filled with moths and dust mites and who knows what else? In juvie she'd be spending the same time in group therapy (always interesting) and watching *The View* (interesting enough). There'd be other girls to hang with. As it is she'll have Dina at home and this old lady here watching her every move.

Molly looks at her watch. They're five minutes early, thanks to Jack, who hustled her out the door.

"Remember: eye contact," he says. "And be sure to smile."

"You are such a *mom.*"

"You know what your problem is?"

"That my boyfriend is acting like a mom?"

"No. Your problem is you don't seem to realize your ass is on the line here."

"What line? Where?" She looks around, wiggling her butt in the seat.

"Listen." He rubs his chin. "My ma didn't tell Vivian about juvie and all that. As far as she knows, you're doing a community service project for school."

"So she doesn't know about my criminal past? Sucker."

"Ay diablo," he says, opening the door and getting out.

"Are you coming in with me?"

He slams the door, then walks around the back of the car to the passenger side and opens the door. "No, I am escorting you to the front step."

"My, what a gentleman." She slides out. "Or is it that you don't trust me not to bolt?"

"Truthfully, both," he says.

Standing before the large walnut door, with its oversized brass knocker, Molly hesitates. She turns to look at Jack, who is already back in his car, headphones in his ears, flipping through what she knows is a dog-eared collection of Junot Díaz stories he keeps in the glove compartment. She stands straight, shoulders back, tucks her hair behind her ears, fiddles with the collar of her blouse (When's the last time she wore a collar? A dog collar, maybe), and raps the knocker. No answer. She raps again, a little louder. Then she notices a buzzer to the left of the door and pushes it. Chimes gong loudly in the house, and within seconds she can see Jack's mom, Terry, barreling toward her with a worried expression. It's always startling to see Jack's big brown eyes in his mother's wide, soft-featured face.

Though Jack has assured Molly that his mother is on board — "That damn attic project has been hanging over her head for so long, you have no idea" — Molly knows the reality is more complicated. Terry adores her only son, and would do just about anything to make him happy. However much Jack wants to believe that Terry's fine and dandy with this plan, Molly knows that he steamrollered her into it.

When Terry opens the door, she gives Molly a once-over. "Well, you clean up nice."

"Thanks. I guess," Molly mutters. She can't tell if Terry's outfit is a uniform or if it's just so boring that it looks like one: black pants, clunky black shoes with rubber soles, a matronly peach-colored T-shirt.

Molly follows her down a long hallway lined with oil paintings and etchings in gold frames, the Oriental runner beneath their

30

feet muting their footsteps. At the end of the hall is a closed door.

Terry leans with her ear against it for a moment and knocks softly. "Vivian?" She opens the door a crack. "The girl is here. Molly Ayer. Yep, okay."

She opens the door wide onto a large, sunny living room with views of the water, filled with floor-to-ceiling bookcases and antique furniture. An old lady, wearing a black cashmere crewneck sweater, is sitting beside the bay window in a faded red wing-back chair, her veiny hands folded in her lap, a wool tartan blanket draped over her knees.

When they are standing in front of her, Terry says, "Molly, this is Mrs. Daly."

"Hello," Molly says, holding out her hand as her father taught her to do.

"Hello." The old woman's hand, when Molly grasps it, is dry and cool. She is a sprightly, spidery woman, with a narrow nose and piercing hazel eyes as bright and sharp as a bird's. Her skin is thin, almost translucent, and her wavy silver hair is gathered at the nape of her neck in a bun. Light freckles — or are they age spots? — are sprinkled across her face. A topographical map of veins runs up her hands and over her wrists, and she has dozens of tiny

31

creases around her eyes. She reminds Molly of the nuns at the Catholic school she attended briefly in Augusta (a quick stopover with an ill-suited foster family), who seemed ancient in some ways and preternaturally young in others. Like the nuns, this woman has a slightly imperious air, as if she is used to getting her way. And why wouldn't she? Molly thinks. She *is* used to getting her way.

"All right, then. I'll be in the kitchen if you need me," Terry says, and disappears through another door.

The old woman leans toward Molly, a slight frown on her face. "How on earth do you achieve that effect? The skunk stripe," she says, reaching up and brushing her own temple.

"Umm . . ." Molly is surprised; no one has ever asked her this before. "It's a combination of bleach and dye."

"How did you learn to do it?"

"I saw a video on YouTube."

"YouTube?"

"On the Internet."

"Ah." She lifts her chin. "The computer. I'm too old to take up such fads."

"I don't think you can call it a fad if it's changed the way we live," Molly says, then smiles contritely, aware that she's already gotten herself into a disagreement with her potential boss.

"Not the way *I* live," the old woman says. "It must be quite time-consuming."

"What?"

"Doing that to your hair."

"Oh. It's not so bad. I've been doing it for a while now."

"What's your natural color, if you don't mind my asking?"

"I don't mind," Molly says. "It's dark brown."

"Well, my natural color is red." It takes Molly a moment to realize she's making a little joke about being gray.

"I like what you've done with it," she parries. "It suits you."

The old woman nods and settles back in her chair. She seems to approve. Molly feels some of the tension leave her shoulders. "Excuse my rudeness, but at my age there's no point in beating around the bush. Your appearance is quite stylized. Are you one of those — what are they called, gothics?"

Molly can't help smiling. "Sort of."

"You borrowed that blouse, I presume."

"Uh . . ."

"You needn't have bothered. It doesn't suit you." She gestures for Molly to sit across from her. "You may call me Vivian. I never liked being called Mrs. Daly. My husband is no longer alive, you know."

"I'm sorry."

"No need to be sorry. He died eight years ago. Anyway, I am ninety-one years old. Not many people I once knew are still alive."

Molly isn't sure how to respond — isn't it polite to tell people they don't look as old as they are? She wouldn't have guessed that this woman is ninety-one, but she doesn't have much basis for comparison. Her father's parents died when he was young; her mother's parents never married, and she never met her grandfather. The one grandparent Molly remembers, her mother's mother, died of cancer when she was three.

"Terry tells me you're in foster care," Vivian says. "Are you an orphan?"

"My mother's alive, but — yes, I consider myself an orphan."

"Technically you're not, though."

"I think if you don't have parents who look after you, then you can call yourself whatever you want."

Vivian gives her a long look, as if she's considering this idea. "Fair enough," she says. "Tell me about yourself, then."

Molly has lived in Maine her entire life. She's never even crossed the state line. She remembers bits and pieces of her childhood on Indian Island before she went into foster care: the gray-sided trailer she lived in with her parents, the community center with pickups parked all around, Sockalexis Bingo Palace, and St. Anne's Church. She remembers an Indian corn-husk doll with black hair and a traditional native costume that she kept on a shelf in her room — though she preferred the Barbies donated by charities and doled out at the community center at Christmas. They were never the popular ones, of course — never Cinderella or Beauty Queen Barbie, but instead one-off oddities that bargain hunters could find on clearance: Hot Rod Barbie, Jungle Barbie. It didn't matter. However peculiar Barbie's costume, her features were always reliably the same: the freakish stiletto-ready feet, the oversized rack and ribless midsection, the ski-slope nose and shiny plastic hair . . .

But that's not what Vivian wants to hear. Where to start? What to reveal? This is the problem. It's not a happy story, and Molly has learned through experience that people either recoil or don't believe her or, worse, pity her. So she's learned to tell an abridged version. "Well," she says, "I'm a Penobscot Indian on my father's side. When I was young, we lived on a reservation near Old Town."

"Ah. Hence the black hair and tribal

makeup."

Molly is startled. She's never thought to make that connection — is it true?

Sometime in the eighth grade, during a particularly rough year — angry, screaming foster parents; jealous foster siblings; a pack of mean girls at school — she got a box of L'Oreal ten-minute hair color and Cover Girl ebony eyeliner and transformed herself in the family bathroom. A friend who worked at Claire's at the mall did her piercings the following weekend — a string of holes in each ear, up through the cartilage, a stud in her nose, and a ring in her eyebrow (though that one didn't last; it soon got infected and had to be taken out, the remaining scar a spiderweb tracing). The piercings were the straw that got her thrown out of that foster home. Mission accomplished.

Molly continues her story — how her father died and her mother couldn't take care of her, how she ended up with Ralph and Dina.

"So Terry tells me you were assigned some kind of community service project. And she came up with the brilliant idea for you to help me clean my attic," Vivian says. "Seems like a bad bargain for you, but who am I to say?"

"I'm kind of a neat freak, believe it or not. I like organizing things."

"Then you are even stranger than you appear." Vivian sits back and clasps her hands together. "I'll tell you something. By your definition I was orphaned, too, at almost exactly the same age. So we have that in common."

Molly isn't sure how to respond. Does Vivian want her to ask about this, or is she just putting that out there? It's hard to tell. "Your parents . . ." she ventures, "didn't look after you?"

"They tried. There was a fire . . ." Vivian shrugs. "It was all so long ago, I barely remember. Now — when do you want to begin?"

New York City, 1929

Maisie sensed it first. She wouldn't stop crying. Since she was a month old, when our mother got sick, Maisie had slept with me on my narrow cot in the small windowless room we shared with our brothers. It was so dark that I wondered, as I had many times before, if this was what blindness felt like — this enveloping void. I could barely make out, or perhaps only sense, the forms of the boys, stirring fitfully but not yet awake: Dominick and James, six-year-old twins, huddled together for warmth on a pallet on the floor.

Sitting on the cot with my back against the wall, I held Maisie the way Mam had shown me, cupped over my shoulder. I tried everything I could think of to comfort her, all the things that had worked before: stroking her back, running two fingers down the bridge of her nose, humming our father's favorite song, "My Singing Bird," softly in her ear: *I have heard the blackbird pipe his note, the thrush and the linnet too / But there's none of them can sing so sweet, my singing bird, as you.* But she only shrieked louder, her body convulsing in spasms.

Maisie was eighteen months old, but her weight was like a bundle of rags. Only a few weeks after she was born, Mam came down with a fever and could no longer feed her, so we made do with warm sweetened water, slow-cooked crushed oats, milk when we could afford it. All of us were thin. Food was scarce; days went by when we had little more than rubbery potatoes in weak broth. Mam wasn't much of a cook even in the best of health, and some days she didn't bother to try. More than once, until I learned to cook, we ate potatoes raw from the bin.

It had been two years since we left our home on the west coast of Ireland. Life was hard there, too; our da held and lost a string of jobs, none of which were enough to support us. We lived in a tiny unheated house made of stone in a small village in County Galway called Kinvara. People all around us were fleeing to America: we heard tales of oranges the size of baking potatoes; fields of grain waving under sunny skies; clean, dry timber houses with indoor plumbing and electricity. Jobs as plentiful as the fruit on the trees. As one final act of kindness toward us — or perhaps to rid themselves of the nuisance of constant worry — Da's parents and sisters scraped together the money for ocean passage for our family of five, and on a warm spring day we boarded the *Agnes Pauline,* bound for Ellis Island. The only link we had to our future was a name scrawled on a piece of paper my father tucked in his shirt pocket as we boarded the ship: a man who had emigrated ten years earlier and now, according to his Kinvara relatives, owned a respectable dining establishment in New York City.

Despite having lived all our lives in a seaside village, none of us had ever been on a boat, much less a ship in the middle of the ocean. Except for my brother Dom, fortified with the constitution of a bull, we were ill for much of the voyage. It was worse for Mam, who discovered on the boat she was again with child and could hardly keep any food down. But even with all of this, as I stood on the lower deck outside our dark, cramped rooms in steerage, watching the oily water churn beneath the *Agnes Pauline,* I felt my spirits lift. Surely, I thought, we would find a place for ourselves in America.

The morning that we arrived in New York

harbor was so foggy and overcast that though my brothers and I stood at the railing, squinting into the drizzle, we could barely make out the ghostly form of the Statue of Liberty a short distance from the docks. We were herded into long lines to be inspected, interrogated, stamped, and then set loose among hundreds of other immigrants, speaking languages that sounded to my ears like the braying of farm animals.

There were no waving fields of grain that I could see, no oversized oranges. We took a ferry to the island of Manhattan and walked the streets, Mam and I staggering under the weight of our possessions, the twins clamoring to be held, Da with a suitcase under each arm, clutching a map in one hand and the tattered paper with *Mark Flannery, The Irish Rose, Delancey Street,* written in his mother's crabbed cursive, in the other. After losing our way several times, Da gave up on the map and began asking people on the street for directions. More often than not they turned away without answering; one man spit on the ground, his face twisted with loathing. But finally we found the place — an Irish pub, as seedy as the roughest ones on the backstreets of Galway.

Mam and the boys and I waited on the sidewalk while Da went inside. The rain had stopped; steam rose from the wet street into the humid air. We stood in our damp clothing, stiffened from sweat and ground-in dirt, scratching our scabbed heads (from lice on the ship, as pervasive as sea-sickness), our feet blistering in the new shoes Gram had bought before we left but Mam didn't let us wear until we walked on American soil — and wondered what we had gotten ourselves into. Except for this sorry reproduction of an Irish pub before us, nothing in this new land bore the slightest resemblance to the world we knew.

Mark Flannery had received a letter from his sister and was expecting us. He hired our da as a dishwasher and took us to a neighborhood like no place I'd ever seen — tall brick buildings packed together on narrow streets teeming with people. He knew of an apartment for rent, ten dollars a month, on the third floor of a five-story tenement on Elizabeth Street. After he left us at the door, we followed the Polish landlord, Mr. Kaminski, down the tiled hallway and up the stairs, struggling in the heat and the dark with our bags while he lectured us on the virtues of cleanliness and civility and industriousness, all of which he clearly suspected we lacked. "I have no trouble with the Irish, as long as you stay out of trouble," he told us in his booming voice. Glancing at Da's face, I saw an expression I'd never seen before, but instantly understood: the shock of realization that here, in this foreign place, he'd be judged harshly as soon as he opened his mouth.

The landlord called our new home a railroad apartment: each room leading to the next, like railway cars. My parents' tiny bedroom, with a window facing the back of another building, was at one end; the room I shared with the boys and Maisie was next, then the kitchen, and then the front parlor, with two windows overlooking the busy street. Mr. Kaminski pulled a chain hanging from the pressed-metal kitchen ceiling, and light seeped from a bulb, casting a wan glow over a scarred wooden table, a small stained sink with a faucet that ran cold water, a gas stove. In the hall, outside the apartment door, was a lavatory we shared with our neighbors — a childless German couple called the Schatzmans, the landlord told us. "They keep quiet, and will expect you to do the same," he said, frowning as my brothers, restless and fidgety, made a game of shoving each other.

Despite the landlord's disapproval, the sweltering heat, the gloomy rooms, and the cacophony of strange noises, so unfamiliar to my country ears, I felt another swell of hope. As I looked around our four rooms, it did seem that we were off to a fresh start, having left behind the many hardships of life in Kinvara: the damp that sank into our bones, the miserable, cramped hut, our father's drinking — did I mention that? — that threw every small gain into peril. Here, our da had the promise of a job. We could pull a chain for light; the twist of a knob brought running water. Just outside the door, in a dry hallway, a toilet and bathtub. However modest, this was a chance for a new beginning.

I don't know how much of my memory of this time is affected by my age now and how much is a result of the age I was then — seven when we left Kinvara, nine on that night when Maisie wouldn't stop crying, that night that, even more than leaving Ireland, changed the course of my life forever. Eighty-two years later, the sound of her crying still haunts me. If only I had paid closer attention to why she was crying instead of simply trying to quiet her. If only I had paid closer attention.

I was so afraid that our lives would fall apart again that I tried to ignore the things that frightened me most: our da's continued love affair with drink, which a change in country did not change; Mam's black moods and rages; the incessant fighting between them. I wanted everything to be all right. I held Maisie to my chest and whispered in her ear — *there's none of them can sing so sweet, my singing bird, as you* — trying to silence her. When she finally stopped, I was only relieved, not understanding that Maisie was like a canary in a mine, warning us of danger, but it was too late.

New York City, 1929

Three days after the fire, Mr. Schatzman wakes me from sleep to tell me that he and Mrs. Schatzman have figured out a perfect solution (yes, he says "perfect," *parr-fec,* in his German accent; I learn, in this instant, the terrible power of superlatives). They will take me to the Children's Aid Society, a place staffed by friendly social workers who keep the children in their care warm and dry and fed.

"I can't go," I say. "My mother will need me when she gets out of the hospital." I know that my father and brothers are dead. I saw them in the hallway, covered with sheets. But Mam was taken away on a stretcher, and I saw Maisie moving, whimpering, as a man in a uniform carried her down the hall.

He shakes his head. "She won't be coming back."

"But Maisie, then —"

46

"Your sister, Margaret, didn't make it," he says, turning away.

My mother and father, two brothers, and a sister as dear to me as my own self — there is no language for my loss. And even if I find words to describe what I feel, there is no one to tell. Everyone I am attached to in the world — this new world — is dead or gone.

The night of the fire, the night they took me in, I could hear Mrs. Schatzman in her bedroom, fretting with her husband about what to do with me. "I didn't ask for this," she hissed, the words as distinct to my ears as if she'd been in the same room. "Those Irish! Too many children in too small a space. The only surprise is that this kind of thing doesn't happen more."

As I listened through the wall, a hollow space opened within me. *I didn't ask for this.* Only hours earlier, my da had come in from his job at the bar and changed his clothes, as he always did after work, shedding rank smells with each layer. Mam mended a pile of clothes she'd taken in for money. Dominick peeled potatoes. James played in a corner. I drew on a piece of paper with Maisie, teaching her letters, the hot-water-bottle weight and warmth of her on my lap, her sticky fingers in my hair.

I try to forget the horror of what happened. Or — perhaps *forget* is the wrong word. How can I forget? And yet how can I move forward even a step without tamping down the despair I feel? When I close my eyes, I hear Maisie's cries and Mam's screams, smell the acrid smoke, feel the heat of the fire on my skin, and heave upright on my pallet in the Schatzmans' parlor, soaked in a cold sweat.

My mother's parents are dead, her brothers in Europe, one having followed the other to serve in the military, and I know nothing about how to find them. But it occurs to me, and I tell Mr. Schatzman, that someone might try to get in touch with my father's mother and his sister back in Ireland, though we haven't had contact with them since we came to this country. I never saw a letter from Gram, nor did I ever see my father writing one. Our life in New York was so bleak, and we clung to it with such an unsteady grip, that I doubt my da had much he would want to report. I don't know much more than the name of our village and my father's family name — though perhaps this information would be enough.

But Mr. Schatzman frowns and shakes his head, and it's then that I realize just how alone I am. There is no adult on this side of the Atlantic who has reason to take any interest in me, no one to guide me onto a boat or pay for my passage. I am a burden to society, and nobody's responsibility.

"You — the Irish girl. Over here." A thin, scowling matron in a white bonnet beckons with a bony finger. She must know I'm Irish from the papers Mr. Schatzman filled out when he brought me in to the Children's Aid several weeks ago — or perhaps it is my accent, still as thick as peat. "Humph," she says, pursing her lips, when I stand in front of her. "Red hair."

"Unfortunate," the plump woman beside her says, then sighs. "And those freckles. It's hard enough to get placed out at her age."

The bony one licks her thumb and pushes the hair off my face. "Don't want to scare them away, now, do you? You must keep it pulled back. If you're neat and well mannered, they might not be so quick to jump to conclusions."

She buttons my sleeves, and when she leans down to retie each of my black shoes, a mildewy smell rises from her bonnet. "It is imperative that you look presentable. The kind of girl a woman would want around the house. Clean and well-spoken. But not too —" She shoots the other one a look.

"Too what?" I ask.

"Some women don't take kindly to a comely girl sleeping under the same roof," she says. "Not that you're so. . . . But still." She points at my necklace. "What is that?"

I reach up and touch the small pewter claddagh Celtic cross I have worn since I was six, tracking the grooved outline of the heart with my finger. "An Irish cross."

"You're not allowed to bring keepsakes with you on the train."

My heart is pounding so hard I believe she can hear it. "It was my gram's."

The two women peer at the cross, and I can see them hesitating, trying to decide what to do.

"She gave it to me in Ireland, before we came over. It's — It's the only thing I have left." This is true, but it's also true that I say it because I think it will sway them. And it does.

We hear the train before we can see it. A low hum, a rumble underfoot, a deep-throated whistle, faint at first and then louder as the train gets close. We crane our necks to look down the track (even as one of our sponsors, Mrs. Scatcherd, shouts in her reedy voice, "Chil-dren! Places, chil-

50

dren!"), and suddenly here it is: a black engine looming over us, shadowing the platform, letting out a hiss of steam like a massive panting animal.

I am with a group of twenty children, all ages. We are scrubbed and in our donated clothes, the girls in dresses with white pinafores and thick stockings, the boys in knickers that button below the knee, white dress shirts, neckties, thick wool suit coats. It is an unseasonably warm October day, Indian summer, Mrs. Scatcherd calls it, and we are sweltering on the platform. My hair is damp against my neck, the pinafore stiff and uncomfortable. In one hand I clutch a small brown suitcase that, excepting the cross, contains everything I have in the world, all newly acquired: a bible, two sets of clothes, a hat, a black coat several sizes too small, a pair of shoes. Inside the coat is my name, embroidered by a volunteer at the Children's Aid Society: Niamh Power.

Yes, Niamh. Pronounced "Neev." A common enough name in County Galway, and not so unusual in the Irish tenements in New York, but certainly not acceptable anywhere the train might take me. The lady who sewed those letters several days ago *tsk*ed over the task. "I hope you aren't attached to that name, young miss, because I

51

can promise if you're lucky enough to be chosen, your new parents will change it in a second." *My Niamh,* my da used to call me. But I'm not so attached to the name. I know it's hard to pronounce, foreign, unlovely to those who don't understand — a peculiar jumble of unmatched consonants.

No one feels sorry for me because I've lost my family. Each of us has a sad tale; we wouldn't be here otherwise. The general feeling is that it's best not to talk about the past, that the quickest relief will come in forgetting. The Children's Aid treats us as if we were born the moment we were brought in, that like moths breaking out of their cocoons we've left our old lives behind and, God willing, will soon launch ourselves into new ones.

Mrs. Scatcherd and Mr. Curran, a milquetoast with a brown mustache, line us up by height, tallest to shortest, which generally means oldest to youngest, with the babies in the arms of the children over eight. Mrs. Scatcherd pushes a baby into my arms before I can object — an olive-skinned, cross-eyed fourteen-month-old named Carmine (who, I can already guess, will soon answer to another name). He clings to me like a terrified kitten. Brown suitcase in one hand, the other holding Carmine secure, I navigate the high steps into the train un-steadily before Mr. Curran scurries over to take my bag. "Use some common sense, girl," he scolds. "If you fall, you'll crack your skulls, and then we'll have to leave the both of you behind."

The wooden seats in the train car all face forward except for two groups of seats op-posite each other in the front, separated by a narrow aisle. I find a three-seater for Car-mine and me, and Mr. Curran heaves my suitcase onto the rack above my head. Car-mine soon wants to crawl off the seat, and I am so busy trying to distract him from escaping that I barely notice as the other kids come on board and the car fills.

Mrs. Scatcherd stands at the front of the car, holding on to two leather seat backs, the arms of her black cape draping like the wings of a crow. "They call this an orphan train, children, and you are lucky to be on it. You are leaving behind an evil place, full of ignorance, poverty, and vice, for the nobility of country life. While you are on this train you will follow some simple rules. You will be cooperative and listen to instruc-tions. You will be respectful of your chap-erones. You will treat the train car respect-fully and will not damage it in any way. You will encourage your seatmates to behave appropriately. In short, you will make Mr. Curran and me proud of your behavior." Her voice rises as we settle in our seats. "When you are allowed to step off the train, you will stay within the area we designate. You will not wander off alone at any time. And if your behavior proves to be a problem, if you cannot adhere to these simple rules of common decency, you will be sent straight back to where you came from and discharged on the street, left to fend for yourselves."

The younger children appear bewildered by this litany, but those of us older than six or seven had already heard a version of it several times at the orphanage before we left. The words wash over me. Of more immediate concern is the fact that Carmine is hungry, as am I. We had only a dry piece of bread and a tin cup of milk for breakfast, hours ago, before it was light. Carmine is fussing and chewing on his hand, a habit that must be comforting to him. (Maisie sucked her thumb.) But I know not to ask when food is coming. It will come when the sponsors are ready to give it, and no entreaties will change that.

I tug Carmine onto my lap. At breakfast this morning, when I dropped sugar into my tea, I slipped two lumps into my pocket. Now I rub one between my fingers, crushing it to granules, then lick my index finger and stick it in the sugar before popping it in Carmine's mouth. The look of wonder on his face, his delight as he realizes his good fortune, makes me smile. He clutches my hand with both of his chubby ones, holding on tight as he drifts off to sleep.

Eventually I, too, am lulled to sleep by the steady rumble of the clicking wheels. When I wake, with Carmine stirring and rubbing his eyes, Mrs. Scatcherd is standing over me. She is close enough that I can see the small pink veins, like seams on the back of a delicate leaf, spreading across her cheeks, the downy fur on her jawbone, her bristly black eyebrows.

She stares at me intently through her small round glasses. "There were little ones at home, I gather."

I nod.

"You appear to know what you're doing."

As if on cue, Carmine bleats in my lap. "I think he's hungry," I tell her. I feel his diaper rag, which is dry on the outside but spongy. "And ready for a change."

She turns toward the front of the car, gesturing back at me over her shoulder. "Come on, then."

Holding the baby against my chest, I rise unsteadily from my seat and sway behind her up the aisle. Children sitting in twos and threes look up with doleful eyes as I pass. None of us knows where we are headed, and I think that except for the very youngest, each of us is apprehensive and fearful. Our sponsors have told us little; we know only that we are going to a land where apples grow in abundance on low-hanging branches and cows and pigs and sheep roam freely in the fresh country air. A land where good people — families — are eager to take us in. I haven't seen a cow, or any animal, for that matter, except a stray dog and the occasional hardy bird, since leaving County Galway, and I look forward to seeing them again. But I am skeptical. I know all too well how it is when the beautiful visions you've been fed don't match up with reality.

Many of the children on this train have been at the Children's Aid for so long that they have no memories of their mothers. They can start anew, welcomed into the arms of the only families they'll ever know. I remember too much: my gram's ample bosom, her small dry hands, the dark cottage with a crumbling stone wall flanking its narrow garden. The heavy mist that settled over the bay early in the morning and late in the afternoon, the mutton and potatoes Gram would bring to the house when Mam was too tired to cook or we didn't have money for ingredients. Buying milk and bread at the corner shop on Phantom Street — Sraid a' Phuca, my da called it in Gaelic — so called because the stone houses in that section of town were built on cemetery grounds. My mam's chapped lips and fleeting smile, the melancholy that filled our home in Kinvara and traveled with us across the ocean to take up permanent residence in the dim corners of our tenement apartment in New York.

And now here I am on this train, wiping Carmine's bottom while Mrs. Scatcherd hovers above us, shielding me with a blanket to hide the procedure from Mr. Curran, issuing instructions I don't need. Once I have Carmine clean and dry, I sling him over my shoulder and make my way back to my seat while Mr. Curran distributes lunch pails filled with bread and cheese and fruit, and tin cups of milk. Feeding Carmine bread soaked in milk reminds me of the Irish dish called champ I often made for Maisie and the boys — a mash of potatoes, milk, green onions (on the rare occasion when we had them), and salt. On the nights when we went to bed hungry, all of us dreamed of that champ.

After distributing the food and one wool blanket to each of us, Mr. Curran announces that there is a bucket and a dipper for water, and if we raise our hands we can come forward for a drink. There's an indoor toilet, he informs us (though, as we soon find out, this "toilet" is a terrifying open hole above the tracks).

Carmine, drunk on sweet milk and bread, splays in my lap, his dark head in the crook of my arm. I wrap the scratchy blanket around us. In the rhythmic clacking of the train and the stirring, peopled silence of the car, I feel cocooned. Carmine smells as lovely as a custard, the solid weight of him so comforting it makes me teary. His spongy skin, pliable limbs, dark fringed lashes — even his sighs make me think (how could they not?) of Maisie. The idea of her dying alone in the hospital, suffering painful burns, is too much to bear. Why am I alive, and she dead?

In our tenement there were families who spilled in and out of each other's apartments, sharing child care and stews. The men worked together in grocery stores and blacksmith shops. The women ran cottage industries, making lace and darning socks. When I passed by their apartments and saw them sitting together in a circle, hunched over their work, speaking a language I didn't understand, I felt a sharp pang.

My parents left Ireland in hopes of a brighter future, all of us believing we were on our way to a land of plenty. As it happened, they failed in this new land, failed in just about every way possible. It may have been that they were weak people, ill suited for the rigors of emigration, its humiliations and compromises, its competing demands of self-discipline and adventurousness. But I wonder how things might have been different if my father was part of a family business that gave him structure and a steady paycheck instead of working in a bar, the worst place for a man like him — or if my mother had been surrounded by women, sisters and nieces, perhaps, who could have provided relief from destitution and loneliness, a refuge from strangers.

In Kinvara, poor as we were, and unstable, we at least had family nearby, people who knew us. We shared traditions and a way of looking at the world. We didn't know until we left how much we took those things for granted.

NEW YORK CENTRAL TRAIN, 1929

As the hours pass I get used to the motion of the train, the heavy wheels clacking in their grooves, the industrial hum under my seat. Dusk softens the sharp points of trees outside my window; the sky slowly darkens, then blackens around an orb of moon. Hours later, a faint blue tinge yields to the soft pastels of dawn, and soon enough sun is streaming in, the stop-start rhythm of the train making it all feel like still photography, thousands of images that taken together create a scene in motion.

We pass the time looking out at the evolving landscape, talking, playing games. Mrs. Scatcherd has a checkers set and a bible, and I thumb through it, looking for Psalm 121, Mam's favorite: *I will lift up mine eyes unto the hills, from whence cometh my help. My help cometh from the Lord, which made heaven and earth . . .*

I'm one of few children on the train who

can read. Mam taught me all my letters years ago, in Ireland, then taught me how to spell. When we got to New York, she'd make me read to her, anything with words on it — crates and bottles I found in the street.

"Donner brand car-bonated bev—"

"Beverage."

"Beverage. LemonKist soda. Artifickle —"

"Artificial. The 'c' sounds like 's.' "

"Artificial color. Kitric — citric acid added."

"Good."

When I became more proficient, Mam went into the shabby trunk beside her bed and brought out a hardback book of poems, blue with gold trim. Francis Fahy was a Kinvara poet born into a family of seventeen children. At fifteen he became an assistant teacher at the local boys' school before heading off to England (like every other Irish poet, Mam said), where he mingled with the likes of Yeats and Shaw. She would turn the pages carefully, running her finger over the black lines on flimsy paper, mouthing the words to herself, until she found the one she wanted.

" 'Galway Bay,' " she would say. "My favorite. Read it to me."

And so I did:

61

Had I youth's blood and hopeful mood
        and heart of fire once more,
For all the gold the world might hold I'd
        never quit your shore,
I'd live content whate'er God sent with
        neighbours old and gray,
And lay my bones 'neath churchyard
        stones, beside you, Galway Bay.

Once I looked up from a halting and botched rendition to see two lines of tears rivuleting Mam's cheeks. "Jesus Mary and Joseph," she said. "We should never have left that place."

Sometimes, on the train, we sing. Mr. Curran taught us a song before we left that he stands to lead us in at least once a day:

From the city's gloom to the country's
        bloom
Where the fragrant breezes sigh
From the city's blight to the greenwood
        bright
Like the birds of summer fly
O Children, dear Children
Young, happy, pure . . .

We stop at a depot for sandwich fixings and fresh fruit and milk, but only Mr. Curran gets off. I can see him outside my window in his white wingtips, talking to farmers on the platform. One holds a basket of apples, one a sack full of bread. A man in a black apron reaches into a box and unwraps a package of brown paper to reveal a thick yellow slab of cheese, and my stomach rumbles. They haven't fed us much, some crusts of bread and milk and an apple each in the past twenty-four hours, and I don't know if it's because they're afraid of running out or if they think it's for our moral good.

Mrs. Scatcherd strides up and down the aisle, letting two groups of children at a time get up to stretch while the train is still. "Shake each leg," she instructs. "Good for the circulation." The younger children are restless, and the older boys stir up trouble in small ways, wherever they can find it. I want nothing to do with these boys, who seem as feral as a pack of dogs. Our landlord, Mr. Kaminski, called boys like these "street Arabs," lawless vagrants who travel in gangs, pickpockets and worse.

When the train pulls out of the station, one of these boys lights a match, invoking the wrath of Mr. Curran, who boxes him about the head and shouts, for the whole car to hear, that he's a worthless good-for-nothing clod of dirt on God's green earth and will never amount to anything. This outburst does little but boost the boy's status in the eyes of his friends, who take to devising ingenious ways to irritate Mr. Curran without giving themselves away. Paper airplanes, loud belches, high-pitched, ghostly moans followed by stifled giggles — it drives Mr. Curran mad that he cannot pick out one boy to punish for all this. But what can he do, short of kicking them all out at the next stop? Which he actually threatens, finally, looming in the aisle above the seats of two particularly rowdy boys, only to prompt the bigger one's retort that he'll be happy to make his way on his own, has done it for years with no great harm, you can shine shoes in any city in America, he'll wager, and it's probably a hell of a lot better than being sent to live in a barn with animals, eating only pig slops, or getting carried off by Indians.

Children murmur in their seats. What'd he say?

Mr. Curran looks around uneasily. "You're scaring a whole car full of kids. Happy now?" he says.

"It's true, ain't it?"

"Of course it ain't — isn't — true. Kids, settle down."

"I hear we'll be sold at auction to the highest bidder," another boy stage-whispers.

The car grows silent. Mrs. Scatcherd stands up, wearing her usual thin-lipped scowl and broad-brimmed bonnet. She is far more imposing, in her heavy black cloak and flashing steel-rimmed glasses, than Mr. Curran could ever be. "I have heard enough," she says in a shrill voice. "I am tempted to throw the whole lot of you off this train. But that would not be" — she looks around at us slowly, dwelling on each somber face — "Christian. Would it? Mr. Curran and I are here to escort you to a better life. Any suggestion to the contrary is ignorant and outrageous. It is our fervent hope that each of you will find a path out of the depravity of your early lives, and with firm guidance and hard work transform into respectable citizens who can pull your weight in society. Now. I am not so naive as to believe that this will be the case for all." She casts a withering look at a blond-haired older boy, one of the troublemakers. "But I am hopeful that most of you will view this as an opportunity. Perhaps the only chance you will ever get to make something of yourselves." She adjusts the cape around her shoulders. "Mr. Curran, maybe the young man who spoke to you so impudently should be moved to a seat where his dubious charms will not be so enthusiastically

65

embraced." She lifts her chin, peering out from her bonnet like a turtle from its shell. "Ah — there's a space beside Niamh," she says, pointing a crooked finger in my direction. "With the added bonus of a squirming toddler."

My skin prickles. Oh no. But I can see that Mrs. Scatcherd is in no mood to reconsider. So I slide as close as I can to the window and set Carmine and his blanket next to me, in the middle of the seat.

Several rows ahead, on the other side of the aisle, the boy stands, sighs loudly, and pulls his bright-blue flannel cap down hard on his head. He makes a production of getting out of his seat, then drags his feet up the aisle like a condemned man approaching a noose. When he gets to my row, he squints at me, then at Carmine, and makes a face at his friends. "This should be fun," he says loudly.

"You will not speak, young sir," Mrs. Scatcherd trills. "You will sit down and behave like a gentleman."

He flings himself into his seat, his legs in the aisle, then takes his cap off and slaps it against the seat in front of us, raising a small cloud of dust. The kids in that seat turn around and stare. "Man," he mutters, not really to anybody, "what an old goat." He

66

holds his finger out to Carmine, who studies it and looks at his face. The boy wiggles his finger and Carmine buries his head in my lap.

"Don't get you nowhere being shy," the boy says. He looks over at me, his gaze loitering on my face and body in a way that makes me blush. He has straight sandy hair and pale blue eyes and is twelve or thirteen, from what I can tell, though his manner seems older. "A redhead. That's worse than a bootblack. Who's gonna want you?"

I feel the sting of truth in his words, but I lift my chin. "At least I'm not a criminal."

He laughs. "That's what I am, am I?"

"You tell me."

"Would you believe me?"

"Probably not."

"No point then, is there."

I do not respond and we three sit in silence, Carmine awed into stillness by the boy's presence. I look out at the severe and lonely landscape drifting past the window. It's been raining off and on all day. Gray clouds hang low in a watery sky.

"They took my kit from me," the boy says after a while.

I turn to look at him. "What?"

"My bootblack kit. All my paste and

brushes. How do they expect me to make a living?"

"They don't. They're going to find you a family."

"Ah, that's right," he says with a dry laugh. "A ma to tuck me in at night and a pa to teach me a trade. I don't see it working out like that. Do you?"

"I don't know. Haven't thought about it," I say, though of course I have. I've gleaned bits and pieces: that babies are the first to be chosen, then older boys, prized by farmers for their strong bones and muscles. Last to go are girls like me, too old to be turned into ladies, too young to be serious help around the house, not much use in the field. If we're not chosen, we get sent back to the orphanage. "Anyway, what can we do about it?"

Reaching into his pocket, he pulls out a penny. He rolls it across his fingers, holds it between thumb and forefinger and touches it to Carmine's nose, then clasps it in his closed fist. When he opens his hand, the penny isn't there. He reaches behind Carmine's ear, and — "Presto," he says, handing him the penny.

Carmine gazes at it, astonished.

"You can put up with it," the boy says. "Or you can run away. Or maybe you'll get lucky and live happily ever after. Only the good Lord knows what's going to happen, and He ain't telling."

UNION STATION, CHICAGO, 1929

We become an odd little family, the boy — real name Hans, I learn, called Dutchy on the street — and Carmine and I in our three-seat abode. Dutchy tells me he was born in New York to German parents, that his mother died of pneumonia and his father sent him out on the streets to earn money as a bootblack, beating him with a belt if he didn't bring enough in. So one day he stopped going home. He fell in with a group of boys who slept on any convenient step or sidewalk during the summer, and in the winter months in barrels and doorways, in discarded boxes on iron gratings on the margin of Printing House Square, warm air and steam rising from the engines beneath. He taught himself piano by ear in the back room of a speakeasy, plunked out tunes at night for drunken patrons, saw things no twelve-year-old should see. The boys tried to look after one another, though if one got sick or maimed — catching pneumonia or falling off a streetcar or under the wheels of a truck — there wasn't much any of them could do.

A few kids from Dutchy's gang are on the train with us — he points out Slobbery Jack, who has a habit of spilling on himself, and Whitey, a boy with translucent skin. They were lured off the street with the promise of a hot meal, and here's where they ended up.

"What about the hot meal? Did you get it?"

"Did we ever. Roast beef and potatoes. And a clean bed. But I don't trust it. I wager they're paid by the head, the way Indians take scalps."

"It's charity," I say. "Didn't you hear what Mrs. Scatcherd said? It's their Christian duty."

"All I know is nobody ever did nothing for me out of Christian duty. I call tell by the way they're talking I'm going to end up worked to the bone and not see a dime for it. You're a girl. You might be all right, baking pies in the kitchen or taking care of a baby." He squints at me. "Except for the red hair and freckles, you look okay. You'll be fine and dandy sitting at the table with a napkin on your lap. Not me. I'm too old to

71

be taught manners, or to follow somebody else's rules. The only thing I'm good for is hard labor. Same with all of us newsies and peddlers and bill posters and bootblacks." He nods toward one boy after another in the car.

On the third day we cross the Illinois state line. Near Chicago, Mrs. Scatcherd stands for another lecture. "In a few minutes we will arrive at Union Station, whereupon we will switch trains for the next portion of our journey," she tells us. "If it were up to me, I'd send you in a straight line right across the platform to the other train, without a minute's worry that you'll get yourselves into trouble. But we are not allowed to board for half an hour. Young men, you will wear your suit coats, and young ladies must put on your pinafores. Careful not to muss them now.

"Chicago is a proud and noble city, on the edge of a great lake. The lake makes it windy, hence its appellation: the Windy City. You will bring your suitcases, of course, and your wool blanket to wrap yourself in, as we will be on the platform for at least an hour.

"The good citizens of Chicago no doubt view you as ruffians, thieves, and beggars, hopeless sinners who have not a chance in the world of being redeemed. They are justifiably suspicious of your character. Your task is to prove them wrong — to behave with impeccable manners, and comport yourselves like the model citizens the Children's Aid Society believes you can become."

The wind on the platform rushes through my dress. I wrap my blanket tight around my shoulders, keeping a close eye on Carmine as he staggers around, seemingly oblivious to the cold. He wants to know the names of everything: *Train. Wheel. Mrs. Scatcherd,* frowning at the conductor. *Mr. Curran,* poring over papers with a station agent. *Lights* — which to Carmine's amazement turn on while he's gazing at them, as if by magic.

Contrary to Mrs. Scatcherd's expectations — or perhaps in response to her rebuke — we are a quiet lot, even the older boys. We huddle together, complacent as cattle, stamping our feet to stay warm.

Except for Dutchy. Where did he go?

"Psst. Niamh."

When I hear my name, I turn to glimpse his blond hair in a stairwell. Then he's gone. I look over at the adults, occupied with plans and forms. A large rat scurries along the far brick wall, and as the rest of the children point and shriek I scoop up Carmine, leaving our small pile of suitcases, and slip behind a pillar and a pile of wooden crates.

In the stairwell, out of sight of the platform, Dutchy leans against a curved wall. When he sees me, he turns without expression and bounds up the stairs, vanishing around a corner. With a glance behind, and seeing no one, I hold Carmine close and follow him, keeping my eyes on the wide steps so I don't fall. Carmine tilts his head up and leans back in my arms, floppy as a sack of rice. *"Yite,"* he murmurs, pointing. My gaze follows his chubby finger to what I realize is the enormous, barrel-vaulted ceiling of the train station, laced with skylights.

We step into the huge terminal, filled with people of all shapes and colors — wealthy women in furs trailed by servants, men in top hats and morning coats, shop girls in bright dresses. It's too much to take in all at once — statuary and columns, balconies and staircases, oversized wooden benches. Dutchy is standing in the middle, looking up at the sky through that glass ceiling, and then he takes off his cap and flings it into the air. Carmine struggles to free himself, and as soon as I set him down he races toward Dutchy and grabs his legs. Dutchy reaches down and hoists him on his shoulders, and as I get close I hear him say, "Put your arms out, little man, and I'll spin you." He clasps Carmine's legs and twirls, Carmine stretching out his arms and throwing his head back, gazing up at the skylights, shrieking with glee as they turn, and in that moment, for the first time since the fire, my worries are gone. I feel a joy so strong it's almost painful — a knife's edge of joy.

And then a whistle pierces the air. Three policemen in dark uniforms rush toward Dutchy with their sticks drawn, and everything happens too fast: I see Mrs. Scatcherd at the top of the stairwell pointing her crow wing, Mr. Curran running in those ridiculous white shoes, Carmine clutching Dutchy's neck in terror as a fat policeman shouts, "Get down!" My arm is wrenched behind my back and a man spits in my ear, "Trying to get away, were yeh?" his breath like licorice. It's hopeless to respond, so I keep my mouth shut as he forces me to my knees.

A hush falls over the cavernous hall. Out of the corner of my eye I see Dutchy on the floor, under a policeman's truncheon. Carmine is howling, his cries puncturing the stillness, and every time Dutchy moves, he gets jammed in the side. Then he's in handcuffs and the fat policeman yanks him to his feet, pushing him roughly so he stumbles forward, tripping over his feet.

In this moment I know that he's been in scrapes like this before. His face is blank; he doesn't even protest. I can tell what the bystanders think: he's a common criminal; he's broken the law, likely more than one. The police are protecting the good citizens of Chicago, and thank God for them.

The fat policeman drags Dutchy over to Mrs. Scatcherd, and Licorice Breath, following his lead, yanks me roughly by the arm.

Mrs. Scatcherd looks as if she's bitten into a lime. Her lips are puckered in a quivering O, and she appears to be trembling. "I placed this young man with you," she says to me in a terrible quiet voice, "in the hopes that you might provide a civilizing influence. It appears that I was gravely mistaken."

My mind is racing. If only I can convince her that he means no harm. "No, ma'am, I —"

"Do not interrupt."

I look down.

"So what do you have to say for yourself?"

I know that nothing I can say will change

76

her opinion of me. And in that realization I feel oddly free. The most I can hope for is to keep Dutchy from being sent back to the streets.

"It's my fault," I say. "I asked Dutchy — I mean Hans — to escort me and the baby up the stairs." I look over at Carmine, trying to squirm out of the arms of the policeman holding him. "I thought . . . maybe we could get a glimpse of that lake. I thought the baby would like to see it."

Mrs. Scatcherd glares at me. Dutchy looks at me with surprise. Carmine says, "Yake?"

"And then — Carmine saw the lights." I point up and look at Carmine, and he throws his head back and shouts, "Yite!"

The policemen aren't sure what to do. Licorice Breath lets go of my arm, apparently persuaded that I'm not going to flee.

Mr. Curran glances at Mrs. Scatcherd, whose expression has ever so slightly softened.

"You are a foolish and headstrong girl," she says, but her voice has lost its edge, and I can tell she's not as angry as she wants to appear. "You flouted my instructions to stay on the platform. You put the entire group of children at risk, and you have disgraced yourself. Worse, you have disgraced me. And Mr. Curran," she adds, turning toward him.

He winces, as if to say *Leave me out of it.* "But this is not, I suppose, a matter for the police. A civil, not a legal, matter," she clarifies.

The fat policeman makes a show of unlocking Dutchy's handcuffs and clipping them to his belt. "Sure you don't want us to take him in, ma'am?"

"Thank you, sir, but Mr. Curran and I will devise a sufficient punishment."

"As you say." He touches the brim of his cap, backs away, and turns on his heels.

"Make no mistake," Mrs. Scatcherd says gravely, staring down her nose at us. "You will be punished."

Mrs. Scatcherd raps Dutchy's knuckles several times with a long wooden ruler, though it seems to me a halfhearted penalty. He barely winces, then shakes his hands twice in the air and winks at me. Truly, there isn't much more she can do. Stripped of family and identity, fed meager rations, consigned to hard wooden seats until we are to be, as Slobbery Jack suggested, sold into slavery — our mere existence is punishment enough. Though she threatens to separate the three of us, in the end she leaves us together — not wanting to infect the others with Dutchy's delinquency, she says, and apparently having decided that taking care of Carmine would've extended my punishment to her. She tells us not to speak to or even look at each other. "If I hear as much as a murmur, so help me . . ." she says, the threat losing air over our heads like a pricked balloon.

By the time we leave Chicago, it is evening. Carmine sits on my lap with his hands on the window, face pressed against the glass, gazing out at the streets and buildings, all lit up. "Yite," he says softly as the city recedes into the distance. I look out the window with him. Soon all is dark; it's impossible to tell where land ends and the sky begins.

"Get a good night's rest," Mrs. Scatcherd calls from the front of the car. "In the morning you will need to be at your very best. It is vital that you make a good impression. Your drowsiness might well be construed as laziness."

"What if nobody wants me?" one boy asks, and the entire car seems to hold its breath. It is the question on everyone's mind, the question none of us are sure we want the answer to.

Mrs. Scatcherd looks down at Mr. Curran as if she's been waiting for this. "If it happens that you are not chosen at the first

79

stop, you will have several additional opportunities. I cannot think of an instance . . ." She pauses and purses her lips. "It is uncommon for a child to be with us on the return trip to New York."

"Pardon me, ma'am," a girl near the front says. "What if I don't want to go with the people who choose me?"

"What if they beat us?" a boy cries out.

"Children!" Mrs. Scatcherd's small glasses flash as she turns her head from side to side. "I will not have you interrupting!" She seems poised to sit down without addressing these questions, but then changes her mind. "I will say this: There is no accounting for taste and personalities. Some parents are looking for a healthy boy to work on the farm — as we all know, hard work is good for children, and you would be lucky to be placed with a God-fearing farm family, all you boys — and some people want babies. People sometimes think they want one thing, but later change their minds. Though we dearly hope all of you will find the right homes at the first stop, it doesn't always work that way. So in addition to being respectable and polite, you must also keep your faith in God to guide you forward if the way is not clear. Whether your journey is long or short, He will help you as long as you place your trust in Him."

I look over at Dutchy, and he looks back at me. Mrs. Scatcherd knows as little as we do about whether we'll be chosen by people who will treat us with kindness. We are headed toward the unknown, and we have no choice but to sit quietly in our hard seats and let ourselves be taken there.

Spruce Harbor, Maine, 2011

Walking back to the car, Molly sees Jack through the windshield, eyes closed, grooving out to a song she can't hear.

"Hey," she says loudly, opening the passenger door.

He opens his eyes and yanks the buds out of his ears. "How'd it go?"

She shakes her head and climbs in. Hard to believe she was only in there for twenty minutes. "Vivian's an odd one. Fifty hours! My God."

"But it's going to work out?"

"I guess so. We made a plan to start on Monday."

Jack pats her leg. "Awesome. You'll knock out those hours in no time."

"Let's not count our chickens."

She's always doing this, crabbily countering his enthusiasm, but it's become something of a routine. She'll tell him, "I'm nothing like you, Jack. I'm bitchy and spiteful,"

82

but is secretly relieved when he laughs it off. He has an optimistic certainty that she's a good person at her core. And if he has this faith in her, then she must be all right, right?

"Just keep telling yourself — better than juvie," he says.

"Are you sure about that? It'd probably be easier to serve my time and get it over with."

"Except for that small problem of having a record."

She shrugs. "That'd be kind of badass, though, don't you think?"

"Really, Moll?" he says with a sigh, turning the ignition key.

She smiles to let him know she's kidding. Sort of. " 'Better than juvie.' That would make a good tattoo." She points to her arm. "Right here across my bicep, in twenty-point script."

"Don't even joke," he says.

Dina plunks the skillet of Hamburger Helper on the trivet in the middle of the table and sits heavily in her chair. "Oof. I'm exhausted."

"Tough day at work, huh, babe?" Ralph says, as he always does, though Dina never asks him about his day. Maybe plumbing isn't as exciting as being a police dispatcher in thrill-a-minute Spruce Harbor. "Molly, hand me your plate."

"My back is killing me from that crappy chair they make me sit in," Dina says. "I swear if I went to a chiropractor, I'd have a lawsuit."

Molly gives her plate to Ralph and he drops some casserole on it. Molly has learned to pick around the meat — even in a dish like this, where you can hardly tell what's what and it's all mixed together — because Dina refuses to acknowledge that she's a vegetarian.

Dina listens to conservative talk radio, belongs to a fundamentalist Christian church, and has a "Guns don't kill people — abortion clinics do" bumper sticker on her car. She and Molly are about as opposite as it is possible to be, which would be fine if Dina didn't take Molly's choices as a personal affront. Dina is constantly rolling her eyes, muttering under her breath about Molly's various infractions — didn't put away her laundry, left a bowl in the sink, can't be bothered to make her bed — all of which are part and parcel of the liberal agenda that's ruining this country. Molly knows she should ignore these comments — "water off a duck's back," Ralph says —

84

but they irk her. She's overly sensitive to them, like a tuning fork pitched too high. It's all part of Dina's unwavering message: Be grateful. Dress like a normal person. Don't have opinions. Eat the food that's put in front of you.

Molly can't quite figure out how Ralph fits into all of this. She knows he and Dina met in high school, followed a predictable football player/cheerleader story arc, and have been together ever since, but she can't tell if Ralph actually buys Dina's party line or just toes it to make his life easier. Sometimes she sees a glimmer of independence — a raised eyebrow, a carefully worded, possibly ironic observation, like, "Well, we can't make a decision on that till the boss gets home."

Still — all things considered, Molly knows she has it pretty good: her own room in a tidy house, employed and sober foster parents, a decent high school, a nice boyfriend. She isn't expected to take care of a passel of kids, as she was at one of the places she lived, or clean up after fifteen dirty cats, as she was at another. In the past nine years she's been in over a dozen foster homes, some for as little as a week. She's been spanked with a spatula, slapped across the face, made to sleep on an unheated sun porch in the winter, taught to roll a joint by a foster father, fed lies for the social worker. She got her tatt illegally at sixteen from a twenty-three-year-old friend of the Bangor family, an "ink expert-in-training," as he called himself, who was just starting out and did it for free — or, well . . . sort of. She wasn't so attached to her virginity anyway.

With the tines of her fork, Molly mashes the hamburger into her plate, hoping to grind it into oblivion. She takes a bite and smiles at Dina. "Good. Thanks."

Dina purses her lips and cocks her head, clearly trying to gauge whether Molly's praise is sincere. Well, Dina, Molly thinks, it is and it isn't. Thank you for taking me in and feeding me. But if you think you can quash my ideals, force me to eat meat when I told you I don't, expect me to care about your aching back when you don't seem the slightest bit interested in my life, you can forget it. I'll play your fucking game. But I don't have to play by your rules.

Spruce Harbor, Maine, 2011

Terry leads the way to the third floor, bustling up the stairs, with Vivian moving more slowly behind her and Molly taking up the rear. The house is large and drafty — much too large, Molly thinks, for an old woman who lives alone. It has fourteen rooms, most of which are shuttered during the winter months. During the Terry-narrated tour on the way to the attic, Molly gets the story: Vivian and her husband owned and ran a department store in Minnesota, and when they sold it twenty years ago, they took a sailing trip up the East Coast to celebrate their retirement. They spied this house, a former ship captain's estate, from the harbor, and on an impulse decided to buy it. And that was it: they packed up and moved to Maine. Ever since Jim died, eight years ago, Vivian has lived here by herself.

In a clearing at the top of the stairs, Terry,

panting a bit, puts her hand on her hip and looks around. "Yikes! Where to start, Vivi?"

Vivian reaches the top step, clutching the banister. She is wearing another cashmere sweater, gray this time, and a silver necklace with an odd little charm on it.

"Well, let's see."

Glancing around, Molly can see that the third floor of the house consists of a finished section — two bedrooms tucked under the slope of the roof and an old-fashioned bathroom with a claw-foot tub — and a large, open attic part with a rough-planked floor half covered in patches of ancient linoleum. It has visible rafters with insulation packed between the beams. Though the rafters and floor are dark, the space is surprisingly light. Levered windows nestle in each dormer, providing a clear view of the bay and the marina beyond.

The attic is filled with boxes and furniture packed so tightly it's hard to move around. In one corner is a long clothes rack covered with a plastic zippered case. Several cedar chests, so large that Molly wonders how they got up here in the first place, are lined up against a wall next to a stack of steamer trunks. Overhead, several bare bulbs glow like tiny moons.

Wandering among the cardboard boxes,

Vivian trails her fingertips across the tops of them, peering at their cryptic labels: *The store, 1960–. The Nielsens. Valuables.* "I suppose this is why people have children, isn't it?" she muses. "So somebody will care about the stuff they leave behind."

Molly looks over at Terry, who is shaking her head with grim resignation. It occurs to her that maybe Terry's reluctance to take on this project has as much to do with avoiding this kind of maudlin moment as avoiding the work itself.

Glancing surreptitiously at her phone, Molly sees it's 4:15 — only fifteen minutes since she arrived. She's supposed to stay until six today, and then come for two hours four days a week, and four hours every weekend until — well, until she finishes her time or Vivian drops dead, whichever comes first. According to her calculations, it should take about a month. To finish the hours, not to kill Vivian.

Though if the next forty-nine hours and forty-five minutes are this tedious, she doesn't know if she'll be able to stand it.

In American History they've been studying how the United States was founded on indentured servitude. The teacher, Mr. Reed, said that in the seventeenth century nearly two-thirds of English settlers came over that way, selling years of their freedom for the promise of an eventual better life. Most of them were under the age of twenty-one.

Molly has decided to think of this job as indentured servitude: each hour she works is another hour closer to freedom.

"It'll be good to clear out this stuff, Vivi," Terry is saying. "Well, I'm going to get started on the laundry. Call if you need me!" She nods to Molly as if to say *All yours!* and retreats down the stairs.

Molly knows all about Terry's work routine. "You're like me at the gym, hey, Ma?" Jack says, teasing her about it. "One day biceps, next day quads." Terry rarely deviates from her self-imposed schedule; with a house this size, she says, you have to tackle a different section every day: bedrooms and laundry on Monday, bathrooms and plants on Tuesday, kitchen and shopping on Wednesday, other main rooms on Thursday, cooking for the weekend on Friday.

Molly wades through stacks of boxes sealed with shiny beige tape to get to the window, which she opens a crack. Even up here, at the top of this big old house, she can smell the salty air. "They're not in any particular order, are they?" she asks Vivian, turning back around. "How long have they been here?"

"I haven't touched them since we moved in. So that must be —"

"Twenty years."

Vivian gives her a flinty smile. "You were listening."

"Were you ever tempted to just toss it all in a Dumpster?"

Vivian purses her lips.

"I didn't mean — sorry." Molly winces, realizing she's pushed a little far.

All right, it's official, she needs an attitude adjustment. Why is she so hostile? Vivian hasn't done anything to her. She should be grateful. Without Vivian she'd be sliding down a dark path toward nowhere good. But it kind of feels nice to nurture her resentment, to foster it. It's something she can savor and control, this feeling of having been wronged by the world. That she has fulfilled her role as a thieving member of the underclass, now indentured to this genteel midwestern white lady, is too perfect for words.

Deep breath. Smile. As Lori, the court-ordered social worker she meets with bi-weekly always tells her to do, Molly decides to make a mental list of all the positive things about her situation. Let's see. One, if she can stick it out, this whole incident will be stricken from her record. Two, she has a place — however tense and tenuous at the moment — to live. Three, if you must spend fifty hours in an uninsulated attic in Maine, spring is probably the best time of year to do it. Four, Vivian is ancient, but she doesn't appear to be senile.

Five — who knows? Maybe there actually will be something interesting in these boxes.

Bending down, Molly scans the labels around her. "I think we should go through them in chronological order. Let's see — this one says 'WWII.' Is there anything before that?"

"Yes." Vivian squeezes between two stacks and makes her way toward the cedar chests. "The earliest stuff I have is over here, I think. These crates are too heavy to move, though. So we'll have to start in this corner. Is that okay with you?"

Molly nods. Downstairs, Terry handed her a cheap serrated knife with a plastic handle, a slippery stack of white plastic garbage bags, and a wire-bound notebook with a pen clipped to it to keep track of "inventory," as she called it. Now Molly takes the knife and pokes it through the tape of the box Vivian has chosen: 1929–1930. Vivian, sitting on a wooden chest, waits patiently. After opening the flaps, Molly lifts out a mustard-colored coat, and Vivian scowls. "Mercy sake," she says. "I can't believe I saved that coat. I always hated it."

Molly holds the coat up, inspecting it. It's interesting, actually, sort of a military style with bold black buttons. The gray silk lining is disintegrating. Going through the pockets, she fishes out a folded piece of lined paper, almost worn away at the creases. She unfolds it to reveal a child's careful cursive in faint pencil, practicing the same sentence over and over again: *Upright and do right make all right. Upright and do right make all right. Upright and do right . . .*

Vivian takes it from her and spreads the paper open on her knee. "I remember this. Miss Larsen had the most beautiful penmanship."

"Your teacher?"

Vivian nods. "Try as I might, I could never form my letters like hers."

Molly looks at the perfect swoops hitting the broken line in exactly the same spot. "Looks pretty good to me. You should see my scrawl."

"They barely teach it anymore, I hear."

"Yeah, everything's on computer." Molly is suddenly struck by the fact that Vivian wrote these words on this sheet of paper more than eighty years ago. *Upright and do*

93

right make all right. "Things have changed a lot since you were my age, huh?"

Vivian cocks her head. "I suppose. Most of it doesn't affect me much. I still sleep in a bed. Sit in a chair. Wash dishes in a sink."

Or Terry washes dishes in a sink, to be accurate, Molly thinks.

"I don't watch much television. You know I don't have a computer. In a lot of ways my life is just as it was twenty or even forty years ago."

"That's kind of sad," Molly blurts, then immediately regrets it. But Vivian doesn't seem offended. Making a "who cares?" face, she says, "I don't think I've missed much."

"Wireless Internet, digital photographs, smartphones, Facebook, YouTube . . ." Molly taps the fingers of one hand. "The entire world has changed in the past decade."

"Not my world."

"But you're missing out on so much."

Vivian laughs. "I hardly think FaceTube — whatever that is — would improve my quality of life."

Molly shakes her head. "It's Face*book.* And YouTube."

"Whatever!" Vivian says breezily. "I don't care. I like my quiet life."

"But there's a balance. Honestly, I don't

94

know how you can just exist in this —
bubble."

Vivian smiles. "You don't have trouble
speaking your mind, do you?"

So she's been told. "Why did you keep
this coat, if you hated it?" Molly asks,
changing the subject.

Vivian picks it up and holds it out in front
of her. "That's a very good question."

"So should we put it in the Goodwill
pile?"

Folding the coat in her lap, Vivian says,
"Ah . . . maybe. Let's see what else is in
this box."

THE MILWAUKEE TRAIN, 1929

I sleep badly the last night on the train. Carmine is up several times in the night, irritable and fidgety, and though I try to soothe him, he cries fitfully for a long time, disturbing the children around us. As dawn emerges in streaks of yellow, he finally falls asleep, his head on Dutchy's curled leg and his feet in my lap. I am wide-awake, so filled with nervous energy that I can feel the blood pumping through my heart.

I've been wearing my hair pulled back in a messy ponytail, but now I untie the old ribbon and let it fall to my shoulders, combing through it with my fingers and smoothing the tendrils around my face. I pull it back as tightly as I can.

Turning, I catch Dutchy looking at me.

"Your hair is pretty." I squint at him in the gloom to see if he's teasing, and he looks back at me sleepily.

"That's not what you said a few days ago."

"I said you'll have a hard time."

I want to push away both his kindness and his honesty.

"Can't help what you are, can you," he says.

I crane my neck to see if Mrs. Scatcherd might have heard us, but there's no movement up front.

"Let's make a promise," he says. "To find each other."

"How can we? We'll probably end up in different places."

"I know."

"And my name will be changed."

"Mine too, maybe. But we can try."

Carmine flops over, tucking his legs beneath him and stretching his arms, and both of us shift to accommodate him.

"Do you believe in fate?" I ask.

"What's that again?"

"That everything is decided. You're just — you know — living it out."

"God has it all planned in advance."

I nod.

"I dunno. I don't like the plan much so far."

"Me either."

We both laugh.

"Mrs. Scatcherd says we should make a clean slate," I say. "Let go of the past."

"I can let go of the past, no problem." He picks up the wool blanket that has fallen to the floor and tucks it around the lump of Carmine's body, covering the parts that are exposed. "But I don't want to forget everything."

Outside the window I see three sets of tracks paralleling the one we are on, brown and silver, and beyond them broad flat fields of furrowed soil. The sky is clear and blue. The train car smells of diaper rags and sweat and sour milk.

At the front of the car Mrs. Scatcherd stands up, bends down to confer with Mr. Curran, and stands up again. She is wearing her black bonnet.

"All right, children. Wake up!" she says, looking around, clapping her hands several times. Her eyeglasses glint in the morning light.

Around me I hear small grunts and sighs as those lucky enough to have slept stretch out their cramped limbs.

"It is time to make yourselves presentable. Each of you has a change of clothing in your suitcase, which as you know is on the rack overhead. Big ones, please assist the little ones. I cannot stress enough how important it is to make a good first impression. Clean

98

faces, combed hair, shirts tucked in. Bright eyes and smiles. You will not fidget or touch your face. And you will say what, Rebecca?"

We're familiar with the script: "Please and thank you," Rebecca says, her voice barely audible.

"Please and thank you what?"

"Please and thank you, ma'am."

"You will wait to speak until you are spoken to, and then you will say please and thank you, ma'am. You will wait to do what, Andrew?"

"Speak until you are spoken to?"

"Exactly. You will not fidget or what, Norma?"

"Touch your face. Ma'am. Ma'am madam."

Titters erupt from the seats. Mrs. Scatcherd glares at us. "This amuses you, does it? I don't imagine you'll think it's quite so funny when all the adults say no thank you, I do not want a rude, slovenly child, and you'll have to get back on the train and go to the next station. Do you think so, Mr. Curran?"

Mr. Curran's head jerks up at the sound of his name. "No indeed, Mrs. Scatcherd."

The train is silent. Not getting chosen isn't something we want to think about. A little girl in the row behind me begins to cry, and soon I can hear muffled sniffs all around me. At the front of the train, Mrs. Scatcherd clasps her hands together and curls her lips into something resembling a smile. "Now, now. No need for that. As with almost everything in life, if you are polite and present yourself favorably, it is probable that you will succeed. The good citizens of Minneapolis are coming to the meeting hall today with the earnest intention of taking one of you home — possibly more than one. So remember, girls, tie your hair ribbons neatly. Boys, clean faces and combed hair. Shirts buttoned properly. When we disembark, you will stand in a straight line. You will speak only when spoken to. In short, you will do everything in your power to make it easy for an adult to choose you. Is that clear?"

The sun is so bright that I have to squint, so hot that I edge to the middle seat, out of the glare of the window, scooping Carmine onto my lap. As we go under bridges and pull through stations the light flickers and Carmine makes a shadow game of moving his hand across my white pinafore.

"You should make out all right," Dutchy says in a low voice. "At least you won't be breaking your back doing farm work."

"You don't know that I won't," I say. "And you don't know that you will."

Milwaukee Road Depot, Minneapolis, 1929

The train pulls into the station with a high-pitched squealing of brakes and a great gust of steam. Carmine is quiet, gaping at the buildings and wires and people outside the window, after hundreds of miles of fields and trees.

We stand and begin to gather our belongings. Dutchy reaches up for our bags and sets them in the aisle. Out the window I can see Mrs. Scatcherd and Mr. Curran on the platform talking to two men in suits and ties and black fedoras, with several policemen behind them. Mr. Curran shakes their hands, then sweeps his hand toward us as we step off the train.

I want to say something to Dutchy, but I can't think of what. My hands are clammy. It's a terrible kind of anticipation, not knowing what we're walking into. The last time I felt this way I was in the waiting rooms at Ellis Island. We were tired, and Mam wasn't well, and we didn't know where we were going or what kind of life we would have. But now I can see all I took for granted: I had a family. I believed that whatever happened, we'd be together.

A policeman blows a whistle and holds his arm in the air, and we understand that we're to line up. The solid weight of Carmine is in my arms, his hot breath, slightly sour and sticky from his morning milk, on my cheek. Dutchy carries our bags.

"Quickly, children," Mrs. Scatcherd says. "In two straight lines. That's good." Her tone is softer than usual, and I wonder if it's because we're around other adults or because she knows what's next. "This way." We proceed behind her up a wide stone staircase, the clatter of our hard-soled shoes on the steps echoing like a drumroll. At the top of the stairs we make our way down a corridor lit by glowing gas lamps, and into the main waiting room of the station — not as majestic as the one in Chicago, but impressive nonetheless. It's big and bright, with large, multipaned windows. Up ahead, Mrs. Scatcherd's black robe billows behind her like a sail.

People point and whisper, and I wonder if they know why we're here. And then I spot a broadside affixed to a column. In black block letters on white papers, it reads:

WANTED
Homes for Orphan Children
A Company of Homeless Children
from the East Will
Arrive at
Milwaukee Road Depot, Friday,
October 18.
Distribution will take place at 10 a.m.
These children are of various ages
and both sexes,
having been thrown friendless upon
the world . . .

"What did I say?" Dutchy says, following my glance. "Pig slops."

"You can read?" I ask with surprise, and he grins.

As if someone has turned a crank in my back, I am propelled forward, one foot in front of the other. The cacophony of the station becomes a dull roar in my ears. I smell something sweet — candy apples? — as we pass a vendor's cart. The hair on my neck is limp, and I feel a trickle of sweat down my back. Carmine is impossibly heavy. How strange, I think — that I am in a place my parents have never been and will never see. How strange that I am here and

104

they are gone.

I touch the claddagh cross around my neck.

The older boys no longer seem so rough. Their masks have slipped; I see fear on their faces. Some of the children are sniffling, but most are trying very hard to be quiet, to do what's expected of them.

Ahead of us, Mrs. Scatcherd stands beside a large oak door, hands clasped in front of her. When we reach her, we gather around in a semi-circle, the older girls holding babies and the younger children holding hands, the boys' hands stuffed in their pockets.

Mrs. Scatcherd bows her head. "Mary, Mother of God, we beseech you to cast a benevolent eye over these children, to guide them and bless them as they make their way in the world. We are your humble servants in His name. Amen."

"Amen," the pious few say quickly, and the rest of us follow.

Mrs. Scatcherd takes off her glasses. "We have reached our destination. From here, the Lord willing, you will disperse to families who need you and want you." She clears her throat. "Now remember, not everyone will find a match right away. This is to be expected, and nothing to worry about. If you do not match now you will simply board the train with Mr. Curran and me, and we will travel to another station about an hour from here. And if you do not find placement there, you will come with us to the next town."

The children around me move like a skittish herd. My stomach is hollow and trembly.

Mrs. Scatcherd nods. "All right, Mr. Curran, are we ready?"

"We are, Mrs. Scatcherd," he says, and leans against the large door with his shoulder, pushing it open.

We're at the back of a large, wood-paneled room with no windows, filled with people milling about and rows of empty chairs. As Mrs. Scatcherd leads us down the center aisle toward a low stage at the front, a hush falls over the crowd, and then a swelling murmur. People in the aisle move aside to let us pass.

Maybe, I think, someone here will want me. Maybe I'll have a life I've never dared to imagine, in a bright, snug house where there is plenty to eat — warm cake and milky tea with as much sugar as I please. But I am quaking as I make my way up the stairs to the stage.

We line up by height, smallest to tallest, some of us still holding babies. Though Dutchy is three years older than me, I'm tall for my age, and we're only separated by one boy in the line.

Mr. Curran clears his throat and begins to make a speech. Looking over at him, I notice his flushed cheeks and rabbity eyes, his droopy brown mustache and bristly eyebrows, the stomach that protrudes from the bottom of his vest like a barely hidden balloon. "A simple matter of paperwork," he tells the good people of Minnesota, "is all that stands between you and one of the children on this stage — strong, healthy, good for farm work and helping around the house. You have the chance to save a child from destitution, poverty, and I believe Mrs. Scatcherd would agree that it is not too great an exaggeration to add sin and depravity."

Mrs. Scatcherd nods.

"So you have the opportunity both to do a good deed and get something in return," he continues. "You will be expected to feed, clothe, and educate the child until the age of eighteen, and provide a religious education as well, of course, and it is our deepest hope that you will grow to feel not only fondness for your child, but to embrace him as your own.

"The child you select is yours for free," he adds, "on a ninety-day trial. At which point, if you so choose, you may send him back."

The girl beside me makes a low noise like a dog's whine and slips her hand into mine. It's as cold and damp as the back of a toad. "Don't worry, we'll be all right . . ." I begin, but she gives me a look of such desperation that my words trail off. As we watch people line up and begin to mount the steps to the stage, I feel like one of the cows in the agricultural show my granddad took me to in Kinvara.

In front of me now stands a young blond woman, slight and pale, and an earnest-looking man with a throbbing Adam's apple and wearing a felt hat. The woman steps forward. "May I?"

"Excuse me?" I say, not understanding.

She holds out her arms. Oh. She wants Carmine.

He looks at the woman before hiding his face in the crook of my neck. "He's shy," I tell her.

"Hello, little boy," she says. "What's your name?"

He refuses to lift his head. I jiggle him.

The woman turns to the man and says softly, "The eyes can be fixed, don't you think?" and he says, "I don't know. I would reckon so."

Another man and woman are watching us. She's heavyset, with a furrowed brow and a soiled apron, and he's got thin strips of hair across his bony head.

"What about that one?" the man says, pointing at me.

"Don't like the look of her," the woman says with a grimace.

"She don't like the look of you, neither," Dutchy says, and all of us turn toward him in surprise. The boy between us shrinks back.

"What'd you say?" The man goes over and plants himself in front of Dutchy.

"Your wife's got no call to talk like that." Dutchy's voice is low, but I can hear every word.

"You stay out of it," the man says, lifting Dutchy's chin with his index finger. "My wife can talk about you orphans any way she goddamn wants."

There's a rustling, a flash of black cape, and like a snake through the underbrush Mrs. Scatcherd is upon us. "What is the problem here?" Her voice is hushed and forceful.

"This boy talked back to my husband," the wife says.

109

Mrs. Scatcherd looks at Dutchy and then at the couple. "Hans is — spirited," she says. "He doesn't always think before he speaks. I'm sorry, I didn't catch your name —"

"Barney McCallum. And this here's my wife, Eva."

Mrs. Scatcherd nods. "What do you have to say to Mr. McCallum, then, Hans?"

Dutchy looks down at his feet. I know what he wants to say. I think we all do. "Apologize," he mumbles without looking up.

While this is unfolding, the slim blond woman in front of me has been stroking Carmine's arm with her finger, and now, still nestled against me, he is looking through his lashes at her. "Sweet thing, aren't you?" She pokes him gently in his soft middle, and he gives her a tentative smile.

The woman looks at her husband. "I think he's the one."

I can feel Mrs. Scatcherd's eyes on us. "Nice lady," I whisper in Carmine's ear. "She wants to be your mam."

"Mam," he says, his warm breath on my face. His eyes are round and shining.

"His name is Carmine." Reaching up, I pry his monkey arms from around my neck,

110

clasping them in my hand.

The woman smells of roses — like the lush white blooms along the lane at my gram's house. She is as finely boned as a bird. She puts her hand on Carmine's back and he clings to me tighter. "It's all right," I start, but the words crumble in my mouth.

"No, no, *no,*" Carmine says. I think I may faint.

"Do you need a girl to help with him?" I blurt. "I could" — I think wildly, trying to remember what I am good at — "mend clothes. And cook."

The woman gives me a pitying look. "Oh, child," she says. "I am sorry. We can't afford two. We just — we came here for a baby. I'm sure you'll find . . ." Her voice trails off. "We just want a baby to complete our family."

I push back tears. Carmine feels the change in me and starts to whimper. "You must go to your new mam," I tell him and peel him off me.

The woman takes him awkwardly, jostling him in her arms. She isn't used to holding a baby. I reach out and tuck his leg under her arm. "Thank you for taking care of him," she says.

Mrs. Scatcherd herds the three of them off the stage toward a table covered with forms, Carmine's dark head on the woman's shoulder.

One by one, the children around me are chosen. The boy beside me wanders away with a short, round woman who tells him it's high time she has a man around the house. The dog-whine girl goes off with a stylish couple in hats. Dutchy and I are standing together talking quietly when a man approaches with skin as tanned and scuffed as old shoe leather, trailed by a sour-looking woman. The man stands in front of us for a minute, then reaches out and squeezes Dutchy's arm.

"What're you doing?" Dutchy says with surprise.

"Open your mouth."

I can see that Dutchy wants to haul off and hit him, but Mr. Curran is watching us closely, and he doesn't dare. The man sticks a dirty-looking finger in his mouth. Dutchy jerks his head around.

"Ever work as a hay baler?" the man asks.

Dutchy stares straight ahead.

"You hear me?"

"No."

"No, you didn't hear me?"

Dutchy looks at him. "Never worked as a hay baler. Don't even know what that is."

112

"Whaddaya think?" the man says to the woman. "He's a tough one, but we could use a kid this size."

"I reckon he'll fall in line." Stepping up to Dutchy, she says, "We break horses. Boys aren't that different."

"Let's load 'im up," the man says. "We got a drive ahead of us."

"You're all set?" Mr. Curran says, coming toward us with a nervous laugh.

"Yep. This is the one."

"Well, all right! If you'll just follow me over here, we can sign those papers."

It's just as Dutchy predicted. Coarse country people looking for a field hand. They don't even walk him down off the stage.

"Maybe it won't be that bad," I whisper.

"If he lays a hand on me . . ."

"You can get placed somewhere else."

"I'm labor," he says. "That's what I am."

"They have to send you to school."

He laughs. "And what'll happen if they don't?"

"You'll make them send you. And then, in a few years —"

"I'll come and find you," he says.

I have to fight to control my voice. "Nobody wants me. I have to get back on the train."

"Hey, boy! Stop yer dallying," the man calls, clapping his hands so loudly that everyone turns to look.

Dutchy walks across the stage and down the steps. Mr. Curran pumps the man's hand, pats him on the shoulder. Mrs. Scatcherd escorts the couple out the door, Dutchy trailing behind. In the doorway he turns and finds my face. And then he's gone.

It's hard to believe, but it's not yet noon. Two hours have passed since we pulled into the station. There are about ten adults milling around, and a half-dozen train riders left — me, a few sickly looking teenage boys, and some homely children — undernourished, walleyed, beetle browed. It's obvious why we weren't chosen.

Mrs. Scatcherd mounts the stage. "All right, children. The journey continues," she says. "It is impossible to know what combination of factors makes a child suitable for a certain family, but to be perfectly frank, you would not want to be with a family that doesn't welcome you wholeheartedly. So — though this may not seem like the desired outcome, I tell you that it is for the best. And if, after several more attempts, it becomes clear that . . ." Her voice wavers. "For now, let's just worry about our next destination. The good people of Albans, Minnesota, are waiting."

ALBANS, MINNESOTA, 1929

It's early afternoon when we arrive in Albans, which, I can see as we pull up to the depot, is barely a town at all. The mayor is standing on the open-air platform, and as soon as we disembark we are herded in a ragtag line to a Grange Hall a block from the station. The brilliant blue of the morning sky has faded, as if left out too long in the sun. The air has cooled. I am no longer nervous or worried. I just want to get this over with.

There are fewer people here, about fifty, but they fill the small brick building. There's no stage, so we walk to the front and turn to face the crowd. Mr. Curran gives a less florid version of the speech he gave in Minneapolis and people begin to inch forward. They generally appear both poorer and kindlier; the women are wearing country dresses and the men seem uncomfortable in their Sunday clothes.

Expecting nothing makes the whole experience easier to bear. I fully believe that I will end up on the train again, to be unloaded at the next town, paraded with the remaining children, and shuttled back on the train. Those of us who aren't chosen will likely return to New York to grow up in an orphanage. And maybe that wouldn't be so bad. At least I know what to expect — hard mattresses, rough sheets, strict matrons. But also friendship with other girls, three meals a day, school. I can go back to that life. I don't need to find a family here, and perhaps it will be for the best if I don't.

As I am thinking this, I become aware of a woman looking at me closely. She is about my mother's age, with wavy brown hair cropped close to her head and plain, strong features. She wears a high-necked white blouse with vertical pleats, a dark paisley scarf, and a plain gray skirt. Heavy black shoes are on her feet. A large oval locket hangs on a gold chain around her neck. The man standing behind her is stout and florid, with shaggy auburn hair. The buttons of his waistcoat strain to confine his drumlike girth.

The woman comes close to me. "What's your name?"

"Niamh."

"Eve?"

"No, Niamh. It's Irish," I say.

"How do you spell it?"

"N-I-A-M-H."

She looks back at the man, who breaks into a grin. "Fresh off the boat," he says. "Ain't that right, missy?"

"Well, not —" I begin, but the man interrupts me.

"Where you from?"

"County Galway."

"Ah, right." He nods, and my heart jumps. He knows it!

"My people're from County Cork. Came over long ago, during the famine."

These two are a peculiar pair — she circumspect and reserved, he bouncing on his toes, humming with energy.

"The name would have to change," she says to her husband.

"Whatever you want, m'dear."

She cocks her head at me. "How old are you?"

"Nine, ma'am."

"Can you sew?"

I nod.

"Do you know how to cross-stitch? Hem? Can you do backstitching by hand?"

"Fairly well." I learned stitches sitting in our apartment on Elizabeth Street, helping

Mam when she took in extra work darning and mending and the occasional full dress from a bolt of cloth. Much of her work came from the sisters Rosenblum downstairs, who did fine finish work and gladly passed along to Mam the more tedious tasks. I stood beside her as she traced patterns in chalk on chambray and calico, and I learned to make the wide simple chain stitches to guide the emerging shape of the garment.

"Who taught you?"

"My mam."

"Where is she now?"

"Passed away."

"And your father?"

"I'm an orphan." My words hang in the air.

The woman nods at the man, who puts his hand on her back and guides her to the side of the room. I watch as they talk. He shakes his floppy head and rubs his belly. She touches the bodice of her blouse with a flat hand, gestures toward me. He stoops, hands on his belt, and bends close to whisper in her ear. She looks me up and down. Then they come back over.

"I am Mrs. Byrne," she says. "My husband works as a women's clothier, and we employ several local women to make garments to order. We are looking for a girl who is good with a needle."

This is so different from what I was expecting that I don't know what to say.

"I will be honest with you. We do not have any children and have no interest in being surrogate parents. But if you are respectful and hardworking, you will be treated fairly."

I nod.

The woman smiles, her features shifting. For the first time, she seems almost friendly. "Good." She shakes my hand. "We'll sign the papers, then."

The hovering Mr. Curran descends, and we are led to the table where the necessary forms are signed and dated.

"I think you'll find that Niamh is mature for her years," Mrs. Scatcherd tells them. "If she is brought up in a strict, God-fearing household, there is no reason to believe she can't become a woman of substance." Taking me aside, she whispers, "You are lucky to have found a home. Do not disappoint me, or the Society. I don't know if you'll get another chance."

Mr. Byrne hoists my brown suitcase onto his shoulder. I follow him and his wife out of the Grange Hall, down the quiet street, and around the corner to where their black Model A is parked in front of a modest storefront with hand-lettered signs advertising sales: NORWEGIAN SARDINES IN OIL 15 CENTS, ROUND STEAK, 36 CENTS/LB. Wind rustles through the tall sparse trees that line the road. After laying my suitcase flat in the trunk, Mr. Byrne opens the rear door for me. The interior of the car is black, the leather seats cool and slippery. I feel very small in the backseat. The Byrnes take their places in the front and don't glance back.

Mr. Byrne reaches over and touches his wife's shoulder, and she smiles at him. With a loud rumble the car springs to life and we set off. The Byrnes are having an animated conversation in the front seat, but I can't hear a word.

Several minutes later, Mr. Byrne pulls into the driveway of a modest beige stucco house with brown trim. As soon as he turns off the car, Mrs. Byrne looks back at me and says, "We've decided on Dorothy."

"You like that name?" Mr. Byrne asks.

"For goodness' sake, Raymond, it doesn't matter what she thinks," Mrs. Byrne snaps as she opens her car door. "Dorothy is our choice, and Dorothy she will be."

I turn the name over in my mind: *Dorothy.* All right. I'm Dorothy now.

The stucco is chipped and paint is peeling off the trim. But the windows are sparkling clean, and the lawn is short and neat. A domed planter of rust-colored mums sits on either side of the steps.

"One of your tasks will be to sweep the front porch, steps, and walkway every day until the snow comes. Rain or shine," Mrs. Byrne says as I follow her to the front door. "You will find the dustpan and broom inside the hall closet on the left." She turns around to face me, and I nearly bump into her. "Are you paying attention? I don't like to repeat myself."

"Yes, Mrs. Byrne."

"Call me ma'am. Ma'am will suffice."

"Yes, ma'am."

The small foyer is gloomy and dark. Shadows from the white crocheted curtains on every window cast lacy shapes on the floor. To the left, through a slightly open door, I glimpse the red-flocked wallpaper and mahogany table and chairs of a dining room. Mrs. Byrne pushes a button on the wall and the overhead light springs on as Mr. Byrne comes through the front door, having retrieved my bag from the truck. "Ready?" she says. Mrs. Byrne opens the door to the right onto a room that, to my surprise, is full of people.

ALBANS, MINNESOTA, 1929

Two women in white blouses sit in front of black sewing machines with the word *Singer* spelled out in gold along the body, pumping one foot on the iron lattice step that moves the needle up and down. They don't look up as we enter, just keep watching the needle, tucking the thread under the foot and pressing the fabric flat. A round young woman with frizzy brown hair kneels on the floor in front of a cloth mannequin, stitching tiny pearls onto a bodice. A gray-haired woman sits on a brown chair, perfectly erect, hemming a calico skirt. And a girl who appears only a few years older than me is cutting a pattern out of thin paper on a table. On the wall above her head is a framed needlepoint that says, in tiny black-and-yellow cross-stitching, KEEP ME BUSY AS A BEE.

"Fanny, can you stop a minute?" Mrs. Byrne says, touching the gray-haired woman on the shoulder. "Tell the others."

"Break," the old woman says. They all look up, but the only one who changes position is the girl, who puts down her shears.

Mrs. Byrne looks around the room, leading with her chin. "As you know, we have needed extra help for quite some time, and I am pleased to report that we have found it. This is Dorothy." She lifts her hand in my direction. "Dorothy, say hello to Bernice" — the woman with frizzy hair — "Joan and Sally" — the women at the Singers — "Fanny" — the only one who smiles at me — "and Mary. Mary," she says to the young girl, "you will help Dorothy get acquainted with her surroundings. She can do some of your scut work and free you up for other things. And, Fanny, you will oversee. As always."

"Yes, ma'am," Fanny says.

Mary's mouth puckers, and she gives me a hard look.

"Well, then," Mrs. Byrne says. "Let's get back to work. Dorothy, your suitcase is in the foyer. We'll discuss sleeping arrangements at supper." She turns to leave, then adds, "We keep strict hours for mealtimes. Breakfast at eight, lunch at twelve, supper at six. There is no snacking between meals. Self-discipline is one of the most important

124

qualities a young lady can possess."

When Mrs. Byrne leaves the room, Mary jerks her head at me and says, "Come on, hurry up. You think I got all day?" Obediently I go over and stand behind her. "What do you know about stitching?"

"I used to help my mam with the mending."

"Have you ever used a sewing machine?"

"No."

She frowns. "Does Mrs. Byrne know that?"

"She didn't ask."

Mary sighs, clearly annoyed. "I didn't expect to have to teach the basics."

"I'm a fast learner."

"I hope so." Mary holds up a flimsy sheet of tissue paper. "This is a pattern. Ever heard of it before?"

I nod and Mary continues, describing the various features of the work I'll be doing. The next few hours are spent doing tasks no one else wants to do — snipping stitches, basting, sweeping up, collecting pins and putting them in pincushions. I keep pricking myself and have to be careful not to get blood on the cloth.

Throughout the afternoon the women pass the time with small talk and occasional humming. But mostly they are quiet. After a while I say, "Excuse me, I need to use the lavatory. Can you tell me where it is?"

Fanny looks up. "Reckon I'll take her. My fingers need a rest." Getting up with some difficulty, she motions toward the door. I follow her down the hall into a spare and spotless kitchen and out the back door. "This is our privy. Don't ever let Mrs. Byrne catch you using the one in the house." She pronounces *catch* "kitch."

At the back of the yard, tufted with grass like sparse hair on a balding head, is a weathered gray shed with a slit cut out of the door. Fanny nods toward it. "I'll wait."

"You don't have to."

"The longer you're in there, the longer my fingers get a break."

The shed is drafty, and I can see a sliver of daylight through the slit. A black toilet seat, worn through to wood in some places, is set in the middle of a rough-hewn bench. Strips of newspaper hang on a roll on the wall. I remember the privy behind our cottage in Kinvara, so the smell doesn't shock me, though the seat is cold. What will it be like out here in a snow-storm? Like this, I suppose, only worse.

When I'm finished, I open the door, pulling down my dress.

"You're pitiful thin," Fanny says. "I'll bet

126

you're hungry." *Hongry.*

She's right. My stomach feels like a cavern. "A little," I admit.

Fanny's face is creased and puckered, but her eyes are bright. I can't tell if she's seventy or a hundred. She's wearing a pretty purple flowered dress with a gathered bodice, and I wonder if she made it herself.

"Mrs. Byrne don't give us much for lunch, but it's prolly more'n you had." She reaches into the side pocket of her dress and pulls out a small shiny apple. "I always save something for later, case I need it. She locks up the refrigerator between meals."

"No," I say.

"Oh yes she does. Says she don't want us rooting around in there without her permission. But I usually manage to save something." She hands me the apple.

"I can't —"

"Go ahead. You got to learn to take what people are willing to give."

The apple smells so fresh and sweet it makes my mouth water.

"You best eat it here, before we go back in." Fanny looks at the door to the house, then glances up at the second-floor windows. "Whyn't you take it back in the privy."

As unappetizing as this sounds, I am so hungry I don't care. I step back inside the

127

little shed and devour the apple down to the core. Juice runs down my chin, and I wipe it with the back of my hand. My da used to eat the apple core and all — "where all the nutrients are. It's plain ignorant to throw it out," he'd say. But to me the hard cartilage is like eating the bones of a fish.

When I open the door, Fanny strokes her chin. I look at her, puzzled. "Evidence," she says, and I wipe my sticky jaw.

Mary scowls when I step back into the sewing room. She shoves a pile of cloth at me and says, "Pin these." I spend the next hour pinning edge to edge as carefully as I can, but each time I put a completed one down she grabs it, inspects it hastily, and flings it back at me. "It's a sloppy mess. Do it again."

"But —"

"Don't argue. You should be ashamed of this work."

The other women look up and silently return to their sewing.

I pull out the pins with shaking hands. Then I slowly repin the cloth, measuring an inch apart with a metal sewing gauge. On the mantelpiece an ornate gold clock with a domed glass front ticks loudly. I hold my breath as Mary inspects my work. "This has some irregularity," she says finally, holding it up.

"What's wrong with it?"

"It's uneven." She won't look me in the eye. "Maybe you're just . . ." Her voice trails off.

"What?"

"Maybe you aren't cut out for this kind of work."

My bottom lip trembles, and I press my lips together hard. I keep thinking someone — maybe Fanny? — will step in, but no one does. "I learned how to sew from my mother."

"You're not mending a rip in your father's trousers. People are paying good money —"

"I know how to sew," I blurt. "Maybe better than you."

Mary gapes at me. "You . . . you are *nothing,*" she sputters. "Don't even have a — a family!"

My ears are buzzing. The only thing I can think to say is, "And you don't have any manners." I stand up and leave the room, pulling the door shut behind me. In the dark hall, I contemplate my options. I could run away, but where would I go?

After a moment the door opens, and Fanny slips out. "Goodness, child," she whispers. "Why you have to be so mouthy?"

"That girl is mean. What'd I do to her?"

Fanny puts a hand on my arm. Her fingers are rough, calloused. "It don't do you any good to squabble."

"But my pins were straight."

She sighs. "Mary's only hurting herself by making you do the work over. She's paid by the piece, so I don't know what she thinks she's doing. But you — well, let me ask you this. Are they paying you?"

"Paying me?"

"Fanny!" a voice rings out above us. We look up to see Mrs. Byrne at the top of the stairs. Her face is flushed. "What on earth is going on?" I can't tell if she heard what we were saying.

"Nothing to concern you, ma'am," Fanny says quickly. "A little spat between the girls is all."

"Over what?"

"Honest, ma'am, I don't think you want to know."

"Oh, but I do."

Fanny gazes at me and shakes her head. "Well . . . You seen that boy who delivers the afternoon paper? They got to arguing over whether he has a sweetheart. You know how girls can be."

I exhale slowly.

"The foolishness, Fanny," Mrs. Byrne says.

"I didn't want to tell you."

"You two get back in there. Dorothy, I don't want to hear another word of this nonsense, you understand?"

"Yes, ma'am."

"There is work to be done."

"Yes, ma'am."

Fanny opens the door and walks ahead of me into the sewing room. Mary and I don't speak for the rest of the afternoon.

That night at supper Mrs. Byrne serves chopped beef, potato salad stained pink by beets, and rubbery cabbage. Mr. Byrne chews noisily. I can hear every click of his jaw. I know to put my napkin in my lap — Gram taught me that. I know how to use a knife and fork. Though the beef tastes as dry and flavorless as cardboard, I'm so ravenous that it's all I can do not to shove it into my mouth. Small, ladylike bites, Gram said.

After a few minutes, Mrs. Byrne puts down her fork and says, "Dorothy, it's time to discuss the rules of the house. As you already know, you are to use the privy in the back. Once a week, on Sunday evenings, I will draw a bath for you in the tub in the washroom off the kitchen. Sunday is also washday, which you'll be expected to help with. Bedtime is at nine P.M., with lights out. There's a pallet for you in the hall closet. You'll bring it out in the evenings and roll it up neatly in the morning, before the girls arrive at eight thirty."

"I'll be sleeping — in the hallway?" I ask with surprise.

"Mercy, you don't expect to sleep on the second floor with us, do you?" she says with a laugh. "Heaven forbid."

When dinner is over, Mr. Byrne announces that he is going for a stroll.

"And I have work to do," Mrs. Byrne says. "Dorothy, you will clean up the dishes. Pay careful attention to where things belong. The best way for you to learn our ways is to observe closely, and teach yourself. Where do we keep the wooden spoons? The juice glasses? It should be a fun game for you." She turns to leave. "You are not to disturb Mr. Byrne and me after dinner. You will put yourself to bed at the appropriate time and turn out your light." With a curt smile, she says, "We expect to have a positive experience with you. Don't do anything to threaten our trust."

I look around at the dishes piled in the sink, the strips of beet peel staining a wooden cutting board, a saucepan half full of translucent cabbage, a roasting pan charred and waxed with grease. Glancing at the door to be sure the Byrnes are gone, I spear a hunk of the flavorless cabbage on a fork and swallow it greedily, barely chewing. I eat the rest of the cabbage this way, listening for Mrs. Byrne's foot on the stairs.

As I wash the dishes I look out the window over the sink at the yard behind the house, murky now in the fading evening light; there are a few spidery trees, their thin trunks flayed into branches. By the time I've finished scrubbing the roasting pan, the sky is dark and the yard has faded from view. The clock above the stove says 7:30.

I pour myself a glass of water from the kitchen faucet and sit at the table. It feels too early to go to bed, but I don't know what else to do. I don't have a book to read, and I haven't seen any in the house. We didn't have many books in the apartment on Elizabeth Street, either, but the twins were always getting old papers from the newsies. In school it was poems I liked best — Wordsworth and Keats and Shelley. Our teacher made us memorize the words to "Ode on a Grecian Urn," and alone in the kitchen now I close my eyes and whisper *Thou still unravish'd bride of quietness, Thou foster-child of Silence and slow Time . . .* but

133

that's all I can remember.

I need to look on the bright side, as Gram always said. It's not so bad here. The house is austere, but not uncomfortable. The light above the kitchen table is warm and cheery. The Byrnes don't want to treat me like a child, but I'm not so sure I want to be treated like one. Work that keeps my hands and mind busy is probably just what I need. And soon I will go to school.

I think of my own home on Elizabeth Street — so different, but truthfully no better than this. Mam in bed in midafternoon, in the sweltering heat, lying in her room past dark, with the boys whining for food and Maisie sobbing and me thinking I'll go mad with the heat and the hunger and the noise. Da up and gone — at work, he said, though the money he brought home was less each week, and he'd stumble in after midnight reeking of hops. We'd hear him tramping up the stairs, belting out the Irish national anthem — "We're children of a fighting race, / That never yet has known disgrace, / And as we march, the foe to face, / We'll chant a soldier's song" — then bursting into the apartment, to Mam's shushing and scolding. He'd stand silhouetted in the grainy light of the bedroom, and though all of us were supposed to be asleep, and pretended to be, we were rapt, awed by his cheer and bravado.

In the hall closet I find my suitcase and a pile of bedding. I unroll a horsehair pallet and place a thin yellowed pillow at the top. There's a white sheet, which I spread on the mattress and tuck around the edges, and a moth-eaten quilt.

Before going to bed I open the back door and make my way to the privy. The light from the kitchen window casts a dull glow for about five feet, and then it's dark.

The grass is brittle underfoot. I know my way, but it's different at night, the outline of the shed barely visible ahead. I look up into the starless sky. My heart pounds. This silent blackness scares me more than night-time in the city, with its noise and light.

I open the latch and go inside the shed. Afterward, shaking, I pull my knickers up and flee, the door knocking behind me as I run across the yard and up the three steps to the kitchen. I lock the door as instructed and lean against it, panting. And then I notice the padlock on the refrigerator. When did that happen? Mr. or Mrs. Byrne must have come downstairs while I was outside.

Spruce Harbor, Maine, 2011

Sometime in the second week it becomes clear to Molly that "cleaning out the attic" means taking things out, fretting over them for a few minutes, and putting them back where they were, in a slightly neater stack. Out of the two dozen boxes she and Vivian have been through so far, only a short pile of musty books and some yellowed linen have been deemed too ruined to keep.

"I don't think I'm helping you much," Molly says.

"Well, that's true," Vivian says. "But I'm helping you, aren't I?"

"So you came up with a fake project as a favor to me? Or, I suppose, Terry?" Molly says, playing along.

"Doing my civic duty."

"You're very noble."

Sitting on the floor of the attic, Molly lifts the pieces out of a cedar chest one by one, Vivian perched on a wooden chair beside her. Brown wool gloves. A green velvet dress with a wide ribbon sash. An off-white cardigan. *Anne of Green Gables.*

"Hand me that book," Vivian says. She takes the hardbound green volume, with gold lettering and a line drawing of a girl with abundant red hair in a chignon on the front, and opens it. "Ah, yes, I remember," she says. "I was almost exactly the heroine's age when I read this for the first time. A teacher gave it to me — my favorite teacher. You know, Miss Larsen." She leafs through the book slowly, stopping at a page here and there. "Anne talks so much, doesn't she? I was much shyer than that." She looks up. "What about you?"

"Sorry, I haven't read it," Molly says.

"No, no. I mean, were you shy as a girl? What am I saying, you're still a girl. But I mean when you were young?"

"Not exactly shy. I was — quiet."

"Circumspect," Vivian says. "Watchful."

Molly turns these words over in her mind. Circumspect? Watchful? Is she? There was a time after her father died and after she was taken away, or her mother was taken away — it's hard to know which came first, or if they happened at the same time — that she stopped talking altogether. Everyone was talking at and about her, but nobody asked her opinion, or listened when she gave it. So she stopped trying. It was during this period that she would wake in the night and get out of bed to go to her parents' room, only to realize, standing in the hall, that she had no parents.

"Well, you're not exactly effervescent now, are you?" Vivian says. "But I saw you outside earlier when Jack dropped you off, and your face was" — Vivian lifts her knobby hands, splaying her fingers — "all lit up. You were talking up a storm."

"Were you spying on me?"

"Of course! How else am I going to find out anything about you?"

Molly has been pulling things out of the chest and putting them in piles — clothes, books, knickknacks wrapped in old newspaper. But now she sits back on her heels and looks at Vivian. "You are funny," she says.

"I've been called many things in my life, my dear, but I'm not sure anyone has ever called me funny."

"I'll bet they have."

"Behind my back, perhaps." Vivian closes the book. "You strike me as a reader. Am I right?"

Molly shrugs. The reading part of her feels

private, between her and the characters in a book.

"So what's your favorite novel?"

"I dunno. I don't have one."

"Oh, I think you probably do. You're the type."

"What's that supposed to mean?"

Vivian spreads a hand across her chest, her pink-tinged fingernails as delicate seeming as a baby's. "I can tell that you feel things. Deeply."

Molly makes a face.

Vivian presses the book into Molly's hand. "No doubt you'll find this old-fashioned and sentimental, but I want you to have it."

"You're giving it to me?"

"Why not?"

To her surprise Molly feels a lump in her throat. She swallows, pushing it down. How ridiculous — an old lady gives her a moldy book she has no use for, and she chokes up. She must be getting her period.

She fights to keep her expression neutral. "Well, thanks," she says non-chalantly. "But does this mean I have to read it?"

"Absolutely. There will be a quiz," Vivian says.

For a while they work in near silence, Molly holding up an item — a sky-blue cardigan with stained and yellowed flowers, a brown dress with several missing buttons, a periwinkle scarf and one matching mitten — and Vivian sighing, "I suppose there's no reason to keep that," then inevitably adding, "Let's put it in the 'maybe' pile." At one point, apropos of nothing, Vivian says, "So where is that mother of yours, anyway?"

Molly has gotten used to this kind of non sequitur. Vivian tends to pick up discussions they started a few days earlier right where they left off, as if it's perfectly natural to do so.

"Oh, who knows." She's just opened a box that, to her delight, looks easy to dispose of — dozens of dusty store ledgers from the 1940s and '50s. Surely Vivian has no reason to hang on to them. "These can go, don't you think?" she says, holding up a slim black book.

Vivian takes it from her and flips through it. "Well . . ." Her voice trails off. She looks up. "Have you looked for her?"

"No."

"Why not?"

Molly gives Vivian a sharp look. She's not used to people asking such blunt questions — asking any questions at all, really. The only other person who speaks this bluntly to her is Lori the social worker, and she already knows the details of her story. (And

140

anyway, Lori doesn't ask "why" questions. She's only interested in cause, effect, and a lecture.) But Molly can't snap at Vivian, who has, after all, given her a get-out-of-jail-free card. If "free" means fifty hours of pointed questions. She brushes the hair out of her eyes. "I haven't looked for her because I don't care."

"Really."

"Really."

"You're not curious at all."

"Nope."

"I'm not sure I believe that."

Molly shrugs.

"Hmm. Because actually, you seem kind of . . . angry."

"I'm not angry. I just don't care." Molly lifts a stack of ledgers out of the box and thumps it on the floor. "Can we recycle these?"

Vivian pats her hand. "I think maybe I'll hang on to this box," she says, as if she hasn't said that about everything they've gone through so far.

"She's all up in my business!" Molly says, burying her face in Jack's neck. They're in his Saturn, and she's straddling him in the pushed-back front seat.

Laughing, his stubble rough against her

141

cheek, he says, "What do you mean?" He slips his hands under her shirt and strokes her ribs with his fingers.

"That tickles," she says, squirming.

"I like it when you move like that."

She kisses his neck, the dark patch on his chin, the corner of his lip, a thick eyebrow, and he pulls her closer, running his hands up her sides and under her small breasts, cupping them.

"I don't know a damn thing about her life — not that I care! But she expects me to tell her everything about mine."

"Oh, come on, what can it hurt? If she knows a little more about you, maybe she's nicer to you. Maybe the hours go a little faster. She's probably lonely. Just wants someone to talk to."

Molly screws up her face.

"Try a little tenderness," Jack croons.

She sighs. "I don't need to entertain her with stories about my shitty life. We can't all be rich as hell and live in a mansion."

He kisses her shoulder. "So turn it around. Ask her questions."

"Do I care?" She sighs, tracing her finger along his ear until he turns his head and bites it, takes it in his mouth.

He reaches down and grabs the lever, and the seat falls back with a jolt. Molly lands sloppily on top of him and they both start to laugh. Sliding over to make room for her in the bucket seat, Jack says, "Just do what it takes to get those hours over with, right?" Turning sideways, he runs his fingers along the waistband of her black leggings. "If you can't stick it out, I might have to figure out a way to go to juvie with you. And that would suck for both of us."

"Doesn't sound so bad to me."

Pushing her waistband down over her hip, he says, "That's what I'm looking for." He traces the inky black lines of the turtle on her hip. Its shell is a pointy oval, bisected at an angle, like a shield with a daisy on one side and a tribal flourish on the other, its flippers extending in pointy arcs. "What's this little guy's name again?"

"It doesn't have a name."

Leaning down and kissing her hip, he says, "I'm going to call him Carlos."

"Why?"

"He looks like a Carlos. Right? See his little head? He's kind of wagging it, like 'What's up?' Hey, Carlos," he says in a Dominican-accented falsetto, tapping the turtle with his index finger. "What's happening, man?"

"It's not a Carlos. It's an Indian symbol,"

she says, a little irritated, pushing his hand away.

"Oh, come on, admit it — you were drunk and got this random-ass turtle. It could just as easily have been a heart dripping blood or some fake Chinese words."

"That's not true! Turtles mean something very specific in my culture."

"Oh yeah, warrior princess?" he says. "Like what?"

"Turtles carry their homes on their backs." Running her finger over the tattoo, she tells him what her dad told her: "They're exposed and hidden at the same time. They're a symbol of strength and perseverance."

"That's very deep."

"You know why? Because I'm very deep."

"Oh yeah?"

"Yeah," she says, kissing him on the mouth. "Actually, I did it because when we lived on Indian Island we had this turtle named Shelly."

"Hah, Shelly. I get it."

"Yup. Anyway, I don't know what happened to it."

Jack curls his hand around her hip bone. "I'm sure it's fine," he says. "Don't turtles live, like, a hundred years?"

"Not in a tank with no one to feed them they don't."

He doesn't say anything, just puts his arm around her shoulder and kisses her hair.

She settles in beside him on the bucket seat. The windshield is fogged and the night is dark, and in Jack's hard-domed little Saturn she feels co-cooned, protected. Yeah, that's right. Like a turtle in a shell.

SPRUCE HARBOR, MAINE, 2011

No one comes to the door when Molly rings the buzzer. The house is quiet. She looks at her phone: 9:45 A.M. It's a teacher enrichment day and there's no school, so she figured, why not knock out some hours?

Molly rubs her arms and tries to decide what to do. It's an unseasonably cool and misty morning, and she forgot to bring a sweater. She took the Island Explorer, the free bus that makes a continuous loop of the island, and got off at the closest stop to Vivian's, about a ten-minute walk. If no one's home, she'll have to go back to the stop and wait for the next bus, which could take a while. But despite the goose bumps, Molly has always liked days like this. The stark gray sky and bare tree limbs feel more suited to her than the uncomplicated promise of sunny spring days.

In the little notebook she carries around, Molly has carefully recorded her time: four hours one day, two the next. Twenty-three so far. She made an Excel spreadsheet on her laptop that lays it all out. Jack would laugh if he knew, but she's been in the system long enough to understand that it all comes down to documentation. Get your papers in order, with the right signatures and record keeping, and the charges will be dropped, money released, whatever. If you're disorganized, you risk losing everything.

Molly figures she can kill at least five hours today. That'll be twenty-eight, and she'll be more than half finished.

She rings the bell again, cups her hands against the glass to peer into the dim hallway. Trying the doorknob, she finds that it turns and the door opens.

"Hello?" she says as she steps inside, and, when she gets no response, tries again, a bit louder, as she walks down the hall.

Yesterday, before she left, Molly told Vivian that she'd be coming early today, but she hadn't given a time. Now, standing in the living room with the shades drawn, she wonders if she should leave. The old house is full of noises. Its pine floors creak, windowpanes rattle, flies buzz near the ceiling, curtains flap. Without the distraction of human voices, Molly imagines she can hear

147

sounds in other rooms: bedsprings groaning, faucets dripping, fluorescent lights humming, pull chains rattling.

She takes a moment to look around — at the ornate mantelpiece above the fireplace, the decorated oak moldings and brass chandelier. Out of the four large windows facing the water she can see the sine curve of the coastline, the serrated firs in the distance, the glittery amethyst sea. The room smells of old books and last night's fire and, faintly, something savory from the kitchen — it's Friday; Terry must be cooking for the weekend.

Molly is gazing at the old hardcovers on the tall bookshelves when the door to the kitchen opens and Terry bustles in.

Molly turns. "Hi there."

"Ack!" Terry shrieks, clutching the rag she's holding to her chest. "You scared the hell out of me! What are you doing here?"

"Umm, well," Molly stammers, beginning to wonder the same thing, "I rang the buzzer a few times and then I just let myself in."

"Vivian knew you were coming?"

Did she? "I'm not sure that we settled on an exact —"

Terry narrows her eyes and frowns. "You can't just show up when you feel like it.

148

She's not available any old time."

"I know," Molly says, her face warming. "I'm sorry."

"Vivian would never have agreed to start this early. She has a routine. Gets up at eight or nine, comes downstairs at ten."

"I thought old people got up early," Molly mumbles.

"Not all old people." Terry puts her hands on her hips. "But that's not the point. You broke in."

"Well, I didn't —"

Sighing, Terry says, "Jack may have told you I wasn't crazy about this idea. About you doing your hours this way."

Molly nods. Here comes the lecture.

"He went out on a limb for you, don't ask me why."

"I know, and I appreciate it." Molly is aware that it's when she's defensive that she gets in trouble. But she can't resist saying, "And I hope I'm proving worthy of that trust."

"Not by showing up unannounced like this, you're not."

All right, she deserved that. What was it the teacher in her Legal Issues class said the other day? Never bring up a point you don't have an answer for.

"And another thing," Terry continues. "I

149

was in the attic this morning. I can't tell what you're doing up there."

Molly bounces on the balls of her feet, pissed that she's being called out for this thing she can't control and even more pissed at herself for not convincing Vivian to get rid of things. Of course it looks to Terry like Molly is just twiddling her thumbs, letting the time slide like a government worker punching a clock.

"Vivian doesn't want to get rid of anything," she says. "I'm cleaning out the boxes and labeling them."

"Let me give you some advice," Terry says. "Vivian is torn between her heart" — and here she again holds the wadded-up rag to her heart — "and her head." As if Molly might not make the connection, she moves the rag to her head. "Letting go of her stuff is like saying good-bye to her life. And that's tough for anybody to do. So your job is to make her. Because I promise you this: I will not be happy if you spend fifty hours up there shuffling things around with nothing to show for it. I love Jack, but . . ." She shakes her head. "Honestly, enough is enough." At this point Terry seems to be talking to herself, or possibly to Jack, and there's little Molly can do but bite her lip and nod to show she gets it.

After Terry grudgingly allows that it might actually be a good idea to get going earlier today, and that if Vivian doesn't show up in half an hour maybe she'll go up and rouse her, she tells Molly to make herself at home; she has work to do. "You've got something to occupy yourself with, right?" she says before heading back to the kitchen.

The book Vivian gave Molly is in her backpack. She hasn't bothered to crack it yet, mainly because it seems like homework for a job that's already punishment, but also because she's rereading *Jane Eyre* for English class (ironically, the teacher, Mrs. Tate, handed out school-issued copies the week after Molly tried to pilfer it) and that book is huge. It's always a shock to the system to reenter it; just to read a chapter she finds she has to slow down her breathing and go into a trance, like a hibernating bear. All her classmates are complaining about it — Brontë's protracted digressions about human nature, the subplots about Jane's friends at Lowood School, the long-winded, "unrealistic" dialogue. "Why can't she just tell the freaking story?" Tyler Baldwin grumbled in class. "I fall asleep every time I start to read it. What's that called, narcolopsy?"

This complaint evinced a chorus of agreement, but Molly was silent. And Mrs. Tate — on alert, no doubt, for the slightest spark in the damp woodpile of her class — noticed.

"So what do *you* think, Molly?"

Molly shrugged, not wanting to appear overeager. "I like the book."

"What do you like about it?"

"I don't know. I just like it."

"What's your favorite part?"

Feeling the eyes of the class on her, Molly shrank a little in her chair. "I don't know."

"It's just a boring romance novel," Tyler said.

"No, it isn't," she blurted.

"Why not?" Mrs. Tate pressed.

"Because . . ." She thought for a moment. "Jane's kind of an outlaw. She's passionate and determined and says exactly what she thinks."

"Where do you get that? Because I'm definitely not feeling it," Tyler said.

"Okay, well — like this line," Molly said. Riffling through the book, she found the scene she was thinking of. " 'I assured him I was naturally hard — very flinty, and that he would often find me so; and that, moreover, I was determined to show him divers rugged points in my character . . . he should know fully what sort of a bargain he had

152

made, while there was yet time to rescind it.' "

Mrs. Tate raised her eyebrows and smiled. "Sounds like someone I know."

Now, sitting alone in a red wingback chair, waiting for Vivian to come down, Molly takes out *Anne of Green Gables*.

She opens to the first page:

Mrs. Rachel Lynde lived just where the Avonlea main road dipped down into a little hollow, fringed with alders and ladies' eardrops and traversed by a brook that had its source away back in the woods of the old Cuthbert place . . .

It's clearly a book intended for young girls, and at first Molly isn't sure she can relate. But as she reads she finds herself caught up in the story. The sun moves higher in the sky; she has to tilt the book out of the glare and then, after several minutes, switch to the other wingback so she doesn't have to squint.

After an hour or so, she hears the door to the hall open, and she looks up. Vivian comes into the room, glances around, focuses on Molly, and smiles, seemingly unsurprised to see her.

"Bright and early!" she says. "I like your

153

enthusiasm. Maybe I'll let you empty out a box today. Or two, if you're lucky."

ALBANS, MINNESOTA, 1929

On Monday morning I get up early and wash my face in the kitchen sink before Mr. and Mrs. Byrne are up, then braid my hair carefully and attach two ribbons I found in the scrap pile in the sewing room. I put on my cleanest dress and the pinafore, which I hung on a branch by the side of the house to dry after we did the washing on Sunday.

At breakfast — lumpy oats with no sugar — when I ask how to get to school and what time I'm expected to be there, Mrs. Byrne looks at her husband and then back at me. She pulls her dark paisley scarf tight around her shoulders. "Dorothy, Mr. Byrne and I feel that you are not ready for school."

The oats taste like congealed animal fat in my mouth. I look at Mr. Byrne, who is bending to tie his shoelaces. His frizzy curls flop over his forehead, hiding his face.

"What do you mean?" I ask. "The Children's Aid —"

Mrs. Byrne clasps her hands together and gives me a tight-lipped smile. "You are no longer a ward of the Children's Aid Society, are you? We are the ones to determine what's best for you now."

My heart skips. "But I'm supposed to go."

"We'll see how you progress over the next few weeks, but for now we think it best for you to take some time to adjust to your new home."

"I am — adjusted," I say, warmth rising to my cheeks. "I've done everything you've asked of me. If you're concerned I won't have time to do the sewing . . ."

Mrs. Byrne fixes me with a steady eye, and my voice falters. "School has been in session for more than a month," she says. "You are impossibly behind, with no chance of catching up this year. And Lord knows what your schooling was like in the slum."

My skin prickles. Even Mr. Byrne is startled by this. "Now, now, Lois," he says under his breath.

"I wasn't in a — *slum.*" I choke out the word. And then, because she hasn't asked, because neither of them has asked, I add, "I was in the fourth grade. My teacher was Miss Uhrig. I was in the Chorus, and we performed an operetta, 'Polished Pebbles.' "

They both look at me.

"I like school," I say.

Mrs. Byrne gets up and starts to stack our dishes. She takes my plate even though I haven't finished my toast. Her actions are jerky, and the silverware clanks against the china. She runs water in the sink and dumps the plates and utensils into it with a loud clatter. Then she turns around, wiping her hands on her apron. "You insolent girl. I don't want to hear another word. We are the ones who decide what's best for you. Is that clear?"

And that's the end of it. The subject of school doesn't come up again.

Several times a day Mrs. Byrne materializes in the sewing room like a phantom, but she never picks up a needle. Her duties, as far as I can see, consist of keeping track of orders, handing out assignments to Fanny, who then doles them out to us, and collecting the finished garments. She asks Fanny for progress reports, all the while scanning the room to be sure the rest of us are hard at work.

I am full of questions for the Byrnes that I'm afraid to ask. What is Mr. Byrne's business, exactly? What does he do with the clothes the women make? (I could say *we* make, but the work I do, basting and hemming, is like peeling potatoes and calling yourself a cook.) Where does Mrs. Byrne go all day, and what does she do with her time? I can hear her upstairs now and then, but it's impossible to know what she's up to.

Mrs. Byrne has many rules. She scolds me in front of the other girls for minor infractions and mistakes — not folding my bed linen as tightly as I should have or leaving the door to the kitchen ajar. All doors in the house are supposed to be shut at all times, unless you're entering or leaving. The way the house is closed off — the door to the sewing room, the doors to the kitchen and dining room, even the door at the top of the stairs — makes it a forbidding and mysterious place. At night, on my pallet in that dark hall at the foot of the stairs, rubbing my feet together for warmth, I am frightened. I've never been alone like this. Even at the Children's Aid Society, in my iron bed on the ward, I was surrounded by other girls.

I'm not allowed to help in the kitchen — I think Mrs. Byrne is afraid I might steal food. And, indeed, like Fanny, I have taken to slipping a slice of bread or an apple into my pocket. The food Mrs. Byrne makes is bland and unappealing — soft gray peas from a can, starchy boiled potatoes, watery stews — and there's never enough of it. I

158

can't tell if Mr. Byrne really doesn't notice how dreadful the food is, or whether he doesn't care — or if his mind is simply elsewhere.

When Mrs. Byrne isn't around, Mr. Byrne is friendly. He likes to talk with me about Ireland. His own family, he tells me, is from Sallybrook, near the east coast. His uncle and cousins were Republicans in the War of Independence; they fought with Michael Collins and were there at the Four Courts building in Dublin in April of 1922, when the Brits stormed the building and killed the insurgents, and they were there when Collins was assassinated a few months later, near Cork. Collins was the greatest hero Ireland ever had, don't you know?

Yes, I nod. I know. But I'm skeptical his cousins were there. My da used to say every Irishman you meet in America swears to have a relative who fought alongside Michael Collins.

My da loved Michael Collins. He sang all the revolutionary songs, usually loudly and out of tune, until Mam would tell him to be quiet, that the babies were sleeping. He told me lots of dramatic stories — about the Kilmainham jail in Dublin, for instance, where one of the leaders of the 1916 uprising, Joseph Plunkett, married his sweetheart Grace

Gifford in the tiny chapel just hours before being executed by firing squad. Fifteen were executed in all that day, even James Connolly, who was too ill to stand, so they strapped him to a chair and carried him out into the courtyard and riddled his body with bullets. "Riddled his body with bullets" — my da talked like that. Mam was always shushing him, but he waved her off. "It's important they know this," he said. "It's their history! We might be over here now, but by God, our people are over there."

Mam had her reasons for wanting to forget. It was the 1922 treaty, leading to the formation of the Free State, that pushed us out of Kinvara, she said. The Crown Forces, determined to crush the rebels, raided towns in County Galway and blew up railway lines. The economy was in ruins. Little work was to be had. My da couldn't find a job.

Well, it was that, she said, and the drink.

"You could be my daughter, you know," Mr. Byrne tells me. "Your name — Dorothy . . . we always said we'd give to our own child someday, but alas it didn't come to pass. And here you are, red hair and all."

I keep forgetting to answer to Dorothy. But in a way I'm glad to have a new identity. It makes it easier to let go of so much else.

I'm not the same Niamh who left her gram and aunties and uncles in Kinvara and came across the ocean on the *Agnes Pauline,* who lived with her family on Elizabeth Street. No, I am Dorothy now.

"Dorothy, we need to talk," Mrs. Byrne says at dinner one evening. I glance at Mr. Byrne, who is studiously buttering a baked potato.

"Mary says that you are not — how should I put this? — a particularly quick learner. She says that you seem — resistant? Defiant? She's not sure which."

"It's not true."

Mrs. Byrne's eyes blaze. "Listen closely. If it were up to me, I would contact the committee immediately and return you for a replacement. But Mr. Byrne convinced me to give you a second chance. However — if I hear one more complaint about your behavior or comportment, you will be returned."

She pauses and takes a sip of water. "I am tempted to attribute this behavior to your Irish blood. Yes, it is true that Mr. Byrne is Irish — indeed, that's why we gave you a chance at all — but I would also point out that Mr. Byrne did not, as he might have, marry an Irish girl, for good reason."

161

The next day Mrs. Byrne comes into the sewing room and says she needs me to go on an errand into the center of town, a mile's walk. "It's not complicated," she says testily when I ask for directions. "Weren't you paying attention when we drove you here?"

"I can go with her this first time, ma'am," Fanny says.

Mrs. Byrne does not look happy about this. "Don't you have work to do, Fanny?"

"I just finished this pile," Fanny says, placing a veined hand on a stack of ladies' skirts. "All hemmed and ironed. My fingers are sore."

"All right, then. This once," Mrs. Byrne says.

We walk slowly, on account of Fanny's hip, through the Byrnes' neighborhood of small houses on cramped lots. At the corner of Elm Street we turn left onto Center and cross Maple, Birch, and Spruce before turning right onto Main. Most of the houses seem fairly new and are variations of the same few designs. They're painted different colors, landscaped neatly with shrubs and bushes. Some front walkways go straight to the door, and others meander in a curvy path. As we get closer to town we pass multifamily dwellings and some outlying

162

businesses — a gas station, a corner shop, a nursery stocked with flowers the colors of autumn leaves: rust and gold and crimson.

"I can't imagine why you didn't memorize this route on the drive home," Fanny says. "My, girl, you are slow." I look at her sideways and she gives me a sly smile.

The general store on Main Street is dimly lit and very warm. It takes a moment for my eyes to adjust. When I look up, I see cured hams hanging from the ceiling and shelves and shelves of dry goods. Fanny and I pick up several packs of sewing needles, some pattern papers, and a bolt of cheese-cloth, and after she pays, Fanny takes a penny from the change she gets and slides it toward me across the counter. "Get yourself a stick of candy for the walk back."

The jars of hard candy sticks lined up on a shelf hold dazzling combinations of colors and flavors. After deliberating for a long mo-ment, I choose a swirl of pink watermelon and green apple.

I unwrap my candy stick and offer to break off a piece, but Fanny refuses it. "I don't have a sweet tooth anymore."

"I didn't know you could outgrow that."

"It's for you," she says.

On the way back we walk slowly. Neither of us, I think, is eager to get there. The hard, grooved candy stick is both sweet and sour, a jolt of flavor so intense I almost swoon. I suck it so that it tapers to a point, savoring each taste. "You'll have to get rid of that before we reach the house," Fanny says. She doesn't need to explain.

"Why does Mary hate me?" I ask when we're nearly there.

"Pish. She doesn't hate you, child. She's scared."

"Of what?"

"What do you think?"

I don't know. Why would Mary be scared of me?

"She's sure you're going to take her job," Fanny says. "Mrs. Byrne holds her money tight in her fist. Why would she pay Mary to do the work you can be trained to do for nothing?"

I try not to betray any emotion, but Fanny's words sting. "That's why they picked me."

She smiles kindly. "You must know that already. Any girl who can hold a needle and thread would've sufficed. Free labor is free labor." As we climb the steps to the house, she says, "You can't blame Mary for being afraid."

From then on, instead of worrying about Mary, I concentrate on the work. I focus on making my stitches identically sized and spaced. I carefully iron each garment until it's smooth and crisp. Each piece of clothing that moves from my basket to Mary's — or one of the other women's — gives me a feeling of accomplishment.

But my relationship with her doesn't improve. If anything, as my own work gets better, she becomes harsher and more exacting. I place a basted skirt in my basket and Mary snatches it, looks at it closely, rips the stitches out, and tosses it at me again.

The leaves turn from rose-tinged to candy-apple red to a dull brown, and I walk to the outhouse on a spongy, sweet-smelling carpet. One day Mrs. Byrne looks me up and down and asks if I have any other clothes. I've been alternating between the two dresses I came with, one blue-and-white checked and one gingham.

"No," I say.

"Well, then," she says, "you will make yourself some."

Later that afternoon she drives me to town, one foot hesitantly on the gas pedal and the other, at erratic intervals, on the brake. Proceeding forward in a jerky fashion we end up eventually in front of the general store.

"You may choose three different fabrics," she says. "Let's see — three yards each?" I nod. "The cloth must be sturdy and inexpensive — that's the only kind that makes sense for a . . ." She pauses. "A nine-year-old girl."

Mrs. Byrne leads me over to a section filled with bolts of fabric, directing me to the shelf with the cheaper ones. I choose a blue-and-gray checked cotton, a delicate green print, and a pink paisley. Mrs. Byrne nods at the first two choices and grimaces at the third. "Mercy, not with red hair." She pulls out a bolt of blue chambray.

"A modest bodice is what I'm thinking, with a minimum of frill. Simple and plain. A gathered skirt. You can wear that pinafore on top when you're working. Do you have more than one pinafore?"

When I shake my head, she says, "We have plenty of ticking fabric in the sewing room. You can make it from that. Do you have a coat? Or a sweater?"

"The nuns gave me a coat, but it's too small."

After the fabric is measured, cut, wrapped in brown paper, and tied with twine, I follow Mrs. Byrne down the street to a women's clothes shop. She heads straight for the sale rack at the back and finds a mustard-colored wool coat, several sizes too big for me, with shiny black buttons. When I put it on, she frowns. "Well, it's a good deal," she says. "And there's no sense in getting something you'll outgrow in a month. I think it's fine."

I hate the coat. It's not even very warm. But I'm afraid to object. Luckily, there's a large selection of sweaters on clearance, and I find a navy blue cable-knit and an off-white V-neck in my size. Mrs. Byrne adds a bulky, too-large corduroy skirt that's 70 percent off.

That evening, at dinner, I wear my new white sweater and skirt. "What's that thing around your neck?" Mrs. Byrne says, and I realize that she is talking about my necklace, which is usually hidden by my high-necked dresses. She leans closer to look.

"An Irish cross," I say.

"It's very odd-looking. What are those, hands? And why does the heart have a crown?" She sits back in her chair. "That looks sacrilegious to me."

I tell her the story of how my gram was given this necklace for her First Communion and passed it down to me before I came to America. "The hands clasped

167

together symbolize friendship. The heart is love. And the crown stands for loyalty," I explain.

She sniffs, refolds the napkin in her lap. "I still think it's odd. I have half a mind to make you take it off."

"Come now, Lois," Mr. Byrne says. "It's a trinket from home. No harm to it."

"Perhaps it's time to put away those old-country things."

"It's not bothering anyone, is it?"

I glance over at him, surprised that he's sticking up for me. He winks at me as if it's a game.

"It's bothering me," she says. "There's no reason this girl needs to tell the world far and wide that she's a Catholic."

Mr. Byrne laughs. "Look at her hair. There's no denying she's Irish, is there?"

"So unbecoming in a girl," Mrs. Byrne says under her breath.

Later Mr. Byrne tells me that his wife doesn't like Catholics in general, even though she married one. It helps that he never goes to church. "Works out well for the both of us," he says.

ALBANS, MINNESOTA, 1929–1930

When Mrs. Byrne appears in the sewing room one Tuesday afternoon at the end of October, it's clear that something is wrong. She looks haggard and stricken. Her cropped dark bob, usually in tight waves against her head, is sticking out all over. Bernice jumps up, but Mrs. Byrne waves her away.

"Girls," she says, holding her hand to her throat, "girls! I need to tell you something. The stock market crashed today. It's in free fall. And many lives are . . ." She stops to catch her breath.

"Ma'am, do you want to sit down?" Bernice says.

Mrs. Byrne ignores her. "People lost everything," she mutters, gripping the back of Mary's chair. Her eyes roam the room as if she is looking for something to focus on. "If we can't feed ourselves, we can hardly afford to employ you, now, can we?" Her

169

eyes fill with tears and she backs out of the room, shaking her head.

We hear the front door open and Mrs. Byrne clatter down the steps.

Bernice tells us all to get back to work, but Joan, one of the women at the Singers, stands up abruptly. "I have to get home to my husband. I have to know what's going on. What use is it to keep working if we won't be paid?"

"Leave if you must," Fanny says.

Joan is the only one who leaves, but the rest of us are jittery throughout the afternoon. It's hard to sew when your hands are shaking.

It's hard to tell exactly what's going on, but as the weeks pass we begin to catch glimmers. Mr. Byrne apparently invested quite a bit in the stock market, and the money is gone. The demand for new garments has slowed, and people have taken to mending their own clothes — it's one place they can easily cut corners.

Mrs. Byrne is even more scattered and absent. We've stopped eating dinner together. She takes her food upstairs, leaving a desiccated chicken leg or a bowl of cold brisket in a chunk of brown gelatinous fat on the counter, with strict instructions that

I wash my dish when I'm done. Thanksgiving is like any other day. I never celebrated it with my Irish family, so it doesn't bother me, but the girls mutter under their breath all day long: it's not Christian, it's not American to keep them from their families.

Maybe because the alternative is so bleak, I've grown to like the sewing room. I look forward to seeing the women every day — kind Fanny, simple-minded Bernice, and quiet Sally and Joan. (All except Mary, who can't seem to forgive me for being alive.) And I like the work. My fingers are getting strong and quick; a piece that used to take an hour or more I can do in minutes. I used to be afraid of new stitches and techniques, but now welcome each new challenge — pencil-sharp pleats, sequins, delicate lace.

The others can see that I'm improving, and they've started giving me more to do. Without ever saying it directly, Fanny has taken over Mary's job of supervising my work. "Be careful, dear," she says, running a light finger over my stitches. "Take the time to make them small and even. Remember, somebody will wear this, probably over and over until it's worn through. A lady wants to feel pretty, no matter how much money she has."

Ever since I arrived in Minnesota people have been warning me about the extreme cold that's on the way. I am beginning to feel it. Kinvara is rain soaked much of the year, and Irish winters are cold and wet. New York is gray and slushy and miserable for months. But neither place compares to this. Already we've had two big snowstorms. As the weather gets colder, my fingers are so stiff when I'm sewing that I have to stop and rub them so I can keep going. I notice that the other women are wearing fingerless gloves, and when I ask where they came from, they tell me they made them themselves.

I don't know how to knit. My mam never taught me. But I know I need to get a pair of gloves for my stiff, cold hands.

Several days before Christmas, Mrs. Byrne announces that Christmas Day, Wednesday, will be an unpaid holiday. She and Mr. Byrne will be gone for the day, visiting relatives out of town. She doesn't ask me to come along. At the end of our workday on Christmas Eve, Fanny slips me a small brown-wrapped parcel. "Open this later," she whispers. "Tell them you brought it from home." I put the packet in my pocket and wade through knee-deep snow to the privy, where I open it in the semidarkness, wind slicing through the cracks in the walls and the slit in the door. It's a pair of fingerless gloves knit from a dense navy blue yarn, and a thick pair of brown wool mittens. When I put on the mittens I find that Fanny lined them with heavy wool and reinforced the top of the thumb and other fingers with extra padding.

As with Dutchy and Carmine on the train, this little cluster of women has become a kind of family to me. Like an abandoned foal that nestles against cows in the barnyard, maybe I just need to feel the warmth of belonging. And if I'm not going to find that with the Byrnes, I will find it, however partial and illusory, with the women in the sewing room.

By January, I am losing so much weight that my new dresses, the ones I made myself, swim on my hips. Mr. Byrne comes and goes at odd hours, and I barely see him. We have less and less work. Fanny is teaching me how to knit, and sometimes the other girls bring in work of their own so they won't go crazy with idleness. The heat is turned off as soon as the workers leave at five. The lights go off at seven. I spend nights on my pallet wide-awake and shivering in the dark, listening to the howling of the seemingly endless storms that rage outside. I wonder about Dutchy — if he's sleeping in a barn with animals, eating only pig slops. I hope he's warm.

One day in early February, Mrs. Byrne enters the sewing room silently and unexpectedly. She seems to have stopped grooming. She's worn the same dress all week, and her bodice is soiled. Her hair is lank and greasy, and she has a sore on her lip.

She asks the Singer girl Sally to step out into the hall, and several minutes later Sally returns to the room with red-rimmed eyes. She picks up her belongings in silence.

A few weeks later Mrs. Byrne comes for Bernice. They go out into the hall, and then Bernice returns and gathers her things.

After that it's just Fanny and Mary and me.

It's a windy afternoon in late March when Mrs. Byrne slips into the room and asks for Mary. I feel sorry for Mary then — despite her meanness, despite everything. Slowly she picks up her belongings, puts on her hat and coat. She looks at Fanny and me and nods, and we nod back. "God bless you, child," Fanny says.

When Mary and Mrs. Byrne leave the room, Fanny and I watch the door, straining to hear the indistinct murmuring in the hall. Fanny says, "Lordy, I'm too old for this."

A week later, the doorbell rings. Fanny and I look at each other. This is strange. The doorbell never rings.

We hear Mrs. Byrne rustle down the stairs, undo the heavy locks, open the squeaky door. We hear her talking to a man in the hall.

The door to the sewing room opens, and I jump a little. In comes a heavyset man in a black felt hat and a gray suit. He has a black mustache and jowls like a basset hound.

"This the girl?" he asks, pointing a sausagey finger at me.

Mrs. Byrne nods.

The man takes off his hat and sets it on a small table by the door. Then he pulls a pair of eyeglasses out of the breast pocket of his overcoat and puts them on, perched partway down his bulbous nose. He takes a piece of folded paper out of another pocket and opens it with one hand. "Let's see. Niamh Power." He pronounces it "Nem." Peering over his glasses at Mrs. Byrne, he says, "You changed her name to Dorothy?"

"We thought the girl should have an American name." Mrs. Byrne makes a strangled sound that I interpret as a laugh.

"Not legally, of course," she adds.

"And you did not change her surname."

"Of course not."

"You weren't considering adoption?"

"Mercy, no."

He looks at me over his glasses, then back at the paper. The clock ticks loudly above the mantelpiece. The man folds the paper and puts it back in his pocket.

"Dorothy, I am Mr. Sorenson. I'm a local agent of the Children's Aid Society, and as such I oversee the placement of homeless train riders. Oftentimes the placements work out as they should, and everyone is content. But now and then, unfortunately" — he takes his glasses off and slips them back into his breast pocket — "things don't work out." He looks at Mrs. Byrne. She has, I notice, a jagged run in her beige stockings, and her eye makeup is smeared. "And we need to procure new accommodations." He clears his throat. "Do you understand what I'm saying?"

I nod, though I'm not sure I do.

"Good. There's a couple in Hemingford — well, on a farm outside of that town, actually — who've requested a girl about your age. A mother, father, and four children. Wilma and Gerald Grote."

I turn to Mrs. Byrne. She is gazing off

somewhere in the middle distance. Though she's never been particularly kind to me, her willingness to abandon me comes as a shock. "You don't want me anymore?"

Mr. Sorenson looks back and forth between us. "It's a complicated situation."

As we're talking, Mrs. Byrne drifts over to the window. She pulls aside the lace curtain and gazes out at the street, at the skim-milk sky.

"I'm sure you have heard this is a difficult time," Mr. Sorenson continues. "Not only for the Byrnes but for a lot of people. And — well, their business has been affected."

With a sudden movement, Mrs. Byrne drops the curtain and wheels around. "She eats too much!" she cries. "I have to padlock the refrigerator. It's never enough!" She puts her palms over her eyes and runs past us, out into the hallway and up the stairs, where she slams the door at the top.

We are silent for a moment, then Fanny says, "That woman ought to be ashamed. The girl is skin and bones." She adds, "They never even sent her to school."

Mr. Sorenson clears his throat. "Well," he says, "perhaps this will be for the best for all concerned." He fixes on me again. "The Grotes are good country people, from what I hear."

"Four children?" I say. "Why do they want another?"

"As I understand it — and I could be wrong; I haven't had the pleasure to meet them yet, this is all hearsay, you understand — but what I have gleaned is that Mrs. Grote is once again with child, and she is looking for a mother's helper."

I ponder this. I think of Carmine, of Maisie. Of the twins, sitting at our rickety table on Elizabeth Street waiting patiently for their apple mash. I imagine a white farmhouse with black shutters, a red barn in the back, a post-and-rail fence, chickens in a coop. Anything has to be better than a padlocked refrigerator and a pallet in the hall. "When do they want me?"

"I'm taking you there now."

Mr. Sorenson says he'll give me a few minutes to collect my things and goes out to his car. In the hall I pull my brown suitcase from the back of the closet. Fanny stands in the door of the sewing room and watches me pack. I fold up the three dresses I made, one of which, the blue chambray, I haven't finished, plus my other dress from the Children's Aid. I add the two new sweaters and the corduroy skirt and the mittens and gloves from Fanny. I'd just as soon leave the ugly mustard coat behind, but

Fanny says I'll regret it if I do, that it's even colder out there on those farms than it is here in town.

When I'm done, we go back in the sewing room and Fanny finds a small pair of scissors, two spools of thread, black and white, a pincushion and pins, and a cellophane packet of needles. She adds a cardboard flat of opalescent buttons for my unfinished dress. Then she wraps it all in cheesecloth for me to tuck in the top of my suitcase.

"Won't you get in trouble for giving me these?" I ask her.

"Pish," she says. "I don't even care."

I do not say good-bye to the Byrnes. Who knows where Mr. Byrne is, and Mrs. Byrne doesn't come downstairs. But Fanny gives me a long hug. She holds my face in her small cold hands. "You are a good girl, Niamh," she says. "Don't let anybody tell you different."

Mr. Sorenson's vehicle, parked in the driveway behind the Model A, is a dark-green Chrysler truck. He opens the passenger door for me, then goes around to the other side. The interior smells of tobacco and apples. He backs out of the driveway and points the car to the left, away from town and toward a direction I've never been. We follow Elm Street until it ends, then turn right down another quiet street, where the houses are set back farther from the sidewalks, until we come to an intersection and turn onto a long, flat road with fields on both sides.

I gaze out at the fields, a dull patchwork. Brown cows huddle together, lifting their necks to watch the noisy truck as it passes. Horses graze. Pieces of farm equipment in the distance look like abandoned toys. The horizon line, flat and low, is straight ahead, and the sky looks like dishwater. Black birds pierce the sky like inverse stars.

I feel almost sorry for Mr. Sorenson on our drive. I can tell this weighs on him. It's probably not what he thought he was signing up for when he agreed to be an agent for the Children's Aid Society. He keeps asking if I'm comfortable, if the heat is too low or too high. When he learns I know almost nothing about Minnesota he tells me all about it — how it became a state just over seventy years ago and is now the twelfth largest in the United States. How its name comes from a Dakota Indian word for "cloudy water." How it contains thousands of lakes, filled with fish of all kinds — walleye, for one thing, catfish, largemouth bass, rainbow trout, perch, and pike. The Mississippi River starts in Minnesota, did I know that? And these fields — he waves his fingers toward the window — they feed the whole country. Let's see, there's grain, the biggest export — a thrasher goes from farm to farm, and neighbors get together to bundle the shocks. There's sugar beets and sweet corn and green peas. And those low buildings way over there? Turkey farms. Minnesota is the biggest producer of turkeys in the country. There'd be no Thanksgiving without Minnesota, that's for darn sure. And don't get me started on hunting. We've got pheasants, quail, grouse, whitetail deer, you name it. It's a hunter's paradise.

I listen to Mr. Sorenson and nod politely as he talks, but it's hard to concentrate. I feel myself retreating to someplace deep inside. It is a pitiful kind of childhood, to know that no one loves you or is taking care of you, to always be on the outside looking in. I feel a decade older than my years. I know too much; I have seen people at their worst, at their most desperate and selfish, and this knowledge makes me wary. So I am learning to pretend, to smile and nod, to display empathy I do not feel. I am learning to pass, to look like everyone else, even though I feel broken inside.

HEMINGFORD COUNTY, MINNESOTA, 1930

After about half an hour, Mr. Sorenson turns onto a narrow unpaved road. Dirt rises around us as we drive, coating the windshield and side windows. We pass more fields and then a copse of birch tree skeletons, cross through a dilapidated covered bridge over a murky stream still sheeted with ice, turn down a bumpy dirt road bordered by pine trees. Mr. Sorenson is holding a card with what looks like directions on it. He slows the truck, pulls to a stop, looks back toward the bridge. Then he peers out the grimy windshield at the trees ahead. "No goldarn signs," he mutters. He puts his foot on the pedal and inches forward.

Out of the side window I point to a faded red rag tied to a stick and what appears to be a driveway, overgrown with weeds.

"Must be it," he says.

Hairy branches scrape the truck on either

side as we make our way down the drive. After about fifty yards, we come to a small wooden house — a shack, really — unpainted, with a sagging front porch piled with junk. In the grassless section in front of the house, a baby is crawling on top of a dog with black matted fur, and a boy of about six is poking a stick in the dirt. His hair is so short, and he's so skinny, that he looks like a wizened old man. Despite the cold, he and the baby are barefoot.

Mr. Sorenson parks the truck as far from the children as possible in the small clearing and gets out of the truck. I get out on my side.

"Hello, boy," he says.

The child gapes at him, not answering.

"Your mama home?"

"Who want to know?" the boy says.

Mr. Sorenson smiles. "Did your mama tell you you're getting a new sister?"

"No."

"Well, she should be expecting us. Go on and tell her we're here."

The boy stabs at the dirt with the stick. "She's sleeping. I'm not to bother her."

"You go on and wake her up. Maybe she forgot we were coming."

The boy traces a circle in the dirt.

"Tell her it's Mr. Sorenson from the

Children's Aid Society."

He shakes his head. "Don't want a whupping."

"She's not going to whip you, boy! She'll be glad to know I'm here."

When it's clear the boy isn't going to move, Mr. Sorenson rubs his hands together and, motioning for me to follow, makes his way gingerly up the creaking steps to the porch. I can tell he's worried about what we might find inside. I am too.

He knocks loudly on the door, and it swings open from the force of his hand. There's a hole where the doorknob is supposed to be. He steps into the gloom, ushering me in with him.

The front room is nearly bare. It smells like a cave. The floor is planked with rough boards, and in places I can see clear through to the ground below. Of the three grimy windows, one has a jagged hole in the upper-right corner and one is seamed with spidery cracks. A wooden crate stands between two upholstered chairs, soiled with dirt, stuffing coming out of split seams, and a threadbare gold sofa. On the far left is a dark hallway. Straight ahead, through an open doorway, is the kitchen.

"Mrs. Grote? Hello?" Mr. Sorenson cocks his head, but there's no response. "I'm not

184

going into a bedroom to find her, that's for sure," he mutters. "Mrs. Grote?" he calls, louder.

We hear faint footsteps and a girl of about three, in a dirty pink dress, emerges from the hall.

"Well, hello, little girl!" Mr. Sorenson says, crouching down on his heels. "Is your mama back there?"

"We sleeping."

"That's what your brother said. Is she still asleep?"

A harsh voice comes from the hallway, startling us both: "What do you want?"

Mr. Sorenson stands up slowly. A pale woman with long brown hair steps out of the darkness. Her eyes are puffy and her lips are chapped, and her nightgown is so thin I can see the dark circles of her nipples through the cloth.

The girl sidles over like a cat and puts an arm around her legs.

"I'm Chester Sorenson, from the Children's Aid Society. You must be Mrs. Grote. I'm sorry to bother you, ma'am, but I was told you knew we were coming. You did request a girl, did you not?"

The woman rubs her eyes. "What day is it?"

"Friday, April fourth, ma'am."

185

She coughs. Then she doubles over and coughs again, harder this time, into her fist.

"Would you like to sit down?" Mr. Sorenson goes over and guides her by the elbow to a chair. "Now, is Mr. Grote home?"

The woman shakes her head.

"Are you expecting him soon?"

She lifts her shoulders in a shrug.

"What time does he get off work?" Mr. Sorenson presses.

"He don't go to work no more. Lost his job at the feed store last week." She glances around as if she's lost something. Then she says, "C'mere, Mabel." The little girl slinks over to her, watching us the whole time. "Go check and see that Gerald Junior's okay in there. And where's Harold?"

"Is that the boy outside?" Mr. Sorenson asks.

"He watching the baby? I told him to."

"They're both out there," he says, and though his voice is neutral, I can tell he doesn't approve.

Mrs. Grote chews her lip. She still hasn't said a word to me. She's barely looked in my direction. "I'm just so tired," she says to no one in particular.

"Well, I'm sure you are, ma'am." It's clear Mr. Sorenson is itching to get out of here. "I'm guessing that's why you asked for this here orphan girl. Dorothy. Her papers say she has experience with children. So that should be a help to you."

She nods distractedly. "I got to sleep when they sleep," she mumbles. "It's the only time I get any rest."

"I'm sure it is."

Mrs. Grote covers her face with both hands. Then she pushes her stringy hair back behind her ears. She juts her chin at me. "This is the girl, huh?"

"Yes, ma'am. Name's Dorothy. She's here to be part of your family and be taken care of by you and help you in return."

She focuses on my face, but her eyes are flat. "What's her age?"

"Nine years old."

"I have enough kids. What I need is somebody who can help me out."

"It's all part of the deal," Mr. Sorenson says. "You feed and clothe Dorothy and make sure she gets to school, and she will earn her keep by doing chores around the house." He pulls his glasses and the sheet of paper out of his various pockets, then puts his glasses on and tilts his head back to read it. "I see there's a school four miles down. And there's a ride she can catch at the post road, three-quarter mile from here." He takes his glasses off. "It's required that Dorothy attend school, Mrs. Grote. Do you agree to abide by that?"

She crosses her arms, and for a moment it looks as if she's going to refuse. Maybe I won't have to stay here, after all!

Then the front door creaks open. We turn to see a tall, thin, dark-haired man wearing a plaid shirt with rolled-up sleeves and grungy overalls. "The girl will go to school, whether she wants to or not," he says. "I'll make sure of it."

Mr. Sorenson strides over and extends his hand. "You must be Gerald Grote. I'm Chester Sorenson. And this is Dorothy."

"Nice to meet you." Mr. Grote clasps his hand, nods over toward me. "She'll do just fine."

"All right, then," Mr. Sorenson says, clearly relieved. "Let's make it official."

There's paperwork, but not a lot. It's only a few minutes before Mr. Sorenson has retrieved my bag from the truck and is driving away. I watch him through the cracked front window with the baby, Nettie, whimpering on my hip.

HEMINGFORD COUNTY, MINNESOTA, 1930

"Where will I sleep?" I ask Mr. Grote when it gets dark.

He looks at me, hands on his hips, as if he hasn't considered this question. He gestures toward the hallway. "There's a bedroom yonder," he says. "If you don't want to sleep with the others, I guess you can sleep out here on the couch. We don't stand on ceremony. I been known to doze off on it myself."

In the bedroom, three old mattresses without sheets are laid across the floor, a carpet of bony springs. Mabel, Gerald Jr., and Harold sprawl across them, tugging a tattered wool blanket and three old quilts from each other. I don't want to sleep here, but it's better than sharing the couch with Mr. Grote. In the middle of the night one kid or another ends up under the crook of my arm or spooned against my back. They smell earthy and sour, like wild animals.

Despair inhabits this house. Mrs. Grote doesn't want all these kids, and neither she nor Mr. Grote really takes care of them. She sleeps all the time, and the children come and go from her bed. There's brown paper tacked over the open window in that room, so it's as dark as a hole in the ground. The children burrow in next to her, craving warmth. Sometimes she lets them crawl in and sometimes she pushes them out. When they're denied a spot, their wails penetrate my skin like tiny needles.

There's no running water, and no electricity or indoor plumbing here. The Grotes use gas lights and candles, and there's a pump and an outhouse in the backyard, wood stacked on the porch. The damp logs in the fireplace make the house smoky and give off a tepid heat.

Mrs. Grote barely looks at me. She sends a child out to be fed or calls me to fix her a cup of coffee. She makes me nervous. I do what I'm told and make an effort to avoid her. The children sniff around, trying to get used to me, all except for two-year-old Gerald Jr., who takes to me right away, follows me like a puppy.

I ask Mr. Grote how they found me. He

says he saw a flyer in town — homeless children for distribution. Wilma wouldn't get out of bed, and he didn't know what else to do.

I feel abandoned and forgotten, dropped into misery worse than my own.

Mr. Grote says he'll never get another job if he can manage it. He plans to live off the land. He was born and raised in the woods; it's the only life he knows or cares to know. He built this house with his own two hands, he says, and his goal is to be entirely self-sufficient. He has an old goat in the back-yard and a mule and half a dozen chickens; he can feed his family on what he can hunt and find in the woods and on a handful of seeds, along with the goat's milk and eggs from the chickens, and he can sell things in town if he has to.

Mr. Grote is lean and fit from walking miles every day. Like an Indian, he says. He has a car, but it's rusted and broken down behind the house. He can't afford to get it fixed, so he goes everywhere on foot or sometimes on the old mule that he says wandered off from a horsemeat truck that broke down on the road a few months back. His fingernails are rimmed with grime made up of axle grease and planting soil and animal blood and who knows what else, ground in so deep it can't be washed off. I've only ever seen him in one pair of overalls.

Mr. Grote doesn't believe in government telling him what to do. Tell the truth, he doesn't believe in government at all. He has never been to school a day in his life and doesn't see the point. But he'll send me to school if that's what it takes to keep the authorities out of his hair.

On Monday, three days after I arrive, Mr. Grote shakes my shoulder in the darkness so I can get ready for school. The room is so cold I can see my breath. I put on one of my new dresses with both sweaters layered on top. I wear Fanny's mittens, the thick stockings I wore from New York, my sturdy black shoes.

I run out to the pump and fill a pitcher with cold water, then bring it inside to heat on the stove. After pouring warm water in a tin bowl, I take a rag and scrub my face, my neck, my fingernails. There's an old mirror in the kitchen, spotted with rusty stains and freckled with black specks, so ruined it's almost impossible to see myself in. I divide my unwashed hair into two pigtails, using my fingers as a comb, and then braid them tightly, tying the ends with thread from the packet Fanny made for me. Then I look closely at my reflection. I am as clean as I can manage without taking a bath. My face is pale and serious.

I barely have any breakfast, just some wild rice pudding made with goat's milk and maple syrup Mr. Grote tapped the day before. I am so relieved to be getting out of this dark, fetid cabin for the day that I swing Harold around, joke with Gerald Jr., share my rice pudding with Mabel, who has only just started looking me in the eye. Mr. Grote draws a map for me with a knife in the dirt — you go out the drive, turn left there where you came in, walk till you get to the T section, then go over that bridge back yonder and on till you get to the county road. Half an hour, give or take.

He doesn't offer a lunch pail, and I don't ask for one. I slip the two eggs I boiled the night before when I was making supper into my coat pocket. I have that piece of paper from Mr. Sorenson that says a man named Mr. Post who drives the kids to school in his truck will be at the corner at 8:30 A.M. and bring me back at 4:30 P.M. It's 7:40, but I'm ready to go. Better to wait at the corner than risk missing my ride.

I skip down the driveway, hurry up the

193

road, linger on the bridge for a moment, looking down at the reflection of the sky like mercury on the dark water, the foaming white suds near the rocks. Ice glistens on tree branches, frost webs over dried grasses in a sparkling net. The evergreens are dusted with the light snow that fell last night like a forest of Christmas trees. For the first time, I am struck by the beauty of this place.

I hear the truck before I see it. About twenty yards from me, it slows to a stop with a great screeching of brakes, and I have to run back along the road to get on. An apple-faced man in a tan cap peers out at me. "Come on, darlin'. Don't have all day."

The truck has a tarpaulin over its bed. I climb in the back, laid with two flat planks for passengers to sit on. There's a heap of horse blankets in the corner, and the four kids sitting there are huddled in them, having wrapped the blankets over their shoulders and tucked them around their legs. The canvas cover gives everyone a yellowish tint. Two of the kids appear close to my age. As we bump along, I hang on to the wooden bench with my mittened fingers so I don't fall onto the floor when we hit a rough patch. The driver stops twice more to pick up passengers. The bed is only big enough to seat six comfortably, and eight of us are crammed in here — we're tight on the bench, but our bodies give off much-needed warmth. Nobody speaks. When the truck is moving, wind slices through the gaps in the tarp.

After several miles, the truck makes a turn, brakes squealing, and climbs up a steep driveway before grinding to a stop. We jump out of the truck bed and line up, then walk to the schoolhouse, a small clapboard building with a bell in front. A young woman in a cornflower-blue dress, a lavender scarf wrapped around her neck, is standing at the front door. Her face is pretty and lively: big brown eyes and a wide smile. Her shiny brown hair is pulled back with a white ribbon.

"Welcome, children. Proceed in an orderly fashion, as always." Her voice is high and clear. "Good morning, Michael . . . Bertha . . . Darlene," she says, greeting each child by name. When I reach her, she says, "Now — I haven't met you yet, but I heard you were coming. I'm Miss Larsen. And you must be —"

I say "Niamh" at the same time that she says "Dorothy." Seeing the expression on my face, she says, "Did I get that wrong? Or do you have a nickname?"

"No, ma'am. It's just . . ." I feel my cheeks redden.

"What is it?"

"I used to be Niamh. Sometimes I forget what my name is. Nobody really calls me anything at my new home."

"Well, I can call you Niamh if you like."

"It's all right. Dorothy is fine."

She smiles, studying my face. "As you wish. Lucy Green?" she says, turning to the girl behind me. "Would you mind showing Dorothy to her desk?"

I follow Lucy into an area lined with hooks, where we hang up our coats. Then we enter a large, sunny room smelling of wood smoke and chalk that contains an oil stove, a desk for the teacher, rows of benches and work spaces, and slate blackboards along the east and south walls, with posters of the alphabet and multiplication tables above. The other walls are made up of large windows. Electric lights shine overhead, and low shelves are filled with books.

When everyone is seated, Miss Larsen pulls a loop on a string and a colorful map of the world unfurls on the wall. At her request I go up to the map and identify Ireland. Looking at it closely, I can find County Galway and even the city center. The village of Kinvara isn't named, but I rub the place where it belongs, right under Galway on the jagged line of the west coast. There is New York — and here's Chicago. And here's Minneapolis. Hemingford County isn't on the map, either.

Including me, there are twenty-three of us between the ages of six and sixteen. Most of the kids are from farms themselves and other rural homes and are learning to read and write at all ages. We smell unwashed — and it's worse with the older ones who have hit puberty. There's a heap of rags, a few bars of soap, and a carton of baking soda in the indoor lavatory, Miss Larsen tells me, in case you want to freshen up.

When Miss Larsen talks to me, she bends down and looks me in the eye. When she asks questions, she waits for my answer. She smells of lemons and vanilla. And she treats me like I'm smart. After I take a test to determine my reading level, she hands me a book from the shelf by her desk, a hardcover filled with small black type called *Anne of Green Gables,* without pictures, and tells me she will ask what I think of it when I'm done.

You'd think with all these kids it would be chaotic, but Miss Larsen rarely raises her voice. The driver, Mr. Post, chops wood, tends the stove, sweeps the leaves from the front walkway, and does mechanical repairs on the truck. He also teaches mathematics up to geometry, which he says he never learned because that year was locusts and he was needed on the farm.

At recess Lucy invites me to play games with a group of them — Annie Annie Over; Pump, Pump, Pull Away; Ring Around the Rosie.

When I get out of the truck at four thirty and have to walk the long route back to the cabin, my footsteps are slow.

The food this family subsists on is like nothing I've ever eaten before. Mr. Grote leaves at dawn with his rifle and rod and brings home squirrels and wild turkeys, whiskery fish, now and then a white-tailed deer. He returns in the late afternoon covered in pine-tree gum. He brings home red squirrels most of all, but they aren't as good as the larger fox and gray squirrels, which he calls bushy tails. The fox squirrels are so big that some of them look like orange cats. They chirp and whistle, and he tricks them into showing themselves by clicking two coins together, which sounds like their chatter. The gray squirrels have the most meat, he tells me, but are hardest to see in the woods. They make a harsh *chich-chich* noise

198

when they're angry or scared. That's how he finds them.

Mr. Grote skins and guts the animals in several fluid motions, then hands me tiny hearts and livers, slabs of deep red meat. All I know how to make is boiled cabbage and mutton, I tell him, but he says it's not that different. He shows me how to make a gallimaufry, a stew of diced meat, onion, and vegetables, with mustard, ginger, and vinegar. You cook the meat in animal fat over high heat to sear it, then add potatoes and vegetables and the rest. "It's just a hotchpotch," he says. "Whatever's around."

At first I am horrified by the ghoulish skinned squirrels, as red and muscular as skinless human bodies in Miss Larsen's science book. But hunger cures my qualms. Soon enough, squirrel stew tastes normal.

Out in back is a homely garden that, even now, in mid-April, has root vegetables waiting to be dug — blighted potatoes and yams and tough-skinned carrots and turnips. Mr. Grote takes me out there with a pick and teaches me how to pry them from the earth, then wash them off under the pump. But the ground is still partially frozen, and the vegetables are hard to extract. The two of us spend about four hours in the cold digging for those tough old vegetables, planted

199

last summer, until we have a gnarled and ugly pile. The children wander in and out of the house, sit and watch us from the kitchen window. I am grateful for my fingerless gloves.

Mr. Grote shows me how he grows wild rice in the stream and collects the seeds. The rice is nutty and brown. He plants the seeds after harvest in late summer for the crop the following year. It's an annual plant, he explains, which means that it dies in the autumn. Seeds that fall in autumn take root in spring underwater, and then the shoot grows above the surface. The stalks look like tall grass swaying in the water.

In the summer, he says, he grows herbs in a patch behind the house — mint, rosemary, and thyme — and hangs them to dry in the shed. Even now there's a pot of lavender in the kitchen. It's a strange sight in that squalid room, like a rose in a junkyard.

At school one late-April day Miss Larsen sends me out to the porch to get some firewood, and when I come back in, the entire class, led by Lucy Green, is standing, singing happy birthday to me.

Tears spring to my eyes. "How did you know?"

"The date was in your paperwork." Miss Larsen smiles, handing me a slice of currant bread. "My landlady made this."

I look at her, not sure I understand. "For me?"

"I mentioned that we had a new girl, and that your birthday was coming up. She likes to bake."

The bread, dense and moist, tastes like Ireland. One bite and I am back in Gram's cottage, in front of her warm Stanley range.

"Nine to ten is a big leap," Mr. Post says. "One digit to two. You'll be two digits now for the next ninety years."

Unwrapping the leftover currant bread at the Grotes' that evening, I tell them about my party. Mr. Grote snorts. "How ridiculous, celebrating a birth date. I don't even know the day I was born, and I sure can't remember any of theirs," he says, swinging his hand toward his kids. "But let's have that cake."

Spruce Harbor, Maine, 2011

Looking closely at Molly's file, Lori the social worker settles on a stool. "So you'll be aging out of foster care in . . . let's see . . . you turned seventeen in January, so nine months. Have you thought about what you're going to do then?"

Molly shrugs. "Not really."

Lori scribbles something on the file folder in front of her. With her bright button eyes and pointy snout nosing into Molly's business, Lori reminds her of a ferret. They're sitting at a lab table in an otherwise empty chemistry classroom at the high school during lunch period, as they do every other Wednesday.

"Any problems with the Thibodeaus?"

Molly shakes her head. Dina barely speaks to her; Ralph is pleasant enough — same as always.

Lori taps her nose with an index finger. "You're not wearing this anymore."

"Jack thought it might scare the old lady." She did take the nose ring out for Jack, but the truth is, she hasn't been in a hurry to put it back in. There are things about it she likes — the way it marks her as a rebel, for one thing. Multiple earrings don't have the same punk appeal; every forty-something divorcée on the island has half a dozen hoops in her ears. But the ring takes a lot of maintenance; it's always in danger of infection, and she has to be careful with it when she washes her face or puts on makeup. It's kind of a relief to have a metal-free face.

Flipping slowly through the file, Lori says, "You've logged twenty-eight hours so far. Good for you. What's it like?"

"Not bad. Better than I thought it would be."

"How do you mean?"

Molly's been surprised to find that she looks forward to it. Ninety-one years is a long time to live — there's a lot of history in those boxes, and you never know what you'll find. The other day, for example, they went through a box of Christmas ornaments from the 1930s that Vivian had forgotten she kept. Cardboard stars and snowflakes covered in gold and silver glitter; ornate glass balls, red and green and gold. Vivian told her stories about decorating the family store for the holidays, putting these ornaments on a real pine tree in the window.

"I like her. She's kind of cool."

"You mean the 'old lady'?"

"Yeah."

"Well, good." Lori gives her a tight smile. A ferrety smile. "You've got what, twenty-two hours left, right? Try to make the most of this experience. And I hope I don't need to remind you that you're on probation. If you're caught drinking or doing drugs or otherwise breaking the law, we're back to square one. You clear on that?"

Molly is tempted to say, *Damn, you mean I have to shut down my meth lab? And I gotta delete those naked pictures I posted on Facebook?* But instead she smiles steadily at Lori and says, "I'm clear."

Pulling Molly's transcript out of the file, Lori says, "Look at this. Your SATs are in the 600s. And you have a 3.8 average this semester. That's really good."

"It's an easy school."

"No, it isn't."

"It's not that big a deal."

"It is a big deal, actually. These are applying-to-college stats. Have you thought about that?"

"No."

"Why not?"

Last year, when she transferred from Bangor High, she was close to failing. In Bangor, she'd had no incentive to do homework — her foster parents were partiers, and she'd come home from school to find a house full of drunks. In Spruce Harbor, there aren't so many distractions. Dina and Ralph don't drink or smoke, and they're strict. Jack has a beer now and then, but that's about it. And Molly discovered that she actually likes to study.

No one has ever talked to her about college except the school guidance counselor who halfheartedly recommended nursing school when she got an A last semester in bio. Her grades have kind of shot up without anyone noticing.

"I don't really think I'm college material," Molly says.

"Well, apparently you are," says Lori. "And since you're officially on your own when you turn eighteen, you might want to start looking into it. There are some decent scholarships out there for aged-out foster youth." She shuts the folder. "Or you can apply for a job behind the counter at the Somesville One-Stop. It's up to you."

"So how's that community service working out?" Ralph asks at dinner, pouring himself a big glass of milk.

"It's all right," Molly says. "The woman is really old. She has a lot of stuff."

"Fifty hours' worth?" Dina asks.

"I don't know. But I guess there are other things I can do if I finish cleaning out boxes. The house is huge."

"Yeah, I've done some work over there. Old pipes," Ralph says. "Have you met Terry? The housekeeper?"

Molly nods. "Actually, she's Jack's mother."

Dina perks up. "Wait a minute. Terry Gallant? I went to high school with her! I didn't know Jack was her kid."

"Yep," Molly says.

Waving a chunk of hot dog around on her fork, Dina says, "Oh, how the mighty have fallen."

Molly gives Ralph a *what the fuck?* look, but he just gazes placidly back.

"It's sad what happens to people, y'know?" Dina says, shaking her head. "Terry Gallant used to be Miss Popular. Homecoming Queen and all that. Then she got knocked up by some Mexican scrub — and now look at her, she's a maid."

"Actually, he was Dominican," Molly mumbles.

"Whatever. Those illegals are all the same,

aren't they?"

Deep breath, stay cool, get through dinner. "If you say so."

"I do say so."

"Hey, now, ladies, that's enough." Ralph is smiling, but it's a worried grimace; he knows Molly is pissed. He's always making excuses — "She didn't mean nothing by it," "She's yanking your chain" — when Dina does things like intone "the Tribe has spoken" when Molly expresses an opinion. "You need to stop taking yourself so seriously, little girl," Dina said when Molly asked her to knock it off. "If you can't laugh at yourself, you're going to have a very hard life."

So Molly moves her mouth muscles into a smile, picks up her plate, thanks Dina for dinner. She says she's got a lot of homework, and Ralph says he'll clean up the kitchen. Dina says it's time for some trash TV.

"Housewives of Spruce Harbor," Ralph says. "When are we going to see that?"

"Maybe Terry Gallant could be in it. Show that yearbook photo of her in her tiara, cut to her washing floors." Dina cackles. "I'd watch that one for sure!"

Spruce Harbor, Maine, 2011

For the past few weeks in Molly's American History class they've been studying the Wabanaki Indians, a confederacy of five Algonquian-speaking tribes, including the Penobscot, that live near the North Atlantic coast. Maine, Mr. Reed tells them, is the only state in the nation that requires schools to teach Native American culture and history. They've read Native narratives and contrasting contemporaneous viewpoints and taken a field trip to The Abbe, the Indian museum in Bar Harbor, and now they have to do a research report on the subject worth a third of their final grade.

For this assignment they're supposed to focus on a concept called "portaging." In the old days the Wabanakis had to carry their canoes and everything else they possessed across land from one water body to the next, so they had to think carefully about what to keep and what to discard.

They learned to travel light. Mr. Reed tells students they have to interview someone — a mother or father or grandparent — about their own portages, the moments in their lives when they've had to take a journey, literal or metaphorical. They'll use tape recorders and conduct what he calls "oral histories," asking the person questions, transcribing the answers, and putting it together in chronological order as a narrative. The questions on the assignment sheet are: *What did you choose to bring with you to the next place? What did you leave behind? What insights did you gain about what's important?*

Molly's kind of into the idea of the project, but she doesn't want to interview Ralph or — God forbid — Dina.

Jack? Too young.

Terry? She'd never agree to it.

The social worker, Lori? Ick, no.

So that leaves Vivian. Molly has gleaned some things about her — that she's adopted, that she grew up in the Midwest and inherited the family business from her well-off parents, that she and her husband expanded it and eventually sold it for the kind of profit that allowed them to retire to a mansion in Maine. Most of all, that she's really, really old. Maybe it'll be a stretch to find drama in Vivian's portage — a happy, stable life does not an interesting story make, right? But even the rich have their problems, or so Molly's heard. It will be her task to extract them. If, that is, she can convince Vivian to talk to her.

Molly's own childhood memories are scant and partial. She remembers that the TV in the living room seemed to be on all the time and that the trailer smelled of cigarette smoke and the cat's litterbox and mildew. She remembers her mother lying on the couch chain-smoking with the shades drawn before she left for her job at the Mini-Mart. She remembers foraging for food — cold hot dogs and toast — when her mother wasn't home, and sometimes when she was. She remembers the giant puddle of melting snow just outside the door of the trailer, so large that she had to jump across it from the top step to get to dry ground.

And there are other, better, memories: making fried eggs with her dad, turning them over with a large black plastic spatula. "Not so fast, Molly Molasses," he'd say. "Easy. Otherwise the eggs'll go splat." Going to St. Anne's Church on Easter and choosing a blooming crocus in a green plastic pot covered with foil that was silver on one side, bright yellow on the other. Every Easter she and her mother planted those crocuses near the fence beside the driveway, and soon enough a whole cluster of them, white and purple and pink, sprang annually like magic from the bald April earth.

She remembers third grade at the Indian Island School, where she learned that the name Penobscot is from Panawahpskek, meaning "the place where the rocks spread out" at the head of the tribal river, right where they were. That Wabanaki means "Dawnland," because the tribes live in the region where the first light of dawn touches the American continent. That the Penobscot people have lived in the territory that became Maine for eleven thousand years, moving around season to season, following food. They trapped and hunted moose, caribou, otters, and beavers; they speared fish and clams and mussels. Indian Island, just above a waterfall, became their gathering place.

She learned about Indian words that have been incorporated into American English, like *moose* and *pecan* and *squash,* and Penobscot words like *kwai kwai,* a friendly greeting, and *woliwoni,* thank you. She learned that they lived in wigwams, not teepees, and that they made canoes from the bark of a single white birch tree, removed in one piece so as not to kill it. She learned about the baskets the Penobscots still make out of birch bark, sweet grass, and brown ash, all of which grow in Maine wetlands, and, guided by her teacher, even made a small one herself.

She knows that she was named for Molly Molasses, a famous Penobscot Indian born the year before America declared its independence from England. Molly Molasses lived into her nineties, coming and going from Indian Island, and was said to possess *m'teoulin,* power given by the Great Spirit to a few for the good of the whole. Those who possess this power, her dad said, could interpret dreams, repel disease or death, inform hunters where to find game, and send a spirit helper to harm their enemies.

But she didn't learn until this year, in Mr. Reed's class, that there were over thirty thousand Wabanakis living on the East Coast in 1600 and that 90 percent of them had died by 1620, almost entirely a result of contact with settlers, who brought foreign diseases and alcohol, drained resources, and fought with the tribes for control of the land. She didn't know that Indian women had more power and authority than white women, a fact detailed in captivity stories. That Indian farmers had greater skill and bounty, and more successful yields, than most Europeans who worked the same land. No, they weren't "primitive" — their social networks were highly advanced. And though they were called savages, even a prominent English general, Philip Sheridan, had to admit, "We took away their country and their means of support. It was for this and against this that they made war. Could anyone expect less?"

Molly had always thought the Indians rebelled like guerrillas, scalping and pillaging. Learning that they attempted to negotiate with the settlers, wearing European-style suits and addressing Congress in the assumption of good faith — and were repeatedly lied to and betrayed — enrages her.

In Mr. Reed's classroom there's a photo of Molly Molasses taken near the end of her life. In it she sits ramrod straight, wearing a beaded, peaked headdress and two large silver brooches around her neck. Her face is dark and wrinkled and her expression is fierce. Sitting in the empty classroom after school one day, Molly stares at that face for a long time, looking for answers to questions she doesn't know how to ask.

On the night of her eighth birthday, after ice-cream sandwiches and a Sara Lee cake her mother brought home from the Mini-Mart, after making a fervent wish, eyes squeezed shut as she blew out the tiny pink-striped birthday candles (for a bicycle, she remembers, pink with white and pink streamers like the one the girl across the street got for her birthday several months earlier), Molly sat on the couch waiting for her dad to come home. Her mom paced back and forth, punching redial on the handset, muttering under her breath, *how could you forget your only daughter's birth-day?* But he didn't pick up. After a while they gave up and went to bed.

An hour or so later she was woken by a shake on the shoulder. Her father was sitting in the chair beside her bed, swaying a little, holding a plastic grocery bag and whispering, "Hey there, Molly Molasses, you awake?"

She opened her eyes. Blinked.

"You awake?" he said again, reaching over and switching on the princess lamp he'd bought for her at a yard sale.

She nodded.

"Hold out your hand."

Fumbling with the bag, he pulled out three flat jewelry cards — each gray plastic, covered in gray fuzz on one side, with a small charm wired in place. "Fishy," he said, handing her the small pearly blue-and-green fish; "raven," the pewter bird; "bear," a tiny brown teddy bear. "It's supposed to be a Maine black bear, but this was all they had," he says apologetically. "So here's the dealio; I was trying to think of what I could get for your birthday that would mean something, not just the usual Barbie crap. And I was thinking — you and me are Indian. Your mom's not, but we are. And I've always liked Indian symbols. Know what a symbol is?"

She shook her head.

"Shit that stands for shit. So let's see if I remember this right." Sitting on the bed, he plucked the bird card out of her hand, turning it around in his fingers. "Okay, this guy is magic. He'll protect you from bad spells and other kinds of weirdness you might not even be aware of." Carefully he detached the small charm from its plastic card, unwinding the wire ties and placing the bird on her bedside table. Then he picked up the teddy bear. "This fierce animal is a protector."

She laughed.

"No, really. It may not look like it, but appearances can be deceiving. This dude is a fearless spirit. And with that fearless spirit, he signals bravery to those who require it." He freed the bear from the card and set it on the table next to the bird.

"All right. Now the fish. This one might be the best of all. It gives you the power to resist other people's magic. How cool is that?"

She thought for a moment. "But how is that different from bad spells?"

He took the wire off the card and set the fish beside the other charms, lining them up carefully with his finger. "Very good question. You're half asleep and still sharper than most people when they're wide-awake. Okay, I can see how it sounds the same. But the difference is important, so pay attention."

She sat up straighter.

"Somebody else's magic might not be bad spells. It might be stuff that looks real good and sounds real nice. It might be — oh, I don't know — somebody trying to convince you to do something you know you shouldn't do. Like smoke cigarettes."

"Yuck. I'd never do that."

"Right. But maybe it's something that's

not so yucky, like taking a candy bar from the Mini-Mart without paying."

"But Mommy works there."

"Yeah, she does, but even if she didn't, you know it's wrong to steal a candy bar, right? But maybe this person has a lot of magic and is very convincing. 'Oh, come on, Moll, you won't get caught,' " he says in a gruff whisper, " 'don't you love candy, don't you want some, come on, just one time?' " Picking up the fish, he talks in a stern fishy voice: " 'No, thank you! I know what you're up to. You are not putting your magic on me, no sir, I will swim right away from you, y'hear? Okay, bye now.' " He turned the charm around and made a wave with his hand, up and down.

Feeling around in the bag, he said, "Aw, shit. I meant to get you a chain to clip these on." He patted her knee. "Don't worry about it. That'll be part two."

Two weeks later, coming home late one night, he lost control of his car, and that was that. Within six months, Molly was living somewhere else. It was years before she bought herself that chain.

SPRUCE HARBOR, MAINE, 2011

"Portage." Vivian wrinkles her nose. "It sounds like — oh, I don't know — a pie made of sausage."

A pie made of sausage? Okay, maybe this isn't going to work.

"Carrying my boat between bodies of water? I'm not so good with metaphors, dear," Vivian says. "What's it supposed to mean?"

"Well," Molly says, "I think the boat represents what you take with you — the essential things — from place to place. And the water — well, I think it's the place you're always trying to get to. Does that make sense?"

"Not really. I'm afraid I'm more confused than I was before."

Molly pulls out a list of questions. "Let's just get started and see what happens."

They are sitting in the red wingback chairs in the living room in the waning light of late afternoon. Their work for the day is finished, and Terry has gone home. It was pouring earlier, great sheets of rain, and now the clouds outside the window are crystal tipped, like mountain peaks in the sky, rays emanating downward like an illustration in a children's bible.

Molly pushes the button on the tiny digital tape recorder she signed out from the school library and checks to see that it's working. Then she takes a deep breath and runs a finger under the chain around her neck. "My dad gave me these charms, and each one represents something different. The raven protects against black magic. The bear inspires courage. The fish signifies a refusal to recognize other people's magic."

"I never knew those charms had meaning." Absently, Vivian reaches up and touches her own necklace.

Looking closely at the pewter pendant for the first time, Molly asks, "Is your necklace — significant?"

"Well, it is to me. But it doesn't have any magical qualities." She smiles.

"Maybe it does," Molly says. "I think of these qualities as metaphorical, you know? So black magic is whatever leads people to the dark side — their own greed or insecurity that makes them do destructive things.

And the warrior spirit of the bear protects us not only from others who might hurt us but our own internal demons. And I think other people's magic is what we're vulnerable to — how we're led astray. So . . . my first question for you is kind of a weird one. I guess you could think of it as metaphorical, too." She glances at the tape recorder once more and takes a deep breath. "Okay, here goes. Do you believe in spirits? Or ghosts?"

"My, that is quite a question." Clasping her frail, veined hands in her lap, Vivian gazes out the window. For a moment Molly thinks she isn't going to answer. And then, so quietly that she has to lean forward in her chair to hear, Vivian says, "Yes, I do. I believe in ghosts."

"Do you think they're . . . present in our lives?"

Vivian fixes her hazel eyes on Molly and nods. "They're the ones who haunt us," she says. "The ones who have left us behind."

Hemingford County, Minnesota, 1930

There's hardly any food in the house. Mr. Grote has returned from the woods empty-handed for the past three days, and we're subsisting on eggs and potatoes. It gets so desperate he decides to kill one of the chickens and starts eyeing the goat. He is quiet these days when he comes in. Doesn't speak to the kids, who clamor for him, holding on to his legs. He bats them off like they're flies on honey.

On the evening of the third day, I can feel him looking at me. He has a funny expression on his face, like he's doing math in his head. Finally he says, "So what's that thing you got around your neck?" and it's clear what he's up to.

"There's no value in it," I say.

"Looks like silver," he says, peering at it. "Tarnished."

My heart thumps in my ears. "It's tin."

"Lemme see."

221

Mr. Grote comes closer, then touches the raised heart, the clasped hands, with his dirty finger. "What is that, some kind of pagan symbol?"

I don't know what pagan is, but it sounds wicked. "Probably."

"Who gave it to you?"

"My gram." It's the first time I've mentioned my family to him, and I don't like the feeling. I wish I could take it back. "It was worthless to her. She was throwing it away."

He frowns. "Sure is strange looking. Doubt I could sell it if I tried."

Mr. Grote talks to me all the time — when I'm pulling feathers off the chicken, frying potatoes on the woodstove, sitting by the fire in the living room with a child in my lap. He tells me about his family — how there was some kind of dispute, and his brother killed his father when Mr. Grote was sixteen and he ran away from home and never went back. He met Mrs. Grote around that time, and Harold was born when they were eighteen. They never actually tied the knot until they had a houseful of kids. All he wants to do is hunt and fish, he says, but he has to feed and clothe all these babies. God's honest truth, he didn't want a single one of 'em. God's honest truth, he's afraid he could get mad enough to hurt them.

As the weeks pass and the weather gets warmer, he takes to whittling on the front porch until late in the evening, a bottle of whiskey by his side, and he's always asking me to join him. In the darkness he tells me more than I want to know. He and Mrs. Grote barely say a word to each other anymore, he says. She hates to talk, but loves sex. But he can't stand to touch her — she doesn't bother to clean herself, and there's always a kid hanging off her. He says, "I should've married someone like you, Dorothy. You wouldn't've trapped me like this, would ya?" He likes my red hair. "You know what they say," he tells me. "If you want trouble, find yourself a redhead." The first girl he kissed had red hair, but that was a long time ago, he says, back when he was young and good-looking.

"Surprised I was good-looking? I was a boy once, you know. I'm only twenty-four now."

He has never been in love with his wife, he says.

Call me Gerald, he says.

I know that Mr. Grote shouldn't be saying all this. I am only ten years old.

The children whimper like wounded dogs

and cluster together for comfort. They don't play like normal kids, running and jumping. Their noses are always filled with green mucus, and their eyes are runny. I move through the house like an armored beetle, impervious to Mrs. Grote's sharp tongue, Harold's whining, the cries of Gerald Jr., who will never in his life satisfy his aching need to be held. I see Mabel turning into a sullen girl, all too aware of the ways she has been burdened, ill-treated, abandoned to this sorry lot. I know how it happened to the children, living this way, but it's hard for me to love them. Their misery only makes me more aware of my own. It takes all my energy to keep myself clean, to get up and out the door in the morning to school.

Lying on a mattress at night during a rainstorm, metal ribs poking at me from under the thin ticking, water dripping on my face, my stomach hollow and empty, I remember a time on the *Agnes Pauline* when it was raining and everyone was seasick and my da tried to distract us kids from our misery by getting us to close our eyes and visualize a perfect day. That was three years ago, when I was seven, but the day I imagined is still vivid in my mind. It's a Sunday afternoon and I am going to visit

Gram in her snug home on the outskirts of town. Walking to her house — climbing over stone walls and across fields of wild grass that move in the wind like waves on the sea — I smell the sweet smoke from turf fires and listen to the thrushes and blackbirds practice their wild songs. In the distance I see the thatched-roof house with its white-washed walls, pots of red geraniums blooming on the window-sill, Gram's sturdy black bike propped inside the gate, near the hedge where blackberries and sloe fruit hang in dense blue clusters.

Inside, a goose roasts in the oven and the black-and-white dog, Monty, waits under the table for scraps. Granddad's out fishing for trout in the river with a homemade rod or hunting grouse or partridge across the fields. So it's just Gram and me, alone for a few hours.

Gram is rolling dough for a rhubarb tart, back and forth with the big rolling pin, dusting the yellow dough with handfuls of flour, stretching it to cover the brimming pie dish. Now and then she takes a puff of her Sweet Afton, wisps of smoke rising above her head. She offers me a bull's-eye sweet, which she's stashed in her apron pocket with a half-dozen half-smoked Afton butts — a mix of flavors I'll never forget. On the front of the yellow cigarette box is a poem by Robert Burns that Gram likes to sing to an old Irish tune:

Flow gently, sweet Afton, among thy
    green braes.
Flow gently, I'll sing thee a song in thy
    praise.

I sit on a three-legged stool listening to the crackle and spit of goose skin in the oven while she trims a ribbon of dough from around the rim of the pie dish, making a cross with a remnant for the center and brushing it all with a beaten egg, finishing with a flourish of fork pricks and a sprinkle of sugar. When the tart's safely in the oven we move to the front room, the "good room," she calls it, just the two of us, for afternoon tea, strong and black with plenty of sugar, and currant bread, sliced and warm. Gram chooses two teacups from her collection of rose-patterned china in the glass-front, along with matching saucers and small plates, and sets each piece carefully on a starched linen placemat. Irish lace, hanging in the windows, filters the afternoon light, softening the lines on her face.

From my perch on the cushioned chair I see the wooden footrest with its floral needlepoint cover in front of her rocker, the small shelf of books — prayer books and poetry, mainly — by the stairs. I see Gram singing and humming as she pours the tea. Her strong hands and kind smile. Her love for me.

Now, tossing and turning on this damp, sour-smelling mattress, I try to focus on my perfect day, but these memories lead to other, darker thoughts. Mrs. Grote, back there moaning in her bedroom, isn't so different from my own mam. Both of them overburdened and ill-equipped, weak by nature or circumstance, married to strong-willed, selfish men, addicted to the opiate of sleep. Mam expected me to cook and clean and take care of Maisie and the boys, relied on me to hear her troubles, called me naive when I insisted things would get better, that we would be all right. "You don't know," she'd say. "You don't know the half of it." One time, not long before the fire, she was curled on her bed in the dark and I heard her crying and went in to comfort her. When I put my arms around her, she sprang up, flinging me away. "You don't care about me," she snapped. "Don't pretend you do. You only want your supper."

I shrank back, my face flaming as if I'd been struck. And in that moment something changed. I didn't trust her anymore. When she cried, I felt numb. After that, she called me heartless, unfeeling. And maybe I was.

At the beginning of June, we all come down with lice, every last one of us, even Nettie, who has barely four hairs on her head. I remember lice from the boat — Mam was terrified of us kids getting it, and she checked our heads every day, quarantining us when we heard about outbreaks in other cabins. "Worst thing in the world to get rid of," she said, and told us about the epidemic at the girls' school in Kinvara when she was a boarder. They shaved every head. Mam was vain about her thick, dark hair and refused to cut it ever again. We got it on the boat, just the same.

Gerald won't stop scratching, and when I inspect his scalp I find it's teeming. I check the other two and find bugs on them as well. Every surface in the house probably has lice on it, the couch and chairs and Mrs. Grote. I know what an ordeal this will be: no more school, my hair gone, hours of labor, washing the bedsheets . . .

I feel an overwhelming urge to flee.

Mrs. Grote is lying in bed with the baby. Propped on two soiled pillows, the blanket pulled up to her chin, she just stares at me when I come in. Her eyes are sunk in their sockets.

"The children have lice."

She purses her lips. "Do you?"

"Probably, since they do."

She seems to think about this for a moment. Then she says, "You brung the parasite into this house."

My face colors. "No, ma'am, I don't think so."

"They came from somewhere," she says.

"I think . . ." I start, but it's hard to get the words out. "I think you might need to check the bed. And your hair."

"You brung it!" she says, flinging back the covers. "Come in here, acting all high and mighty, like you're better than us . . ."

Her nightgown is bunched up around her belly. I see a dark triangle of fur between her legs and turn away, embarrassed.

"Don't you dare leave!" she shrieks. She snatches baby Nettie, wailing, off the bed and tucks her under one arm, pointing at the bed with the other. "Sheets need to be boiled. Then you can start going through the kids' hair with a comb. I told Gerald it was too much, bringing a vagrant in this house when Lord knows where she's been."

The next five hours are even more miserable than I imagined — boiling pots of water and emptying it into a big tub without scalding any of the children, pulling every blanket and sheet and piece of clothing I can find into the water and scrubbing them with lye soap, then pushing the sheets through the hand wringer. I'm barely strong enough to load and turn the crank, and my arms ache with the effort.

When Mr. Grote comes home he talks to his wife, who's camped on the living room couch. Snatches of their conversation waft back to me — "trash," "vermin," "dirty Irish bog-trotter" — and in a few minutes he comes through the kitchen door to find me on my knees, trying to turn the wringer. "Lord Jesus," he says, and gets to work helping me.

Mr. Grote agrees that the mattresses are probably infested. He thinks if we drag them out to the porch and pour boiling water over them it will kill the bugs. "I have half a mind to do the same to the kids," he says, and I know he's only barely kidding. He makes quick work of shaving the heads of all four of them with a straight razor. Despite my attempts to hold their heads still, they twitch and fidget, and as a result have little bloody nicks and gashes all over their heads. They remind me of photos of soldiers returning from the Great War, hollow-eyed

230

and bald. Mr. Grote rubs lye over each head, and the children scream and yell. Mrs. Grote sits on the couch, watching.

"Wilma, it's your turn," he says, turning to her with the razor in his hand.

"No."

"We have to check, at least."

"Check the girl. She brought them here." Mrs. Grote turns her face to the back of the couch.

Mr. Grote motions me over. I take my hair out of its tight braids and kneel in front of him while he gently picks through. It's strange to feel this man's breath on my neck, his fingers on my scalp. He pinches something between his fingers and sits back on his heels. "Yep. You got some eggs in there."

I am the only one of my siblings with red hair. When I asked my da where I got it, he joked that there must've been rust in the pipes. His own hair was dark — "cured," he said, through years of toil — but when he was young it was more like auburn. Nothing like yours, he said. Your hair is as vivid as a Kinvara sunset, autumn leaves, the Koi goldfish in the window of that hotel in Galway.

Mr. Grote doesn't want to shave my head. He says it would be a crime. Instead he

231

winds my hair around his fist and slices straight through it at the nape of my neck. A heap of coils slide to the floor, and he cuts the rest of the hair on my head about two inches long.

I spend the next four days in that miserable house, burning logs and boiling water, the children cranky and underfoot as they always are, Mrs. Grote back on damp sheets on the mildewing mattress with her lice-infested hair, and there's nothing I can do about any of it, nothing at all.

"We've missed you, Dorothy!" Miss Larsen says when I return to school. "And my — a brand-new hairstyle!"

I touch the top of my head where my hair is sticking up. Miss Larsen knows why my hair is short — it's in the note I had to give her when I got out of the truck — but she doesn't give away a thing. "Actually," she says, "you look like a flapper. Do you know what that is?"

I shake my head.

"Flappers are big-city girls who cut their hair short and go dancing and do what they please." She gives me a friendly smile. "Who knows, Dorothy? Maybe that's what you'll become."

HEMINGFORD COUNTY, MINNESOTA, 1930

By summer's end, Mr. Grote seems to be having more luck. Whatever he can kill he brings home in a sack and skins right away, then hangs in the shed out back. He built a smoker behind the shed and now he keeps it going all the time, filling it with squirrels and fish and even raccoons. The meat gives off a curdled-sweet smell that turns my stomach, but it's better than going hungry.

Mrs. Grote is pregnant again. She says the baby's due in March. I'm worried I'll be expected to help her when the time comes. When Mam had Maisie there were plenty of neighbors on Elizabeth Street who'd been through it before, and all I had to do was watch the younger kids. Mrs. Schatzman, down the hall, and the Krasnow sisters a floor below, with seven children between them, came into the apartment and took over, closing the bedroom door behind them. My da went out. Maybe he was sent

233

out by them, I don't know. I was in the living room, playing patty-cake and reciting the alphabet and singing all the songs he'd belt out when he came home from the pub late at night, waking the neighbors.

By mid-September, round bales of golden straw dot the yellow fields on my walk to the county road, arranged in geometric formations and stacked in pyramids and scattered in haphazard clumps. In history we learn about the pilgrims in Plymouth Plantation in 1621 and the food they ate, wild turkeys and corn and five deer brought to the feast by the Indians. We talk about family traditions, but like the Byrnes, the Grotes don't take any notice of the holiday. When I mention it to Mr. Grote, he says, "What's the big deal about a turkey? I can bag one of those any old day." But he never does.

Mr. Grote has become even more distant, up at the crack of dawn to go hunting, then skinning and smoking the meat at night. When he's home, he yells at the children or avoids them. Sometimes he shakes the baby until it whimpers and stops crying. I don't even know if he sleeps in the back bedroom anymore. Oftentimes I find him asleep on the couch in the living room, his form under a quilt like the exposed root of an old tree.

■ ■ ■ ■

I wake one November morning coated in a fine cold dust. There must have been a storm in the night; snow piles in small drifts on the mattresses, having blown in through the cracks and crevices in the walls and roof. I sit up and look around. Three of the kids are in the room with me, huddled like sheep. I get up, shaking snow from my hair. I slept in my clothes from yesterday, but I don't want Miss Larsen and the girls at school, Lucy in particular, to see me in the same clothes two days in a row (though other kids, I've noticed, have no shame about this at all). I pull a dress and my other sweater from my suitcase, which I keep open in a corner, and change quickly, pulling them over my head. None of my clothes are ever particularly clean, but I cling to these rituals nevertheless.

It's the promise of the warm schoolhouse, Miss Larsen's friendly smile, and the distraction of other lives, other worlds on the pages of the books we read in class, that get me out the door. The walk to the corner is getting harder; with each snowfall I have to forge a new path. Mr. Grote tells me that when the heavy storms hit in a few weeks I might as well forget it.

At school Miss Larsen takes me aside. She holds my hand and looks into my eyes. "Are things all right at home, Dorothy?"

I nod.

"If there's anything you want to tell me —"

"No, ma'am," I say. "Everything is fine."

"You haven't been handing in your homework."

There's no time or place to read or do homework at the Grotes', and after the sun goes down at five there's no light, either. There are only two candle stubs in the house, and Mrs. Grote keeps one with her in the back room. But I don't want Miss Larsen to feel sorry for me. I want to be treated like everyone else.

"I'll try harder," I say.

"You . . ." Her fingers flutter at her neck, then drop. "Is it difficult to keep clean?"

I shrug, feeling the heat of shame. My neck. I'll have to be more thorough.

"Do you have running water?"

"No, ma'am."

She bites her lip. "Well. Come and see me if you ever want to talk, you hear?"

"I'm fine, Miss Larsen," I tell her. "Everything is fine."

■ ■ ■ ■

I am asleep on a pile of blankets, having been nudged off the mattresses by a fitful child, when I feel a hand on my face. I open my eyes. Mr. Grote, bending over me, puts a finger to his lips, then motions for to me to come. Groggily I get up, wrapping a quilt around myself, and follow him to the living room. In the weak moonlight, filtered through clouds and the dirty windows, I see him sit on the gold sofa and pat the cushion beside him.

I pull the quilt tighter. He pats the cushion again. I go over to him, but I don't sit.

"It's cold tonight," he says in a low voice. "I could use some company."

"You should go back there with her," I say.

"Don't want to do that."

"I'm tired," I tell him. "I'm going to bed."

He shakes his head. "You're gonna stay here with me."

I feel a flutter in my stomach and turn to leave.

He reaches out and grabs my arm. "I want you to stay, I said."

I look at him in the gloom. Mr. Grote has never frightened me before, but something in his voice is different, and I know I need to be careful. His mouth is curled up at the edges into a funny smile.

He tugs the quilt. "We can warm each other up."

I yank it tighter around my shoulders and turn away again, and then I am falling. I hit my elbow on the hard floor and feel a sharp pain as I land heavily on it, my nose to the floor. Twisting in the quilt, I look up to see what happened. I feel a rough hand on my head. I want to move, but am trapped in a cocoon.

"You do what I say." I feel his stubbled face on my cheek, smell his gamy breath. I squirm again and he puts his foot on my back. "Be quiet."

His big rough hand is inside the quilt, and then it's under my sweater, under my dress. I try to pull away but I can't. His hand roams up and down and I feel a jolt of shock as he probes the place between my legs, pushes at it with his fingers. His sandpaper face is still against mine, rubbing against my cheek, and his breathing is jagged.

"Yesss," he gulps into my ear. He is hunched above me like a dog, one hand rubbing hard at my skin and the other unbuttoning his trousers. Hearing the rough snap of each button, I bend and squirm but

238

am trapped in the quilt like a fly in a web. I see his pants open and low on his hips, the engorged penis between his legs, his hard white belly. I've seen enough animals in the yard to know what he's trying to do. Though my arms are trapped, I rock my body to try to seal the quilt around me. He yanks at it roughly and I feel it giving way, and as it does he whispers in my ear, "Easy, now, you like this, don't you," and I start to whimper. When he sticks two fingers inside me, his jagged nails tear at my skin and I cry out. He slaps his other hand over my mouth and rams his fingers deeper, grinding against me, and I make noises like a horse, frantic guttural sounds from deep in my throat.

And then he lifts his hips and takes his hand off my mouth. I scream and feel the blinding shock of a slap across my face.

From the direction of the hallway comes a voice — "Gerald?" — and he freezes, just for a second, before slithering off me like a lizard, fumbling with his buttons, pulling himself off the floor.

"What in the name of Christ —" Mrs. Grote is leaning against the door frame, cupping her rounded stomach with one hand.

I yank my underpants up and my dress and sweater down, sit up and stumble to my feet, clutching the quilt around me.

"Not *her*!" she wails.

"Now, Wilma, it isn't what it looks like —"

"You animal!" Her voice is deep and savage. She turns to me. "And you — you — I knew —" She points at the door. "Get out. *Get out!*"

It takes me a moment to understand what she means — that she wants me to leave, now, in the cold, in the middle of the night.

"Easy, Wilma, calm down," Gerald — Mr. Grote — says.

"I want that girl — that *filth* — out of my house."

"Let's talk about this."

"I want her out!"

"All right, all right." He looks at me with dull eyes, and I can see that as bad as this situation is, it's about to get worse. I don't want to stay here, but how can I survive out there?

Mrs. Grote disappears down the hall. I hear a child crying in the back. She returns a moment later with my suitcase and heaves it across the room. It crashes against the wall, spilling its contents across the floor.

My boots and the mustard coat, with Fanny's precious lined gloves in the pocket, are on a nail by the front door, and I'm

240

wearing my only pair of threadbare socks. I make my way to the suitcase and grab what I can, open the door to a sharp blast of cold air and toss a few scattered pieces of clothing onto the porch, my breath a puff of smoke in front of me. As I put on my boots, fumbling with the laces, I hear Mr. Grote say, "What if something happens to her?" and Mrs. Grote's reply: "If that stupid girl gets it in her head to run away, there's nothing we can do, is there?"

And run I do, leaving almost everything I possess in the world behind me — my brown suitcase, the three dresses I made at the Byrnes', the fingerless gloves and change of underwear and the navy sweater, my schoolbooks and pencil, the composition book Miss Larsen gave me to write in. The sewing packet Fanny made for me, at least, is in the inner pocket of my coat. I leave four children I could not help and did not love. I leave a place of degradation and squalor, the likes of which I will never experience again. And I leave any last shred of my childhood on the rough planks of that living room floor.

HEMINGFORD COUNTY, MINNESOTA, 1930

Trudging forward like a sleepwalker in the bitter cold, I make my way down the driveway, then turn left and plod up the rutted dirt road to the falling-down bridge. In places I have to crunch through the top layer of snow, thick as piecrust. The sharp edges lacerate my ankles. As I gaze up at the crystal stars glittering overhead, cold steals the breath from my mouth.

Once I'm out of the woods and on the main road, a full moon bathes the fields around me in a shimmering, pearly light. Gravel crunches loudly under my boots; I can feel its pebbly roughness through my thin soles. I stroke the soft wool inside my gloves, so warm that not even my fingertips are cold. I'm not afraid — it was more frightening in that shack than it is on the road, with moonlight all around. My coat is thin, but I'm wearing what clothing I could salvage underneath, and as I hurry along I begin to warm up. I make a plan: I will walk to school. It's only four miles.

The dark line of the horizon is far in the distance, the sky above it lighter, like layers of sediment in rock. The schoolhouse is fixed in my mind. I just have to get there. Walking at a steady pace, my boots scuffing the gravel, I count a hundred steps and start again. My da used to say it's good to test your limits now and then, learn what the body is capable of, what you can endure. He said this when we were in the throes of sickness on the *Agnes Pauline,* and again in the bitter first winter in New York, when four of us, including Mam, came down with pneumonia.

Test your limits. Learn what you can endure. I am doing that.

As I walk along I feel as weightless and insubstantial as a slip of paper, lifted by the wind and gliding down the road. I think about the many ways I ignored what was in front of me — how blind I was, how foolish not to be on my guard. I think of Dutchy, who knew enough to fear the worst.

Ahead on the horizon, the first pink light of dawn begins to show. And just before it, the white clapboard building becomes visible halfway up a small ridge. Now that the schoolhouse is within sight my energy drains, and all I want to do is sink down by the side of the road. My feet are leaden and aching. My face is numb; my nose feels frozen. I don't know how I make it to the school, but somehow I do. When I get to the front door, I find that the building is locked. I go around to the back, to the porch where they keep wood for the stove, and I open the door and fall onto the floor. An old horse blanket is folded by the woodpile, and I wrap myself in it and fall into a fitful sleep.

I am running in a yellow field, through a maze of hay bales, unable to find my way . . .

"Dorothy?" I feel a hand on my shoulder, and spring awake. It's Mr. Post. "What in God's name . . . ?"

For a moment I'm not sure myself. I look up at Mr. Post, at his round red cheeks and puzzled expression. I look around at the pile of rough-cut wood, the wide whitewashed planks of the porch walls. The door to the schoolroom is ajar, and it's clear that Mr. Post has come to get wood to start the fire, as he must do every morning before heading out to pick us up.

"Are you all right?"

I nod, willing myself to be.

"Does your family know you're here?"

"No, sir."

"How'd you get to the school?"

"I walked."

He stares at me for a moment, then says, "Let's get you out of the cold."

Mr. Post guides me to a chair in the schoolroom and puts my feet on another chair, then takes the dirty blanket from my shoulders and replaces it with a clean plaid one he finds in a cupboard. He unlaces each of my boots and sets them beside the chair, *tsk*ing over the holes in my socks. Then I watch him make a fire. The room is already getting warm when Miss Larsen arrives a few minutes later.

"What's this?" she says. "Dorothy?" She unwraps her violet scarf and takes off her hat and gloves. In the window behind her I see a car pulling away. Miss Larsen's long hair is coiled in a bun at the nape of her neck, and her brown eyes are clear and bright. The pink wool skirt she's wearing brings out the color in her cheeks.

Kneeling by my chair, she says, "Goodness, child. Have you been here long?"

Mr. Post, having completed his duties, is putting on his hat and coat to make the rounds in the truck. "She was asleep out there on the porch when I arrived." He laughs. "Scared the bejeezus out of me."

"I'm sure it did," she says.

"Says she walked here. Four miles." He shakes his head. "Lucky she didn't freeze to death."

"You seem to have warmed her up nicely."

"She's thawing out. Well, I'm off to get the others." He pats the front of his coat. "See you in a jiff."

As soon as he leaves, Miss Larsen says, "Now then. Tell me what happened."

And I do. I wasn't planning to, but she looks at me with such genuine concern that everything spills out. I tell her about Mrs. Grote lying in bed all day and Mr. Grote in the woods and the snow dust on my face in the morning and the stained mattresses. I tell her about the cold squirrel stew and the squalling children. And I tell her about Mr. Grote on the sofa, his hands on me, and pregnant Mrs. Grote in the hallway, yelling at me to get out. I tell her that I was afraid to stop walking, afraid that I would fall asleep. I tell her about the gloves Fanny knitted for me.

Miss Larsen puts her hand over mine and leaves it there, squeezing it every now and then. "Oh, Dorothy," she says.

And then, "Thank goodness for the gloves. Fanny sounds like a good friend."

"She was."

She holds her chin, tapping it with two fingers. "Who brought you to the Grotes'?"

"Mr. Sorenson from the Children's Aid Society."

"All right. When Mr. Post gets back, I'll send him out to find this Mr. Sorenson." Opening her lunch pail, she pulls out a biscuit. "You must be hungry."

Normally I would refuse — I know this is part of her lunch. But I am so ravenous that at the sight of the biscuit my mouth fills with water. I accept it shamefully and wolf it down. While I'm eating the biscuit Miss Larsen heats water on the stove for tea and cuts an apple into slices, arranging them on a chipped china plate from the shelf. I watch as she spoons loose tea into a strainer and pours the boiling water over it into two cups. I've never seen her offer tea to a child before, and certainly not to me.

"Miss Larsen," I start. "Could you ever — would you ever —"

She seems to know what I'm asking. "Take you home to live with me?" She smiles, but her expression is pained. "I care about you, Dorothy. I think you know that. But I can't — I'm in no position to take care of a girl. I live in a boardinghouse."

I nod, a knob in my throat.

"I will help you find a home," she says gently. "A place that is safe and clean, where you'll be treated like a ten-year-old girl. I promise you that."

When the other kids file in from the truck, they look at me curiously.

"What's she doing here?" one boy, Robert, says.

"Dorothy came in a little early this morning." Miss Larsen smooths the front of her pretty pink skirt. "Take your seats and pull out your workbooks, children."

After Mr. Post has come in from the back with more wood and arranged the logs in the bin by the stove, Miss Larsen signals to him, and he follows her back to the entry vestibule. A few minutes later he heads outside again, still in his coat and cap. The engine roars to life and the brakes screech as he maneuvers his truck down the steep drive.

About an hour later, I hear the truck's distinctive clatter and look out the window. I watch as it slowly makes its way up the steep drive, then comes to a stop. Mr. Post climbs out and comes in the porch door, and Miss Larsen excuses herself from the lesson and goes to the back. A few moments later she calls my name and I rise from my desk, all eyes on me, and make my way to the porch.

Miss Larsen seems worried. She keeps touching her hair in the bun. "Dorothy, Mr. Sorenson is not convinced . . ." She stops and touches her neck, glances beseechingly at Mr. Post.

"I think what Miss Larsen is trying to say," he says slowly, "is that you will need to explain what happened in detail to Mr. Sorenson. Ideally, as you know, they want to make the placements work. Mr. Sorenson wonders if this might simply be a matter of — miscommunication."

I feel light-headed as I realize what Mr. Post is saying. "He doesn't believe me?"

A look passes between them. "It's not a question of believing or not believing. He just needs to hear the story from you," Miss Larsen says.

For the first time in my life, I feel the wildness of revolt. Tears spring to my eyes. "I'm not going back there. I can't."

Miss Larsen puts an arm around my shoulder. "Dorothy, don't worry. You'll tell Mr. Sorenson your story, and I'll tell him what I know. I won't let you go back there."

The next few hours are a blur. I mimic Lucy's movements, pulling out the spelling primer when she does, lining up behind her to write on the board, but I barely register what's going on around me. When she whispers, "Are you all right?" I shrug. She squeezes my hand but doesn't probe further — and I don't know if it's because she senses I don't want to talk about it or if she's afraid of what I might say.

After lunch, when we are back in our seats, I see a vehicle way off in the distance. The sound of the motor fills my head; the dark truck coming toward the school is the only thing I see. And here it is — puttering up the steep drive, screeching to a stop behind Mr. Post's truck.

I see Mr. Sorenson in the driver's seat. He sits there for a moment. Takes off his black felt hat, strokes his black mustache. Then he opens the car door.

"My, my, my," Mr. Sorenson says when I've finished my story. We are sitting on hard chairs on the back porch, warmer now than it was earlier in the day from the sun and the heat of the stove. He reaches out to pat my leg, then seems to think better of it and rests his hand on his hip. With his other hand he strokes his mustache. "Such a long walk in the cold. You must have been very . . ." His voice trails off. "And yet. And yet. I wonder: the middle of the night. Might you perhaps have . . . ?"

I look at him steadily, my heart pounding in my chest.

". . . misconstrued?"

He looks at Miss Larsen. "A ten-year-old girl . . . don't you find, Miss Larsen, that there can be a certain — excitability? A tendency to overdramatize?"

"It depends on the girl, Mr. Sorenson," she says stiffly, lifting her chin. "I have never known Dorothy to lie."

Chuckling, he shakes his head. "Ah, Miss Larsen, that's not at all what I'm saying, of course not! I merely meant that sometimes, particularly if one has been through distressing events in one's young life, one might be inclined to jump to conclusions — to inadvertently blow things out of proportion. I saw with my own eyes that living conditions in the Grote household were, well, less than optimal. But we can't all have storybook families, can we, Miss Larsen? The world is not a perfect place, and when we are dependent on the charity of others, we are not always in a position to complain." He smiles at me. "My recommendation, Dorothy, is to give it another try. I can talk to the Grotes and impress upon them the need to improve conditions."

Miss Larsen's eyes are glittering strangely, and a red rash has crept up her neck. "Did you hear the girl, Mr. Sorenson?" she says in a strained voice. "There was an attempted . . . violation. And Mrs. Grote, coming upon the appalling scene, cast her out. Surely you don't expect Dorothy to return to that situation, now, do you? Frankly, I wonder why you don't ask the police to go out there and take a look. It doesn't sound like a healthy place for the other children there, either."

Mr. Sorenson is nodding slowly, as if to say *Now, now, it was just a thought, don't get shrill, let's all calm down.* But what he says is, "Well, then, you see, we're in a bit of a pickle. There are no families that I know of at the moment seeking orphans. I could inquire farther afield, of course. Contact the Children's Aid in New York. If it comes down to it, Dorothy could go back there, I suppose, on the next train that comes through."

"Surely we won't need to resort to that," Miss Larsen says.

He gives a little shrug. "One would hope not. One doesn't know."

She puts her hand on my shoulder and gives it a squeeze. "Let's explore our options then, Mr. Sorenson, shall we? And in the meantime — for a day or two — Dorothy can come home with me."

I look up at her with surprise. "But I thought —"

"It can't be permanent," she says quickly. "I live in a boardinghouse, Mr. Sorenson, where no children are allowed. But my landlady has a kind heart, and she knows I am a schoolteacher and that not all of my children are" — she appears to pick her words carefully — "housed advantageously. I think she will be sympathetic — as I say, for a day or two."

Mr. Sorenson strokes his mustache. "Very well, Miss Larsen. I will look into other possibilities, and leave you in charge of Dorothy for a few days. Young lady, I trust that you will be appropriately polite and well behaved."

"Yes, sir," I say solemnly, but my heart is swelling with joy. Miss Larsen is taking me home with her! I can't believe my good fortune.

HEMINGFORD, MINNESOTA, 1930

The man who picks Miss Larsen and me up after school signals surprise at my presence with a lift of his eyebrow, but says nothing.

"Mr. Yates, this is Dorothy," she tells him, and he nods at me in the rearview mirror. "Dorothy, Mr. Yates works for my landlady, Mrs. Murphy, and is kind enough to take me to the schoolhouse each day, since I don't drive myself."

"It's a pleasure, miss," he says, and I can see by his pink ears that he means it.

Hemingford is much larger than Albans. Mr. Yates drives slowly down Main Street, and I gaze out at the signs: the Imperial Theatre (whose marquee trumpets NOW WITH THE TALKING, SINGING AND DANCING!); the *Hemingford Ledger;* Walla's Recreational Parlor, advertising BILLIARDS, FOUNTAIN, CANDY, TOBACCO in its plate-glass window; Farmer's State Bank; Shindler's Hardware; and Nielsen's General Store — EVERYTHING TO EAT AND WEAR.

At the corner of Main and Park, several blocks from the town center, Mr. Yates pulls to a stop in front of a light-blue Victorian house with a wraparound porch. An oval placard by the front door announces, HEMINGFORD HOME FOR YOUNG LADIES.

The bell tinkles when Miss Larsen opens the door. She ushers me in but holds a finger to her lips and whispers, "Wait here a moment," before pulling off her gloves, unwrapping the scarf around her neck, and disappearing through a door at the end of the hall.

The foyer is formal, with flocked burgundy wallpaper, a large gilt-framed mirror, and a dark, ornately carved chest of drawers. After looking around a bit, I perch on a slippery horsehair chair. In one corner an imposing grandfather clock ticks loudly, and when it chimes the hour, I nearly slide off in surprise.

After a few minutes, Miss Larsen returns. "My landlady, Mrs. Murphy, would like to meet you," she says. "I told her about your — predicament. I felt I needed to explain why I brought you here. I hope that's all right."

"Yes, of course."

"Just be yourself, Dorothy," she says. "All right, then. This way."

I follow her down the hall and through the door into a parlor, where a plump, bosomy woman with a nimbus of downy gray hair is sitting on a rose velvet sofa next to a glowing fire. She has long lines beside her nose like a marionette and a watchful, alert expression. "Well, my girl, it sounds as if you've had quite a time of it," she says, motioning for me to sit across from her in one of two floral wingback chairs.

I sit in one and Miss Larsen takes the other, smiling at me a little anxiously.

"Yes, ma'am," I say to Mrs. Murphy.

"Oh — you're Irish, are you?"

"Yes, ma'am."

She beams. "I thought so! But I had a Polish girl here a few years ago with hair redder than yours. And of course there are the Scottish, though not as commonly in these parts. Well, and I'm Irish too, if you couldn't tell," she adds. "Came over like you as a wee lass. My people are from Enniscorthy. And yours?"

"Kinvara. In County Galway."

"Indeed, I know the place! My cousin married a Kinvara girl. Are you familiar with the Sweeney clan?"

I've never heard of the Sweeney clan, but

I nod just the same.

"Well, then." She looks pleased. "What's your family name?"

"Power."

"And you were christened . . . Dorothy?"

"No, Niamh. My name was changed by the first family I came to." My face reddens as I realize I'm confessing to having been thrown out of two homes.

But she doesn't seem to notice, or care. "I guessed as much! Dorothy is no Irish name." Leaning toward me, she inspects my necklace. "A claddagh. I haven't seen one of those in an elephant's age. From home?"

I nod. "My gram gave it to me."

"Yes, and see how she guards it," she comments to Miss Larsen.

I'm not aware until she says this that I'm holding it between my fingers. "I didn't mean —"

"Oh, lass, it's all right," she says, patting my knee. "It's the only thing you've got to remind you of your people, now, isn't it?"

When Mrs. Murphy turns her attention to the cabbage-rose tea service on the table in front of her, Miss Larsen gives me a wink. I think we're both surprised that Mrs. Murphy seems to be warming to me so quickly.

Miss Larsen's room is tidy and bright, and

about the size of a storage closet — barely big enough for a single bed, a tall oak dresser, and a narrow pine desk with a brass lamp. The bedspread has neatly tucked-in hospital corners; the pillowcase is clean and white. Several watercolors of flowers hang from hooks on the walls, and a black-and-white photograph of a stern-looking couple sits on the dresser in a gilt frame.

"Are these your parents?" I ask, looking closely at the picture. A bearded man in a dark suit stands stiffly behind a thin woman seated in a straight-backed chair. The woman, wearing a plain black dress, looks like a sterner version of Miss Larsen.

"Yes." She comes closer and gazes at the picture. "They're both dead now, so I suppose that makes me an orphan, too," she says after a moment.

"I'm not really an orphan," I tell her.

"Oh?"

"At least I don't know. There was a fire — my mother went to the hospital. I never saw her again."

"But you think she may be alive?"

I nod.

"Would you hope to find her?"

I think of what the Schatzmans said about my mother after the fire — that she'd gone crazy, lost her mind after losing all those children. "It was a mental hospital. She wasn't — well. Even before the fire." This is the first time I've admitted this to anyone. It's a relief to speak the words.

"Oh, Dorothy." Miss Larsen sighs. "You've been through a lot in your young life, haven't you?"

When we go down to the formal dining room at six o'clock, I am stunned at the bounty: a ham in the middle of the table, roasted potatoes, brussels sprouts glistening with butter, a basket of rolls. The dishes are real china in a pattern of purple forget-me-nots with silver trim. Even in Ireland I never saw a table like this, except on a holiday — and this is an ordinary Tuesday. Five boarders and Mrs. Murphy are standing behind chairs. I take the empty seat beside Miss Larsen.

"Ladies," Mrs. Murphy says, standing at the head of the table. "This is Miss Niamh Power, from County Galway, by way of New York. She came to Minnesota as a train rider — you may have heard about them in the papers. She will be with us for a few days. Let's do our best to make her feel welcome."

The other women are all in their twenties. One works as a counter girl at Nielsen's General Store, one at a bakery, another at the *Hemingford Ledger* as a receptionist. Under the watchful eye of Mrs. Murphy, all of them are polite, even rail-thin and sour-faced Miss Grund, a clerk in a shoe store. ("She's not accustomed to children," Miss Larsen whispers to me after Miss Grund shoots an icy look down the dinner table.) These women are a little afraid of Mrs. Murphy, I can see. Over the course of dinner I notice that she can be snappish and short-tempered, and she likes to be the boss. When one of them expresses an opinion she disagrees with, she looks around at the group and gathers allies for her position. But she is nothing but kind to me.

Last night I barely slept on the cold porch of the school, and before that I was on a soiled mattress in a fetid room with three other children. But tonight I have my own room, the bed neatly made up with crisp white sheets and two clean quilts. When Mrs. Murphy bids me good night, she hands me a gown and undergarments, a towel and hand cloth and a brush for my teeth. She shows me to the bathroom down the hall, with running water in its sink and a WC that flushes and a large porcelain tub, and tells me to draw a bath and stay in it as long as I wish; the others can use a different powder room.

When she leaves, I inspect my reflection in the mirror — the first time since arriving in Minnesota I've looked in a whole piece of mirror unclouded by spots and damage. A girl I barely recognize stares back. She is thin and pale, dull eyed, with sharp cheekbones and matted dark red hair, windchapped cheeks, and a red-rimmed nose. Her lips are scabbed, and her sweater is pilled and soiled with dirt. I swallow — she swallows. My throat hurts. I must be getting sick.

When I shut my eyes in the warm bath, I feel as if I'm floating inside a cloud.

Back in my room, warm and dry and dressed in my new gown, I shut the door and lock it. I stand with my back against it, savoring the feeling. I've never had a room of my own — not in Ireland, on Elizabeth Street, at the Children's Aid Society, in the hallway at the Byrnes', at the Grotes'. I pull back the covers, tucked tightly around the mattress, and slip between the sheets. Even the pillow, with its cotton casing smelling of washing soap, is a marvel. Lying on my back with the electric lamp on, I gaze at the small red and blue flowers in the off-white wallpaper, the white ceiling above, the oak dresser with its bacon pattern and smooth white knobs. I look down at the coiled rag rug and the shiny wood floor underneath. I turn off the light and lie in the dark. As my eyes adjust to the darkness, I can make out the shapes of each object in the room. Electric lamp. Dresser. Bed frame. My boots. For the first time since I stepped off the train in Minnesota more than a year ago, I feel safe.

For the next week, I barely leave my bed. The white-haired doctor who comes to examine me puts a cold metal stethoscope to my chest, listens thoughtfully for a few moments, and announces that I have pneumonia. For days I live in a fever, with the covers pulled up and the shades drawn, the door to my bedroom open so that Mrs. Murphy can hear me call. She puts a small silver bell on the dresser and instructs me to shake it if I need anything. "I'm just downstairs," she says. "I'll come right up." And though she bustles around, muttering about all the things she needs to do and how one girl or another — she calls them girls, though they are all working women — didn't make her bed or left her dishes in the sink or neglected to bring the tea set to the kitchen when she left the parlor, she drops everything when I ring the bell.

The first few days I slip in and out of

sleep, opening my eyes to the soft glow of sunlight through my window shade, and then the room is dark; Mrs. Murphy leans over me with a cup of water, her yeasty breath on my face, the warm hennish bulk of her against my shoulder. Miss Larsen, hours later, placing a cool folded cloth on my forehead with careful fingers. Mrs. Murphy nursing me with chicken soup filled with carrots and celery and potatoes.

In my moments of fevered consciousness I think I am dreaming. Am I really in this warm bed in this clean room? Am I really being taken care of?

And then I open my eyes in the light of a new day, and feel different. Mrs. Murphy takes my temperature and it is under one hundred degrees. Raising the shade, she says, "Look at what you've missed," and I sit up and look outside at snow like swirling cotton, blanketing everything and still falling, the sky white and more white — trees, cars, the sidewalk, the house next door, transformed. My own awakening feels as momentous. I too am blanketed, my harsh edges obscured and transformed.

When Mrs. Murphy learns that I have come with almost nothing, she sets about gathering clothes. In the hall is a large trunk filled with garments that boarders have left behind, chemises and stockings and dresses, sweater sets and skirts, and even a few pairs of shoes, and she lays them out on the double bed in her own large room for me to try on.

Almost everything is too big, but a few pieces will work — a sky-blue cardigan embroidered with white flowers, a brown dress with pearl buttons, several sets of stockings, a pair of shoes. "Jenny Early," Mrs. Murphy sighs, fingering a particularly pretty yellow floral dress. "A slip of a girl, she was, and lovely too. But when she found herself in the family way . . ." She looks at Miss Larsen, who shakes her head. "Water under the bridge. I heard that Jenny had a nice wedding and a healthy baby boy, so all's well that ends well."

As my health improves I begin to worry: this won't last. I will be sent away. I made it through this year because I had to, because I had no options. But now that I've experienced comfort and safety, how can I go back? These thoughts take me to the edge of despair, so I will myself — I force myself — not to have them.

SPRUCE HARBOR, MAINE, 2011

Vivian is waiting by the front door when Molly arrives. "Ready?" she says, turning to head up the stairs as soon as Molly crosses the threshold.

"Hang on." Molly shrugs off her army jacket and hangs it on the black iron coatrack in the corner. "What about that cup of tea?"

"No time," Vivian calls over her shoulder. "I'm old, you know. Could drop dead any minute. We've got to get going!"

"Really? No tea?" Molly grumbles, following behind her.

A curious thing is happening. The stories that Vivian began to tell only with prodding, in dutiful answer to specific questions, are spilling forth unprompted, one after another, so many that even Vivian seems surprised. " 'Who would have thought the old man to have had so much blood in him?' " she said after one session. "*Macbeth,*

265

dear. Look it up."

Vivian has never really talked about her experience on the train with anyone. It was shameful, she says. Too much to explain, too hard to believe. All those children sent on trains to the Midwest — collected off the streets of New York like refuse, garbage on a barge, to be sent as far away as possible, out of sight.

And anyway, how do you talk about losing everything?

"But what about your husband?" Molly asks. "You must have told him."

"I told him some things," Vivian says. "But so much of my experience was painful, and I didn't want to burden him. Sometimes it's easier to try to forget."

Aspects of Vivian's memory are triggered with each box they open. The sewing kit wrapped in cheesecloth evokes the Byrnes' grim home. The mustard-colored coat with military buttons, the felt-lined knit gloves, the brown dress with pearl buttons, a carefully packed set of cabbage-rose china. Soon enough Molly is able to keep the cast of characters straight in her head: Niamh, Gram, Maisie, Mrs. Scatcherd, Dorothy, Mr. Sorenson, Miss Larsen. . . . One story circles back to another. *Upright and do right make all right.* As if joining scraps of fabric

266

to make a quilt, Molly puts them in the right sequence and stitches them together, creating a pattern that was impossible to see when each piece was separate.

When Vivian describes how it felt to be at the mercy of strangers, Molly nods. She knows full well what it's like to tamp down your natural inclinations, to force a smile when you feel numb. After a while you don't know what your own needs are anymore. You're grateful for the slightest hint of kindness, and then, as you get older, suspicious. Why would anyone do anything for you without expecting something in return? And anyway — most of the time they don't. More often than not, you see the worst of people. You learn that most adults lie. That most people only look out for themselves. That you are only as interesting as you are useful to someone.

And so your personality is shaped. You know too much, and this knowledge makes you wary. You grow fearful and mistrustful. The expression of emotion does not come naturally, so you learn to fake it. To pretend. To display an empathy you don't actually feel. And so it is that you learn how to pass, if you're lucky, to look like everyone else, even though you're broken inside.

■ ■ ■ ■

"Eh, I don't know," Tyler Baldwin says one day in American History after they watch a film about the Wabanakis. "What's that saying again — 'to the victor go the spoils'?" I mean, it happens all the time, all over the world, right? One group wins, another loses."

"Well, it's true that humans have been dominating and oppressing each other since time began," Mr. Reed says. "Do you think the oppressed groups should just stop their complaining?"

"Yeah. You lost. I kind of feel like saying 'Deal with it,' " Tyler says.

The rage Molly feels is so overwhelming she sees spots before her eyes. For more than four hundred years Indians were deceived, corralled, forced onto small pieces of land and discriminated against, called dirty Indians, injuns, redskins, savages. They couldn't get jobs or buy homes. Would it compromise her probationary status to strangle this imbecile? She takes a deep breath and tries to calm down. Then she raises her hand.

Mr. Reed looks at her with surprise. Molly rarely raises her hand. "Yes?"

"I'm an Indian." She's never told anyone this except Jack. To Tyler she knows she's just . . . Goth, if he thinks of her at all. "Penobscot. I was born on Indian Island. And I just want to say that what happened to the Indians is exactly like what happened to the Irish under British rule. It wasn't a fair fight. Their land was stolen, their religion was forbidden, they were forced to bend to foreign domination. It wasn't okay for the Irish, and it's not okay for the Indians."

"Jeez, soapbox much?" Tyler mutters.

Megan McDonald, one seat ahead of Molly, raises her hand, and Mr. Reed nods. "She has a point," she says. "My grandpa's from Dublin. He's always talking about what the Brits did."

"Well, my granddad's parents lost everything in the Great Depression. You don't see me crying for handouts. Shit happens, excuse my French," Tyler says.

"Tyler's French aside," Mr. Reed says, raising his eyebrows at the class as if to say he doesn't approve but will deal with it later, "is that what they're doing? Asking for handouts?"

"They just want to be treated fairly," a kid in the back says.

"But what does that mean? And where does it end?" another kid asks.

269

As others join the conversation, Megan turns in her seat and squints at Molly, as if noticing her for the first time. "An Indian, huh. That's cool," she whispers. "Like Molly Molasses, right?"

Weekdays, now, Molly doesn't wait for Jack to take her to Vivian's house. Outside of school she picks up the Island Explorer.

"You have other things to do," she tells him. "I know it's a pain for you to wait on me." But in truth, taking the bus gives her the freedom to stay as long as Vivian will have her without Jack's questions.

Molly hasn't told Jack about the portage project. She knows he'd say it's a bad idea — that she's getting overinvolved in Vivian's life, asking too much of her. Even so, Jack has had an edge in his voice recently. "So hey, you're getting to the end of your hours soon, huh?" he says, and, "Making any progress up there?"

These days Molly slips into Vivian's house, ducks her head with a quick hello to Terry, sidles up the stairs. It seems both too hard to explain her growing relationship with Vivian and beside the point. What does it matter what anyone else thinks?

"Here's my theory," Jack says one day as they're sitting outside on the lawn at school during lunch period.

It's a beautiful morning, and the air is fresh and mild. Dandelions dance like sparklers in the grass.

"Vivian is like a mother figure to you. Grandmother, great-grandmother — whatever. She listens to you, she tells you stories, lets you help her out. She makes you feel needed."

"No," Molly says with irritation. "It's not like that. I have hours to do; she has work that needs to be done. Simple."

"Not really so simple, Moll," he says with exaggerated reasonableness. "Ma tells me there's not a helluva lot going on up there." He pops open a big can of iced tea and takes a long swallow.

"We're making progress. It's just hard to see."

"Hard to see?" He laughs, unwrapping a Subway Italian sandwich. "I thought the whole point was to get rid of the boxes. That seems fairly straightforward. No?"

Molly snaps a carrot stick in half. "We're organizing things. So they'll be easier to find."

"By who? Estate sale people? Because that's who it's going to be, you know. Vivian will probably never set foot up there again."

Is this really any of his business? "Then

271

we're making it easier for the estate sale people." In truth, though she hasn't admitted it out loud until now, Molly has virtually given up on the idea of disposing of anything. After all, what does it matter? Why shouldn't Vivian's attic be filled with things that are meaningful to her? The stark truth is that she will die sooner than later. And then professionals will descend on the house, neatly and efficiently separating the valuable from the sentimental, lingering only over items of indeterminate origin or worth. So yes — Molly has begun to view her work at Vivian's in a different light. Maybe it doesn't matter how much gets done. Maybe the value is in the process — in touching each item, in naming and identifying, in acknowledging the significance of a cardigan, a pair of children's boots.

"It's her stuff," Molly says. "She doesn't want to get rid of it. I can't force her, can I?"

Taking a bite of his sandwich, its fillings spilling out onto the waxy paper below his chin, Jack shrugs. "I don't know. I think it's more the" — he chews and swallows and Molly looks away, annoyed at his passive aggression — "appearance of it, y'know?"

"What do you mean?"

"To Ma it might look a little like you're taking advantage of the situation."

Molly looks down at her own sandwich.

"I just know you'll like it if you give it a chance," Dina said breezily when Molly asked her to stop putting bologna sandwiches in her lunch bag, adding, "or you can make your own damn lunch." So now Molly does — she swallowed her pride, asked Ralph for money, and bought almond butter, organic honey, and nutty bread in the health food store in Bar Harbor. And it's fine, though her little stash is about as welcome in the pantry as a fresh-killed mouse brought in by the cat — or perhaps, being vegetarian, less so — and is quarantined on a shelf in the mudroom "so no one gets confused," as Dina says.

Molly feels anger rising in her chest — at Dina's unwillingness to accept her for who she is, at Terry's judgments and Jack's need to placate her. At all of them. "The thing is — it's not really your mother's business, is it?"

The moment she says this she regrets it.

Jack gives her a sharp look. "Are you kidding me?"

He balls up the Subway wrapper and stuffs it in the plastic bag it came in. Molly has never seen him like this, his jaw tight, his eyes hard and angry. "My mother went out on a limb for you," he says. "She brought you into that house. And do I need to remind you that she lied to Vivian? If anything happens, she could lose her job. Like that." He snaps his fingers hard.

"Jack, you're right. I'm sorry," she says, but he is already on his feet and walking away.

Spruce Harbor, Maine, 2011

"Spring at last!" Ralph beams, pulling on work gloves in the kitchen while Molly pours herself a bowl of cereal. It does feel like spring today — real spring, with leafy trees and blooming daffodils, air so warm you don't need a sweater. "Here I go," he says, heading outside to clear brush. Working in the yard is Ralph's favorite activity; he likes to weed, to plant, to cultivate. All winter he's been like a dog scratching the door, begging to go out.

Dina, meanwhile, is watching HGTV and painting her toenails on the living room couch. When Molly comes into the living room with her raisin bran, she looks up and frowns. "Something I can do for you?" She jabs the tiny brush into the coral bottle, wipes the excess under the rim, and expertly strokes it on her big toe, correcting the line with her thumb. "No food in the living room, remember."

Good morning to you, too. Without a word, Molly turns and heads back to the kitchen, where she speed-dials Jack.

"Hey." His voice is cool.

"What're you up to?"

"Vivian's paying me to do a spring cleanup of her property — get rid of dead branches and all that. You?"

"I'm heading over to Bar Harbor, to the library. I have a research project due in a few days. I was hoping you'd come with me."

"Sorry, can't," he says.

Ever since their conversation at lunch last week, Jack's been like this. Molly knows it is taking great effort on his part to hold this grudge — it runs so counter to his personality. And though she wants to apologize, to make things right between them, she's afraid that anything she says now will ring hollow. If Jack knows she's been interviewing Vivian — that cleaning the attic has morphed into this ongoing conversation — he'll be even more pissed off.

She hears a whisper in her head: *Leave well enough alone. Finish your hours and be done with it.* But she can't leave well enough alone. She doesn't want to.

The Island Explorer is nearly empty. The few passengers greet each other with a nod as they get on. With her earbuds in, Molly knows she looks like a typical teenager, but what she's actually listening to is Vivian's voice. On the tape Molly hears things she didn't when Vivian was sitting in front of her . . .

Time constricts and flattens, you know. It's not evenly weighted. Certain moments linger in the mind and others disappear. The first twenty-three years of my life are the ones that shaped me, and the fact that I've lived almost seven decades since then is irrelevant. Those years have nothing to do with the questions you ask.

Molly flips open her notebook, runs her finger down the names and dates she's recorded. She plays the tape backward and forward, stops and starts, scribbles down identifiers she missed. Kinvara, County Galway, Ireland. The *Agnes Pauline.* Ellis Island, The Irish Rose, Delancey Street. Elizabeth Street, Dominick, James, Maisie Power. The Children's Aid Society, Mrs. Scatcherd, Mr. Curran . . .

What did you choose to take with you? What did you leave behind? What insights did you gain?

Vivian's life has been quiet and ordinary. As the years have passed, her losses have piled one on another like layers of shale:

even if her mother lived, she would be dead now; the people who adopted her are dead; her husband is dead; she has no children. Except for the company of the woman she pays to take care of her, she is as alone as a person can be.

She has never tried to find out what happened to her family — her mother or her relatives in Ireland. But over and over, Molly begins to understand as she listens to the tapes, Vivian has come back to the idea that the people who matter in our lives stay with us, haunting our most ordinary moments. They're with us in the grocery store, as we turn a corner, chat with a friend. They rise up through the pavement; we absorb them through our soles.

Vivian has given Molly's community service sentence meaning. Now Molly wants to give something back. No one else knows Vivian's story. There's no one to read the documents of indenture, of adoption; no one to acknowledge the significance of the things she values, things that would be meaningful only to someone who cares about her. But Molly cares. The gaps in Vivian's stories seem to her mysteries she can help solve. On TV once she heard a relationship expert say that you can't find peace until you find all the pieces. She wants to help Vivian find some kind of peace, elusive and fleeting as it may be.

After being dropped off at the Bar Harbor green, Molly walks over to the library, a brick structure on Mount Desert Street. In the main reading room, she chats with the reference librarian, who helps her find a cache of books on Irish history and immigration in the 1920s. She spends a few hours poring over them and jotting notes. Then she pulls out her laptop and launches Google. Different words together yield different results, so Molly tries dozens of combinations: "1929 fire NYC," "Lower East Side Elizabeth St. fire 1929," "Agnes Pauline," "Ellis Island 1927." On the Ellis Island website she clicks Passenger Records Search. *Search by ship. Now click the name of a ship from the list below . . .* And here it is, the *Agnes Pauline.*

She finds Vivian's parents' full names in the passenger records log — Patrick and Mary Power from County Galway, Ireland — and feels a vertiginous thrill, as if fictional characters have suddenly sprung to life. Searching the names, separately and together, she finds a small notice about the fire noting the deaths of Patrick Power and his sons, Dominick and James. There's no mention of Maisie.

She types "Mary Power." Then "Maisie Power." Nothing. She has an idea: Schatzman. "Schatzman Elizabeth Street." "Schatzman Elizabeth Street NYC." "Schatzman Elizabeth Street NYC 1930." A reunion blog pops up. A Liza Schatzman organized a family reunion in 2010 in upstate New York. Under the "family history" tab, Molly finds a sepia-toned picture of Agneta and Bernard Schatzman, who emigrated from Germany in 1915, resided at 26 Elizabeth Street. He worked as a vendor and she took in mending. Bernard Schatzman was born in 1894 and Agneta in 1897. They had no children until 1929, when he was thirty-five and she was thirty-two.

Then they adopted a baby, Margaret.

Maisie. Molly sits back in her chair. So Maisie didn't die in the fire.

Less than ten minutes after beginning her search, Molly is looking at a year-old photograph of a woman who must be Vivian's white-haired baby sister, Margaret Reynolds née Schatzman, age eighty-two, surrounded by her children, grandchildren, and great-grandchildren at her home in Rhinebeck, New York. Two and a half hours from New York City and just over eight hours from Spruce Harbor.

She types in "Margaret Reynolds, Rhinebeck, NY." An obituary notice from the *Poughkeepsie Journal* pops up. It's five months old.

Mrs. Margaret Reynolds, age 83, died peacefully in her sleep on Saturday after a short illness. She was surrounded by her loving family . . .

Lost — and found — and lost again. How will she ever tell Vivian?

HEMINGFORD, MINNESOTA, 1930

When I get better, I ride to school with Miss Larsen in the black car. Mrs. Murphy gives me something new nearly every day — a skirt she says she found in a closet, a woolen hat, a camel-colored coat, a periwinkle scarf and matching mittens. Some of the clothes have missing buttons or small rips and tears, and others need hemming or taking in. When Mrs. Murphy finds me mending a dress with the needle and thread Fanny gave me, she exclaims, "Why, you're as handy as a pocket in a shirt."

The food she makes, familiar to me from Ireland, evokes a flood of memories: sausages roasting with potatoes in the oven, the tea leaves in Gram's morning cuppa, laundry flapping on the line behind her house, the faint clang of the church bell in the distance. Gram saying, "Now, that was the goat's toe," after a satisfying supper. And other things: quarrels between Mam and

Gram, my da passed out drunk on the floor. Mam's cry: "You spoiled him rotten, and now he'll never be a man" — and Gram's retort: "You keep pecking at him and soon he won't come home at all." Sometimes when I stayed overnight at Gram's, I'd overhear my grandparents whispering at the kitchen table. *What are we to do about it, then? Will we have to feed that family forever?* I knew they were exasperated with Da, but they had little patience for Mam, either, whose people were from Limerick and never lifted a finger to help.

The day Gram gave me the claddagh I was sitting on her bed, tracing the nubby white bedspread like Braille under my fingers, watching her get ready for church. She sat at a small vanity table with an oval mirror, fluffing her hair lightly with a brush she prized — the finest whalebone and horse-hair, she said, letting me touch the smooth off-white handle, the stiff bristles — and kept in a casketlike case. She'd saved for the brush by mending clothes; it took four months, she told me, to earn the money.

After replacing the brush in its case, Gram opened her jewelry box, an off-white faux-leather one with gilt trim and a gold clasp, plush red velvet inside, revealing a trove of treasures — sparkling earrings, heavy necklaces in onyx and pearl, gold bracelets. (My mam later said spitefully that these were cheap costume jewelry from a Galway five-and-dime, but at the time they seemed impossibly luxurious to me.) She picked out a pair of clustered pearl earrings with padded back clasps, clipping first one and then the other to her low-hanging lobes.

In the bottom of the box was the claddagh cross. I'd never seen her wear it. She told me that her da, now long dead, had given it to her for her First Holy Communion when she was thirteen. She'd planned to give it to her daughter, my auntie Brigid, but Brigid wanted a gold birthstone ring instead.

"You are my only granddaughter, and I want you to have it," Gram declared, fastening the chain around my neck. "See the interlaced strands?" She touched the raised pattern with a knobby finger. "These trace a never-ending path, leading away from home and circling back. When you wear this, you'll never be far from the place you started."

Several weeks after Gram gave me the claddagh, she and Mam got into one of their arguments. As their voices rose I took the twins into a bedroom down the hall.

"You tricked him into it; he wasn't ready,"

I heard Gram shout. And then Mam's retort, as clear as day: "A man whose mother won't let him lift a finger is ruined for a wife."

The front door banged; it was Granddad, I knew, stomping out in disgust. And then I heard a crash, a shriek, a cry, and I ran to the parlor to find Gram's whalebone brush shattered in pieces against the hearth, and Mam with a look of triumph on her face.

Not a month later, we found ourselves bound for Ellis Island on the *Agnes Pauline*.

Mrs. Murphy's husband died a decade ago, I learn, leaving her with this big old house and little money. Making the most of the situation, she began to take in boarders. The women have a schedule that rotates once a week: cooking, laundry, cleaning, washing the floors. Soon enough I am helping too: I set the table for breakfast, clear the plates, sweep the hall, wash the dishes after dinner. Mrs. Murphy is the hardest working of all, up early to make scones and biscuits and porridge, last to bed when she shuts off the lights.

At night, in the living room, the women gather to talk about the stockings they wear, whether the best ones have a seam up the back or are smooth, which brands last longest, which are scratchy; the most desirable shade of lipstick (by consensus, Ritz Bonfire Red); and their favorite brands of face powder. I sit silently by the fireplace, listening. Miss Larsen rarely participates; she is busy in the evenings creating lesson plans and studying. She wears small gold glasses when she reads, which seems to be whenever she isn't doing chores. She always has a book or a dishrag in her hand, and sometimes both.

I am beginning to feel at home here. But as much as I hope that Mrs. Murphy has forgotten I don't belong, of course she hasn't. One afternoon, when I come in from the car with Miss Larsen after school, Mr. Sorenson is standing in the foyer, holding his black felt hat in his hands like a steering wheel. My stomach flops.

"Ah, here she is!" Mrs. Murphy exclaims. "Come, Niamh, into the parlor. Join us, please, Miss Larsen. Shut that door, we'll catch our death of cold. Tea, Mr. Sorenson?"

"That would be lovely, Mrs. Murphy," Mr. Sorenson says, lumbering after her through the double doors.

Mrs. Murphy gestures toward the rose velvet sofa and he sits down heavily, like an elephant I once saw in a picture book, his large stomach protruding from rounded thighs. Miss Larsen and I sit in the wing-back chairs. When Mrs. Murphy disappears into the kitchen, he leans forward and smirks. "Niamh again, are you?"

"I don't know." I glance out the window at the street dusted with snow and Mr. Sorenson's dark green truck that I somehow hadn't noticed earlier parked in front of the house. The vehicle, more than his presence, makes me shudder. It's the same one I rode in to the Grotes', with Mr. Sorenson gabbing cheerfully the whole way.

"Let's go back to Dorothy, shall we?" he says. "Easier."

Miss Larsen looks as me, and I shrug. "All right."

He clears his throat. "Why don't we get to it." He pulls his small glasses out of his breast pocket, puts them on, and holds a paper out at arm's length. "There have been two failed attempts at placing out. The Byrnes and the Grotes. Trouble with the woman of the house in both places." He looks at me over the top of his silver rims. "I must tell you, Dorothy, it's beginning to appear that there's some kind of . . . problem with you."

"But I didn't —"

He waves his sausage fingers at me. "The

predicament, you must understand, is that you are an orphan, and that whatever the reality, it looks as if there may be an issue with . . . insubordination. Now, there are several ways to proceed. First, of course, we can send you back to New York. Or we can attempt to find another home." He sighs heavily. "Which, to be frank, may prove difficult."

Mrs. Murphy, who has been in and out of the room with her cabbage-rose tea service and is now pouring tea into delicate, thin-rimmed cups, sets the teapot on a trivet in the middle of the polished coffee table. She hands Mr. Sorenson a cup and offers him the sugar bowl. "Marvelous, Mrs. Murphy," he says, and dumps four spoons of sugar into his cup. He adds milk, stirs it noisily, rests the small silver spoon on the rim of his saucer, and takes a long slurp.

"Mr. Sorenson," Mrs. Murphy says when his cup is back in its resting place. "A thought occurs. May I speak with you in the foyer?"

"Why certainly." He wipes his mouth with a pink napkin and gets up to follow her into the hall.

When the door closes behind them, Miss Larsen takes a sip of tea and places her cup back on its saucer with a little rattle. The brass lamp on the round table between us emits an amber glow. "I'm sorry you have to go through this. But I'm sure you understand that Mrs. Murphy, generous hearted as she is, can't take you in indefinitely. You *do* understand, don't you?"

"Yes." There's a lump in my throat. I don't trust myself to say more.

When Mrs. Murphy and Mr. Sorenson come back into the room, she fixes her steady gaze on him and smiles.

"You are quite a fortunate girl," he tells me. "This extraordinary woman!" He beams at Mrs. Murphy, and she lowers her eyes. "Mrs. Murphy has brought to my attention that a couple named the Nielsens, friends of hers, own the general store on Center Street. Five years ago they lost their only child."

"Diphtheria, I believe it was, poor thing," Mrs. Murphy adds.

"Yes, yes, tragedy," Mr. Sorenson says. "Well, apparently they've been looking for help with the shop. Mrs. Nielsen contacted Mrs. Murphy several weeks ago, asking whether any young woman in residence was seeking employment. And then, when you washed up on her doorstep . . ." Perhaps sensing that this characterization of how I got here might be perceived as insensitive,

289

he chuckles. "Forgive me, Mrs. Murphy! A figure of speech!"

"Quite all right, Mr. Sorenson, we understand you meant no harm by it." Mrs. Murphy pours more tea into his cup and hands it to him, then turns to me. "After speaking with Miss Larsen about your situation, I told Mrs. Nielsen about you. I said that you are a sober-minded and mature almost-eleven-year-old girl, that you have impressed me with your ability to sew and clean, and that I have no doubt you could be of use to her. I explained that while adoption may be the most desirous eventual result, it is not expected." She clasps her hands together. "And so Mr. and Mrs. Nielsen have agreed to meet with you."

I know I am expected to respond, to express gratitude, but it takes a conscious effort to smile, and several moments to form the words. I am not grateful; I am bitterly disappointed. I don't understand why I need to leave, why Mrs. Murphy can't keep me if she thinks I am so well mannered. I don't want to go into another home where I'm treated like a servant, tolerated only for the labor I can provide.

"How kind of you, Mrs. Murphy!" Miss Larsen exclaims, plunging into the silence. "That's wonderful news, isn't it, Dorothy?"

"Yes. Thank you, Mrs. Murphy," I say, choking out the words.

"You're quite welcome, child. Quite welcome." She beams proudly. "Now, Mr. Sorenson. Perhaps you and I should attend this meeting as well?"

Mr. Sorenson drains his teacup and sets it in its saucer. "Indeed, Mrs. Murphy. I am also thinking that the two of us should meet separately to discuss the . . . finer points of this transaction. What would you say to that?"

Mrs. Murphy blushes and blinks; she shifts in her chair, picks up her teacup, and then puts it down without taking a sip. "Yes, that's probably wise," she says, and Miss Larsen looks over and gives me a smile.

Hemingford, Minnesota, 1930

Over the next few days, every time I see her Mrs. Murphy has another suggestion for how I should comport myself on meeting the Nielsens. "A firm handshake, but not a squeeze," she says, passing me on the stairs. "You must be ladylike. They need to know that you can be trusted behind the counter," she lectures at dinner.

The other women chime in. "Don't ask questions," one advises.

"But answer them without hesitation," another adds.

"Make sure your fingernails are clipped and groomed."

"Clean your teeth just before with baking soda."

"Your hair must be" — Miss Grund grimaces and reaches up to her own head, as if patting down soap bubbles — "tamed. You never know how they might feel about a redhead. Especially that tinny shade."

"Now, now," Miss Larsen says. "We're going to scare the poor girl so much she won't know how to act."

On the morning of the meeting, a Saturday in mid-December, there is a light knock on my bedroom door. It's Mrs. Murphy, holding a navy blue velvet dress on a hanger. "Let's see if this fits," she says, handing it to me. I'm not sure whether to invite her in or close the door while I change, but she solves this dilemma by bustling in and sitting on the bed.

Mrs. Murphy is so matter-of-fact that I am not ashamed to take my clothes off and stand there in my knickers. She removes the dress from the hanger, unzips a seam at the side that I hadn't realized was a zipper, and lifts it over my head, helping me with the long sleeves, pulling down the gathered skirt, zipping it up again. She steps back in the small space to inspect me, yanks at one side and then the other. Tugs at a sleeve. "Let's see about that hair," she says, instructing me to turn around so she can take a look. Fishing in her apron pocket, she pulls out bobby pins and a hair clip. For the next few minutes she pokes and prods, pulling the hair back from my face and smoothing it into submission. When she's finished to her satisfaction, she turns me around to look at my reflection in the glass.

Despite my trepidation about meeting the Nielsens, I can't help smiling. For the first time since Mr. Grote butchered my hair months ago, I look almost pretty. I have never worn a velvet dress before. It is heavy and a little stiff, with a full skirt that falls in a lush drape to my midcalf. It gives off a faint scent of mothballs whenever I move. I think it's beautiful, but Mrs. Murphy isn't satisfied. Narrowing her eyes at me and clicking her tongue, she pinches the material. "Wait a minute, I'll be right back," she says, hurrying out and returning a few moments later with a wide black ribbon. "Turn around," she instructs, and when I do, she loops the sash around my waist and ties it in the back with a wide bow. We both inspect her handiwork in the mirror.

"There we are. You look like a princess, my dear," Mrs. Murphy declares. "Are your black stockings clean?"

I nod.

"Put them on, then. And your black shoes will be fine." She laughs, her hands on my waist. "A redheaded Irish princess you are, right here in Minnesota!"

At three o'clock that afternoon, in the early hours of the first heavy snowstorm of the season, I greet Mr. and Mrs. Nielsen in Mrs. Murphy's parlor, with Mr. Sorenson and Miss Larsen standing by.

Mr. Nielsen resembles a large gray mouse, complete with twitching whiskers, pink-tinged ears, and a tiny mouth. He is wearing a gray three-piece suit and a silk striped bow tie, and he walks with a black cane. Mrs. Nielsen is thin, almost frail. Her dark head of hair, streaked with silver, is pulled back in a bun. She has dark eyebrows and eyelashes and deep-set brown eyes, and her lips are stained a dark red. She wears no powder or rouge on her olive skin.

Mrs. Murphy puts the Nielsens at ease, plying them with tea and biscuits and inquiring about their short trip across town in the snow and then remarking generally on the weather: how the temperature dipped in the past few days and snow clouds gathered slowly to the west, how the storm finally began today, as everyone knew it would. They speculate about how much snow we are bound to get tonight, how long it will stay on the ground, when we might expect more snow, and what kind of winter it will be. Surely it won't rival the winter of 1922, when ice storms were followed by blizzards and nobody could get any relief? Or the black-dust blizzard of 1923 —

remember that? — when dirty snow blew down from North Dakota, seven-foot snow-drifts covered entire sections of the city, and people didn't leave their houses for weeks? On the other hand, there's little chance that it will be as mild as 1921, the warmest December on record.

The Nielsens are politely curious about me, and I do my best to answer their questions without sounding either desperate or apathetic. The other three adults watch us with a quivering intensity. I sense them urging me to do well, to sit up straight and answer in complete sentences.

Finally, as one conversational theme after another runs its course, Mr. Sorenson says, "All right then. I believe we all know why we are here — to determine whether the Nielsens might be willing to provide Dorothy with a home, and whether Dorothy is suitable to their needs. To that end, Dorothy — can you tell the Nielsens why you wish to become part of their household, and what you might bring to it yourself?"

If I am honest — which is not, of course, what Mr. Sorenson is asking of me — I will say that I simply need a warm, dry place to live. I want enough food to eat, clothes, and shoes that will protect me from the cold. I want calmness and order. More than anything, I want to feel safe in my bed.

"I can sew, and I am quite neat. I'm good with numbers," I say.

Mr. Nielsen, turning to Mrs. Murphy, asks, "And can the young lady cook and clean? Is she hardworking?"

"Is she a Protestant?" Mrs. Nielsen adds.

"She is a hardworking girl, I can attest to that," Mrs. Murphy says.

"I can cook some things," I tell them, "though at my previous residence I was expected to make stew out of squirrels and raccoons, and I'd rather not do that again."

"Mercy, no," Mrs. Nielsen says. "And the other question — ?"

"The other question?" I'm barely keeping up.

"Do you go to church, dear?" Mrs. Murphy prompts.

"Oh, right. The family I lived with were not churchgoing people," I answer honestly, though in truth I have not been to church since the chapel at the Children's Aid Society, and before that only with Gram. I remember clasping her hand as we walked to St. Joseph's, right in the center of Kinvara, a small church made of stone with jewel-toned stained-glass windows and dark oak pews. The smell of incense and lilies, the candles lit for loved ones passed away, the throaty intonations of the priest, and the majestic trumpeting of the organ. My da said he was allergic to religion, it never did anybody any good; and when Mam got grief from the neighbors on Elizabeth Street about not going to services, she'd say, "You try packing up a swarm of kids on a Sunday morning when one has a fever, one has the colic, and your husband's passed out in the bed." I remember watching other Catholics, girls in their Communion dresses and boys in their spit-shined shoes, walking down the street below our apartment, their mothers pushing prams and fathers strolling along beside.

"She's an Irish girl, Viola, so I suspect she's a Catholic," Mr. Nielsen says to his wife.

I nod.

"You may be a Catholic, child," Mr. Nielsen says — the first thing he has said to me directly — "but we are Protestant. And we will expect you to go to Lutheran services with us on Sundays."

It's been years since I've attended services of any kind, so what does it matter? "Yes, of course."

"And you should know that we will send you to school in town here, a short walk from our home — so you won't attend Miss

Larsen's classes any longer."

Miss Larsen says, "I believe Dorothy was about to outgrow the schoolhouse, anyway, she's such a smart girl."

"And after school," Mr. Nielsen says, "you will be expected to help in the store. We'll pay you an hourly wage, of course. You know about the store, Dorothy, do you not?"

"It's sort of a general-interest, all-purpose place," Mrs. Nielsen says.

I nod and nod and nod. So far they've said nothing that raises an alarm. But I don't feel the spark of connection with them, either. They don't seem eager to learn about me, but then again, few people are. I get the sense that my abandonment, and the circumstances that brought me to them, matter little to them, compared to the need I might fill in their lives.

The following morning, at 9:00 A.M., Mr. Nielsen pulls up in a blue-and-white Studebaker with silver trim and raps on the front door. Mrs. Murphy has been so generous that I now have two suitcases and a satchel filled with clothes and books and shoes. As I'm closing my bags Miss Larsen comes to my room and presses *Anne of Green Gables* into my hands. "It's my own book, not the school's, and I want you to have it," she says, hugging me good-bye.

And then, for the fourth time since I first set foot in Minnesota over a year ago, everything I possess is loaded into a vehicle and I am on my way to somewhere new.

HEMINGFORD, MINNESOTA, 1930–1931

The Nielsens' home is a two-story colonial painted yellow with black shutters and a long slate walkway leading to the front door. It sits on a quiet street several blocks from the center of town. Inside, the floor plan is a circle: a sunny living room on the right leads into the kitchen in the back, which connects to a dining room and back to the foyer.

Upstairs I have my own large room, painted pink, with a window overlooking the street, and even my own bathroom, with a large porcelain sink and pink tiles and a cheerful white curtain with pink piping.

Mr. and Mrs. Nielsen take things for granted that I've never dared to dream of. All the rooms have steel air vents with black-painted scrollwork. Even when no one is home, the water heater is on, so that when they come home after work, they don't have to wait for the water to heat up. A woman named Bess cleans the house and does the washing once a week. The refrigerator is stocked with milk and eggs and cheese and juice, and Mrs. Nielsen notices what I like to eat and buys more of it — oats for breakfast, for instance, and fruits, even exotic ones like oranges and bananas. I find aspirin and store-bought toothpaste in the medicine cabinet and clean towels in the hall closet. Every two years, Mr. Nielsen tells me, he trades in his car for a new model.

On Sunday morning we go to church. Grace Lutheran is different from any place of worship I've ever seen: a simple white building with a steeple, Gothic arched windows, oak pews, and a spare altar. I find the rituals comforting — the tried-and-true hymns, sermons by the mild-mannered, slope-shouldered reverend that emphasize decency and good manners. Mr. Nielsen and other parishioners grumble about the organist, who either plays so fast that we jumble the words or so slow that the songs become dirges, and he can't seem to take his foot off the pedal. But nobody actually protests — they just raise their eyebrows at each other midsong and shrug.

I like the assumption that everyone is trying his best, and we should all just be kind to each other. I like the coffee hour with almond cake and snickerdoodles in the vestry. And I like being associated with the Nielsens, who seem to be generally regarded as fine, upstanding citizens. For the first time in my life, the glow of other people's approval extends to, and envelops, me.

Life with the Nielsens is calm and orderly. Each morning at five thirty, six days a week, Mrs. Nielsen makes breakfast for her husband, usually fried eggs and toast, and he leaves for the store to open for the farmers at six. I get ready for school and leave the house at seven forty-five for the ten-minute walk to the schoolhouse, a brick building that holds sixty children, separated into grades.

On my first day in this new school, the fifth-grade teacher, Miss Buschkowsky, asks the twelve of us in her class to introduce ourselves and list one or two of our hobbies.

I've never heard of a "hobby." But the boy before me says playing stick-ball, and the girl before him says stamp collecting, so when the question comes to me, I say sewing.

"Lovely, Dorothy!" Miss Buschkowsky says. "What do you like to sew?"

"Clothes, mostly," I tell the class.

Miss Buschkowsky smiles encouragingly. "For your dolls?"

"No, for ladies."

"Well, isn't that nice!" she says in a too-bright voice, and in that way it becomes clear to me that most ten-year-olds probably don't sew clothes for ladies.

And so I begin to adjust. The kids know I've come from somewhere else, but as time passes, and with careful effort, I lose any trace of an accent. I note what the girls my age are wearing and the style of their hair and the subject of their conversations, and I work hard to banish my foreignness, to make friends, to fit in.

After school, at three o'clock, I walk directly to the store. Nielsen's is a large open space divided into aisles, with a pharmacy in the back, a candy section up front, clothes, books, and magazines, shampoo, milk, and produce. My job is to stack shelves and help with inventory. When it's busy, I help out at the cash register.

From my place at the counter I see longing in the faces of certain children — the ones who sidle into the store and linger in the candy aisle, eyeing the hard striped sticks with a fierce hunger I remember only too well. I ask Mr. Nielsen if I can use my own earnings to give a child a stick of penny candy now and then, and he laughs. "Use your discretion, Dorothy. I won't take it out of your wages."

Mrs. Nielsen leaves the store at five to start dinner; sometimes I go home with her, and sometimes I stay and help Mr. Nielsen close up. He always leaves at six. At dinner we talk about the weather and my homework and the store. Mr. Nielsen is a member of the chamber of commerce, and conversations often include discussion of initiatives and plans for stimulating business in this "unruly" economy, as he calls it. Late at night, Mr. Nielsen sits in the parlor at his rolltop desk, going over the store ledgers, while Mrs. Nielsen prepares our lunches for the next day, tidies the kitchen, takes care of household tasks. I help wash the dishes, sweep the floor. When chores are done, we play checkers or hearts and listen to the radio. Mrs. Nielsen teaches me to needlepoint; while she's making intricately detailed pillows for the sofa, I work on the floral cover for a stool.

One of my first tasks at the store is to help decorate for Christmas. Mrs. Nielsen and I bring boxes filled with glass balls and china ornaments and ribbon and strings of sparkling beads up from the storage room in the cellar. Mr. Nielsen has his two delivery boys, Adam and Thomas, drive to the outskirts of town to cut a tree for the window, and we spend an afternoon putting swags of greenery with red velveteen bows over the store entrance and decorating the tree, wrapping empty boxes in foil paper and tying them with flocked ribbon and silk cording.

As we work together, Mrs. Nielsen tells me bits and pieces about her life. She is Swedish, though you wouldn't know it — her people were dark-eyed gypsies who came to Gothamberg from central Europe. Her parents are dead, her siblings scattered. She and Mr. Nielsen have been married for eighteen years, since she was twenty-five and he was in his early thirties. They thought they couldn't have children, but about eleven years ago she got pregnant. On July 7, 1920, their daughter, Vivian, was born.

"What is your birth date again, Dorothy?" Mrs. Nielsen asks.

"April twenty-first."

Carefully she threads silver ribbon through the tree branches in the back, ducking her head so I can't see her face. Then she says, "You girls are almost the same age."

"What happened to her?" I venture. Mrs. Nielsen has never mentioned her daughter before and I sense that if I don't ask now, I may not get the chance.

Mrs. Nielsen ties the ribbon to a branch and bends down to find another. She attaches the end of the new ribbon to the same branch to make it look continuous, and begins the process of weaving it through.

"When she was six, she developed a fever. We thought it was a cold. Put her to bed, called the doctor. He said we should let her rest, give her plenty of fluids, the usual advice. But she didn't get better. And next thing we knew it was the middle of the night and she was delirious, out of her mind, really, and we called the doctor again and he looked down her throat and saw the telltale spots. We didn't know what it was, but he did.

"We took her to St. Mary's Hospital in Rochester, and they quarantined her. When they told us there was nothing they could do, we didn't believe them. But it was just a matter of time." She shakes her head, as if to clear the thought.

I think about how hard it must have been for her, losing a daughter. And I think of my brothers and Maisie. We have a lot of sadness inside us, Mrs. Nielsen and I. I feel sorry for the both of us.

■ ■ ■ ■

On Christmas Eve, in a soft snowfall, the three of us walk to church. We light candles on the twenty-foot tree to the right of the altar, all the fair-haired Lutheran children and parents and grandparents singing with songbooks open, the reverend preaching a sermon as elemental as a story in a child's picture book, a lesson about charity and empathy. "People are in dire need," he tells the congregation. "If you have something to give, give. Rise to your best selves."

He talks about some families in crisis: hog farmer John Slattery lost his right arm in a threshing accident; they need canned goods and any manpower you can spare while they try to salvage the farm . . . Mrs. Abel, eighty-seven years old, blind now in both eyes and all alone; if you can see it in your heart to spare a few hours a week it would be greatly appreciated . . . a family of seven, the Grotes, in dire straits; the father out of work, four young children and another born prematurely a month ago, now sickly, the mother unable to get out of bed . . .

"How sad," Mrs. Nielsen murmurs. "Let's put together a package for that poor family."

She doesn't know my history with them. They're just another distant calamity.

After the service we walk back through quiet streets. The snow has stopped and it's a clear, cold night; the gas lamps cast circles of light. As the three of us approach the house I see it as if for the first time — the porch light shining, an evergreen wreath on the door, the black iron railing and neatly shoveled walkway. Inside, behind a curtain, a lamp in the living room glows. It's a pleasant place to return to. A home.

Every other Thursday after supper, Mrs. Nielsen and I join Mrs. Murphy and six other ladies at a quilting group. We meet in the spacious parlor room of the wealthiest lady in the group, who lives in a grand Victorian on the outskirts of town. I am the only child in a room full of women and am immediately at ease. We work together on one quilt, a pattern and fabric that a member of the group has brought in; as soon as that one is finished, we'll move to the next. Each quilt takes about four months to finish. This group, I learn, made the quilt on my bed in the pink bedroom. It's called Irish Wreath, four purple irises with green stems meeting in the middle on a black background. "We'll make a quilt for you someday, too, Dorothy," Mrs. Nielsen tells me. She begins to save cuttings from the fabric station in the store; every scrap goes into a steamer trunk with my name on it. We talk about it at dinner: "A lady bought ten and a half yards of a beautiful blue calico, and I saved the extra half yard for you," she'll say. I've already decided on the pattern: a Double Wedding Ring, a series of interlocking circles made up of small rectangles of fabric.

Once a month, on a Sunday afternoon, Mrs. Nielsen and I polish the silver. From a deep drawer in the cabinet in the dining room she takes out a heavy mahogany box that contains the cutlery she was given by her mother as a wedding present — her only inheritance, she tells me. Removing the pieces one by one, she lines them up on tea towels on the table, while I gather two small silver bowls from the living room mantel, four candlesticks and a serving platter from the sideboard, and a hinged box with her name, *Viola,* in spidery script across the top from her bedroom. We use a heavy, mud-colored paste in a jar, a few small, stiff brushes, water, and lots of rags.

One day, as I am polishing an ornately decorated serving spoon, Mrs. Nielsen points at her clavicle and says, without looking at me, "We could clean that up for you, if you like."

I touch the chain around my neck, following it with my finger down to the claddagh. Reaching back with both hands, I unfasten the clasp.

"Use the brush. Be gentle," she says.

"My gram gave this to me," I tell her.

She looks at me and smiles. "Warm water, too."

As I work the brush along the chain, it is transformed from a dull gray to the color of tinsel. The claddagh charm, its details obscured by tarnish, becomes three-dimensional again.

"There," Mrs. Nielsen says when I've rinsed and dried the necklace and put it on again, "much better," and though she doesn't ask anything about it, I know this is her way of acknowledging that she knows it holds meaning for me.

One night at dinner, after I have been living in their house for several months, Mr. Nielsen says, "Dorothy, Mrs. Nielsen and I have something to discuss with you."

I think Mr. Nielsen is going to talk about the trip they've been planning to Mount Rushmore, but he looks at his wife, and she smiles at me, and I realize it's something else, something bigger.

"When you first came to Minnesota, you were given the name Dorothy," she says. "Are you particularly fond of that name?"

"Not particularly," I say, unsure where this is going.

"You know how much our Vivian meant to us, don't you?" Mr. Nielsen says.

I nod.

"Well." Mr. Nielsen's hands are flat on the table. "It would mean a lot to us if you would take Vivian's name. We consider you our daughter — not legally yet, but we are beginning to think of you that way. And we hope that you are beginning to think of us as your parents."

They look at me expectantly. I don't know what to think. What I feel for the Nielsens — gratitude, respect, appreciation — isn't the same as a child's love for her parents, not quite; though what that love is, I'm not sure I can say. I am glad to be living with this kind couple, whose quiet, self-effacing manner I am coming to understand. I am grateful that they took me in. But I am also aware every day of how different I am from them. They are not my people, and never will be.

I don't know how I feel, either, about taking their daughter's name. I don't know if I can bear the weight of that burden.

"Let's not pressure her, Hank." Turning to me, Mrs. Nielsen says, "Take the time you need, and let us know. You have a place in our home, whatever you decide."

Several days later, in the store stocking shelves in the canned food aisle, I hear a man's voice I recognize but can't place. I stack the remaining cans of corn and peas on the shelf in front of me, pick up the empty cardboard box, and stand up slowly, hoping to determine who it is without being seen.

"I got some fine piecework to barter, if you're amenable," I hear a man say to Mr. Nielsen, standing behind the counter.

Every day people come into the store with reasons why they can't pay, asking for credit or offering goods for trade. Every evening, it seems, Mr. Nielsen brings something home from a customer: a dozen eggs, soft Norwegian flatbread called *lefse,* a long knitted scarf. Mrs. Nielsen rolls her eyes and says, "Mercy," but she doesn't complain. I think she's proud of him — for being kindhearted, and for having the means to be.

"Dorothy?"

I turn around, and with a little shock I realize it's Mr. Byrne. His auburn hair is lank and unkempt, and his eyes are bloodshot. I wonder if he's been drinking. What is he doing here, in the general store of a town thirty miles from his own?

"Well, this is a surprise," he says. "You work here?"

I nod. "The owners — the Nielsens — took me in."

Despite the February cold, sweat is trickling down Mr. Byrne's temple. He wipes it away with the back of his hand. "So you happy with them?"

"Yes, sir." I wonder why he's acting so odd. "How's Mrs. Byrne?" I ask, trying to steer the conversation to pleasantries.

He blinks several times. "You haven't heard."

"Pardon?"

Shaking his head, he says, "She was not a strong woman, Dorothy. Couldn't take the humiliation. Couldn't bear to beg for favors. But what should I have done different? I think about it every day." His face contorts. "When Fanny left, it was the —"

"Fanny left?" I don't know why I'm surprised, but I am.

"A few weeks after you did. Came in one morning and said her daughter up in Park Rapids wanted her to live with them, and she'd decided to go. We'd lost everyone else, you know, and I think Lois just couldn't bear the thought . . ." He wipes his hand across his whole face, as if trying to erase his features. "Remember the freak storm that blew through last spring? Late April it was. Well, Lois walked out into it and kept walking. They found her froze to death about four miles from the house."

I want to feel sympathy for Mr. Byrne. I want to feel something. But I cannot. "I'm sorry," I tell him, and I suppose I *am* sorry — for him, for his tattered life. But I cannot muster any sorrow for Mrs. Byrne. I think of her cold eyes and perpetual scowl, her unwillingness to see me as anything more than a pair of hands, fingers holding a needle and thread. I am not glad she is dead, but I am not sorry she is gone.

At dinner that evening I tell the Nielsens I will take their daughter's name. And in that moment, my old life ends and a new one begins. Though I find it hard to trust that my good fortune will continue, I am under no illusions about what I've left behind. So when, after several years, the Nielsens tell me that they want to adopt me, I readily agree. I will become their daughter, though I never can bring myself to call them Mother and Father — our affiliation feels too formal for that. Even so, from now on it is clear that I belong to them; they are responsible for me and will take care of me.

As time passes, my real family becomes harder and harder to remember. I have no photographs or letters or even books from that former life, only the Irish cross from my gram. And though I rarely take the claddagh off, as I get older I can't escape the realization that the only remaining piece of my blood family comes from a woman who pushed her only son and his family out to sea in a boat, knowing full well she'd probably never see them again.

HEMINGFORD, MINNESOTA, 1935–1939

I am fifteen when Mrs. Nielsen finds a pack of cigarettes in my purse.

It's clear when I walk into the kitchen that I've done something to displease her. She is quieter than usual, with an air of injured aggravation. I wonder if I'm imagining it; I try to remember if I said or did anything to upset her before I left for school. The pack of cigarettes, which my friend Judy Smith's boyfriend bought for her at the Esso station outside of town, and which she passed along to me, doesn't even register in my mind.

After Mr. Nielsen comes in and we sit down to supper, Mrs. Nielsen slides the pack of Lucky Strikes toward me across the table. "I was looking for my green gloves and thought you might have borrowed them," she says. "I found this instead."

I look at her, then at Mr. Nielsen, who lifts his fork and knife and begins cutting his pork chop into small pieces.

"I only smoked one, to try it," I say, though they can clearly see that the pack is half empty.

"Where'd you get it?" Mrs. Nielsen asks.

I am tempted to tell them it was Judy's boyfriend, Douglas, but realize it will only be worse to drag other people in. "It was — an experiment. I didn't like it. They made me cough."

She raises her eyebrows at Mr. Nielsen, and I can tell they've already decided on a punishment. The only thing they can really take away is my weekly Sunday-afternoon trip to the picture show with Judy, so for the next two weeks I stay home instead. And endure their silent reprobation.

After this, I decide that the cost of upsetting them is too much. I don't climb out my bedroom window and down the drainpipe like Judy; I go to school and work in the store and help with dinner and do my homework and go to bed. I go out with boys now and then, always on a double date or in groups. One boy in particular, Ronnie King, is sweet on me and gives me a promise ring. But I am so worried I might do something to disappoint the Nielsens that I avoid any situation that might lead to impropriety. Once, after a date, Ronnie tries to kiss me good night. His lips brush mine and I pull back quickly. Soon after that I give back his ring.

I never lose the fear that any day Mr. Sorenson could be on the doorstep, telling me that the Nielsens have decided I'm too expensive, too much trouble, or merely a disappointment, and they've decided to let me go. In my nightmares I am alone on a train, heading into the wilderness. Or in a maze of hay bales. Or walking the streets of a big city, gazing at lights in every window, seeing the families inside, none of them mine.

One day I overhear a man at the counter talking to Mrs. Nielsen. "My wife sent me in here to get some things for a basket our church is putting together for a boy who came on that orphan train," he says. "Remember those? Used to come through a while ago with all those homeless waifs? I went to the Grange Hall in Albans once to see 'em. Pitiful lot. Anyhow, this kid had one misfortune after another, got beat up pretty bad by the farmer who took him in, and now the elderly lady he went to after that has died, and he's on his own again. It's a scandal, sending those poor kids out here on their own, expecting folks to take care of 'em — as if we don't have our own burdens."

"Ummhmm," Mrs. Nielsen says noncommittally.

I move closer, wondering if he might be talking about Dutchy. But then I realize Dutchy is eighteen now. Old enough to be on his own.

I am nearly sixteen when I look around the store and realize that it has barely changed in all the time I've been here. And there are things we can do to make it nicer. A lot of things. First, after consulting Mr. Nielsen, I move the magazines to the front, near the cash register. The shampoos and lotions and balms that used to be at the back of the store I shift to shelves near the pharmacy, so that people filling prescriptions can also buy plasters and ointments. The women's section is woefully understocked — understandable, given Mr. Nielsen's general ignorance and Mrs. Nielsen's lack of interest (she does wear an occasional coat of lipstick, though it always seems to have been randomly chosen and hurriedly applied). Remembering the long discussions about stockings and garters and makeup rituals at Mrs. Murphy's, I suggest that we increase and expand this section, purchasing, for example, a hosiery carousel with seamed and unseamed stockings from one of the vendors, and advertise it in the paper. The Nielsens are skeptical, but in the first week we go through our entire stock. The following week Mr. Nielsen doubles the order.

Recalling what Fanny said about ladies wanting to feel pretty even when they don't have much money, I convince Mr. Nielsen to order small inexpensive items, sparkling costume jewelry and gloves made of cotton velvet, Bakelite wrist bangles and colorful printed scarves. There are several girls I watch avidly at school, a grade or two above me, whose well-to-do parents take them to the Twin Cities to buy clothes. I notice what they wear and what they eat, what music they listen to, the cars they dream about, and the movie stars they follow. And like a magpie I bring these scraps and twigs back to the store. One of these girls will wear a new color or style of belt or a button-plate hat tilted to one side, and that afternoon I'll pore through our vendors' catalogs to find similar designs. I choose mannequins out of a catalog that look like these girls, with pencil-thin eyebrows and rosebud lips and soft, wavy hairstyles, and dress them in the latest styles and colors. I find out the perfumes they favor, like Blue Grass by Elizabeth Arden, and we stock those as well as standard ladies' favorites such as Joy by Jean Patou and Vol de Nuit by Guerlain.

As business grows, we push the shelves closer together, erect special displays at the ends of the aisles, crowd the lotions. When the shop next door, a jeweler's called Rich's, goes out of business, I convince Mr. Nielsen to remodel and expand. Inventory will be in the basement instead of in the back, and the store will be organized into departments.

We keep prices low, and lower them even more with sales every week and coupons in the paper. We institute a layaway plan so people can buy more expensive items in installments. And we put in a soda fountain as a place people can linger. Before long the store is thriving. It seems as though we are the only business doing well in this terrible economy.

"Did you know your eyes are your best feature?" Tom Price tells me in math class senior year, leaning across my desk to look at them, first one and then the other. "Brown, green, even a little gold in there. I've never seen so many colors in a pair of eyes." I squirm under his gaze, but when I get home that afternoon, I lean in close to the bathroom mirror and stare at my eyes for a long time.

My hair isn't as brassy as it used to be. Over the years it has turned a deep russet, the color of dead leaves. I've had it cut in the fashionable style — fashionable for our town, at least — right above my shoulders. And when I begin to wear makeup, I have a revelation. I've viewed my life until now as a series of unrelated adaptations, from Irish Niamh to American Dorothy to the reincarnated Vivian. Each identity has been projected onto me and fits oddly at first, like a pair of shoes you have to break in before they're comfortable. But with red lipstick I can fashion a whole new — and temporary — persona. I can determine my own next incarnation.

I attend the homecoming dance with Tom. He shows up at the door with a wrist corsage, a fat white carnation and two tiny roses; I've sewn my own dress, a pink chiffon version of one Ginger Rogers wore in *Swing Time,* and Mrs. Nielsen loans me her pearl necklace and matching earrings. Tom is affable and good-natured right up until the moment the whiskey he's tippling from a flask in the pocket of his father's too-big suit coat makes him drunk. Then he gets into a scuffle with another senior on the dance floor and manages to get himself, and me, ejected from the dance.

The next Monday, my twelfth-grade English teacher, Mrs. Fry, takes me aside after class. "Why are you wasting time with a boy like that?" she scolds. She urges me to apply to colleges out of state — Smith College in Massachusetts, for one, her alma mater. "You'll have a bigger life," she says. "Don't you want that, Vivian?" But though I'm flattered by her interest, I know I'll never go that far. I can't leave the Nielsens, who've come to depend on me for so much. Besides, Tom Price notwithstanding, the life I'm living is big enough for me.

As soon as I graduate, I begin to manage the store. I find that I am suited to the task, and that I enjoy it. (I'm taking a class in accounting and business administration at St. Olaf College, but my classes meet in the evenings.) I hire the workers — nine in all, now — and order much of the merchandise. At night, with Mr. Nielsen, I go over the ledgers. Together we manage employees' problems, placate customers, massage vendors. I'm constantly angling for the best price, the most attractive bundle of goods, the newest option. Nielsen's is the first place in the county to carry upright electric vacuum cleaners, blenders, freeze-dried coffee. We've never been busier.

Girls from my graduating class come into the store brandishing solitaire diamonds like Legion of Honor medals, as if they've accomplished something significant — which I guess they think they have, though all I can see is a future of washing some man's clothes stretching ahead of them. I want nothing to do with marriage. Mrs. Nielsen agrees. "You're young. There'll be time for that," she says.

Spruce Harbor, Maine, 2011

"Buying all these fancy vegetables is eating up my whole salary," Dina grumbles. "I don't know if we can keep doing this."

Dina's talking about a stir-fry that Molly has thrown together for the three of them after returning from the library in Bar Harbor: tofu, red and green peppers, black beans, and zucchini. Molly has been cooking quite a bit lately, reasoning that if Dina tries some dishes that don't have animal protein front and center, she'll see how many more options are available. So in the past week Molly has made cheese and mushroom quesadillas, vegetarian chili, and eggplant lasagna. Still Dina complains: it's not filling enough, it's weird. (She'd never tried eggplant in her life before Molly roasted one in the oven.) And now she complains that it costs too much.

"I don't think it's that much more," Ralph says.

"Plus the extra cost in general," Dina says under her breath.

Let it go, Molly tells herself, but . . . fuck it. "Wait a minute. You get paid for having me, right?"

Dina looks up in surprise, her fork in midair. Ralph raises his eyebrows. "I don't know what that has to do with anything," Dina says.

"Doesn't that money cover the cost of having an extra person?" Molly asks. "More than covers it, right? Honestly, isn't that the reason you take in foster kids at all?"

Dina stands abruptly. "Are you kidding me?" She turns to Ralph. "Is she really talking to me like this?"

"Now, you two —" Ralph begins with a tremulous smile.

"It's not *us two*. Don't you dare group me with her," Dina says.

"Well, okay, let's just —"

"No, Ralph, I've had it. Community service, my ass. If you ask me, this girl should be in juvie right now. She's a thief, plain and simple. She steals from the library, who knows what she steals from us. Or from that old lady." Dina marches over to Molly's bedroom, opens the door, and disappears inside.

"Hey," Molly says, getting up.

327

A moment later Dina emerges with a book in her hand. She holds it up like a protest sign. *Anne of Green Gables.* "Where'd you get this?" she demands.

"You can't just —"

"Where'd you get this book?"

Molly sits back in her chair. "Vivian gave it to me."

"Like hell." Dina flips it open, jabs her finger at the inside cover. "Says right here it belongs to Dorothy Power. Who's that?"

Molly turns to Ralph and says slowly, "I did not steal that book."

"Yeah, I'm sure she just 'borrowed' it." Dina points a long pink talon at her. "Listen, young lady. We have had nothing but trouble since you came into this house, and I am so over it. I mean it. I am so. Over. It." She stands with her legs apart, breathing shallowly, tossing her blond frosted mane like a nervous pony.

"Okay, okay, Dina, look." Ralph has his hands out, patting the air like a conductor. "I think this has gone a little far. Can we just take a deep breath and calm down?"

"Are you fucking *kidding* me?" Dina practically spits.

Ralph looks at Molly, and in his expression she sees something new. He looks weary. He looks over it.

328

"I want her out," Dina says.

"Deen—"

"OUT."

Later that evening Ralph knocks on Molly's bedroom door. "Hey, what're you doing?" he says, looking around. The L.L.Bean duffel bags are splayed wide, and Molly's small collection of books, including *Anne of Green Gables,* is piled on the floor.

Stuffing socks into a plastic Food Mart bag, Molly says, "What does it look like I'm doing?" She's not usually rude to Ralph, but now she figures, who cares? He wasn't exactly watching her back out there.

"You can't leave yet. We have to contact Social Services and all that. It'll be a couple of days, probably."

Molly crams the bag o' socks into one end of a duffel, rounding it nicely. Then she starts lining up shoes: the Doc Martens she picked up at a Salvation Army store, black flip-flops, a dog-chewed pair of Birkenstocks that a previous foster mother tossed in the trash and Molly rescued, black Walmart sneakers.

"They'll find you someplace better suited," Ralph says.

She looks up at him, brushes the bangs out of her eyes. "Oh yeah? I won't hold my breath."

"Come on, Moll. Give me a break."

"You give me a break. And don't call me Moll." It's all she can do to restrain herself from flying at his face with her claws out like a feral cat. Fuck him. Fuck him and the bitch he rode in on.

She's too old for this — too old to wait around to be placed with another foster family. Too old to switch schools, move to a new town, submit herself to yet another foster parent's whims. She is so white-hot furious she can barely see. She stokes the fire of her hatred, feeding it tidbits about bigoted idiot Dina and spineless mushmouth Ralph, because she knows that just beyond the rage is a sorrow so enervating it could render her immobile. She needs to keep moving, flickering around the room. She needs to fill her bags and get the hell out of here.

Ralph hovers, uncertain. As always. She knows he's caught between her and Dina, and utterly unequipped to handle either of them. She almost feels sorry for him, the pusillanimous wretch.

"I have somewhere to go, so don't worry about it," she says.

"To Jack's, you mean?"

"Maybe."

Actually, no. She could no more go to

Jack's than she could get a room at the Bar Harbor Inn. (Yes, I'd prefer a water view. And send up a mango smoothie, thanks!) Things between them are still strained. But even if things were fine, Terry would never allow her to stay overnight.

Ralph sighs. "Well, I get why you don't want to stay here."

She gives him a look. No shit, Sherlock.

"Let me know if I can drive you anyplace."

"I'll be fine," she says, dropping a pile of black T-shirts in the bag and standing there with folded arms until he slinks out.

So where the hell can she go?

There's $213 left in Molly's savings account from the minimum-wage job she had last summer scooping ice cream in Bar Harbor. She could take a bus to Bangor or Portland, or maybe even Boston. But what then?

She wonders, not for the first time, about her mother. Maybe she's better. Maybe she's clean and sober now, with some kind of steady job. Molly's always resisted the urge to look for her, dreading what she might find. But desperate times . . . and who knows? The state loves it when biological parents get their shit together. This could be an opportunity for both of them.

Before she can change her mind, she

crawls over to her sleeping laptop, propped open on her bed, and taps the keyboard to nudge it awake. She googles "Donna Ayer Maine."

The first listing is an invitation to view Donna Ayer's professional profile on LinkedIn. (Unlikely.) Next is a PDF of Yarmouth city council members that includes a Donna Ayer. (Even more unlikely.) Third down is a wedding announcement: a Donna Halsey married Rob Ayer, an air force pilot, in Mattawamkeag in March. (Um, no.) And finally, yep, here she is — Molly's mother, in a small item in the *Bangor Daily News.* Clicking through to the article, Molly finds herself staring at her mother's mug shot. There's no question it's her, though she's wan, squinty, and decidedly worse for wear. Arrested three months ago for stealing OxyContin from a pharmacy in Old Town with a guy named Dwayne Bordick, twenty-three, Ayer is being held in lieu of bond, the article says, at the Penobscot County Jail in Bangor.

Well, that was easy enough.

Can't go there.

What now? Looking up homeless shelters online, Molly finds one in Ellsworth, but it says that patrons have to be eighteen or older "unless with a parent." The Sea Coast

Mission in Bar Harbor has a food pantry, though no overnight accommodations.

So what about . . . Vivian? That house has fourteen rooms. Vivian lives in about three of them. She's almost certainly home — after all, she never goes anywhere. Molly glances at the time on her phone: 6:45 P.M. That's not too late to call her, is it? But . . . now that she thinks about it, she's never actually seen Vivian talking on the phone. Maybe it would be better to take the Island Explorer over there to talk with her in person. And if she says no, well, maybe Molly could just sleep in her garage tonight. Tomorrow, with a clear head, she'll figure out what to do.

Spruce Harbor, Maine, 2011

Molly trudges up the road toward Vivian's from the bus stop, her laptop in her backpack, red Braden slung over one shoulder and Hawaiian Ashley on the other. The duffels are knocking into each other like rowdy patrons at a bar, with Molly stuck between. It's slow going.

Before the blowup with Dina, Molly had planned to go to Vivian's tomorrow, to tell her what she found at the library. Well, plans change.

Leaving was anticlimactic. Dina stayed behind her shut bedroom door with the TV blaring while Ralph lamely offered to help Molly with her bags, loan her a twenty, drive her somewhere. Molly almost said thank you, almost gave him a hug, but in the end she just barked, "No, I'm fine, see ya," and propelled herself forward by thinking: This is already over, I am already gone . . .

Occasionally a car lumbers past — this

being the off-season, most cars on the road are sensible Subarus, ten-ton trucks, or clunkers. Molly is wearing her heavy winter coat because, though it's May, this is, after all, Maine. (And who knows, she might end up sleeping in it.) She left behind heaps of stuff for Ralph and Dina to deal with, including a few hideous synthetic sweaters Dina had tossed her way at Christmas. Good riddance.

Molly counts her steps: left, right, left, right. Left right. Left *right.* Her left shoulder hurts, strap digging into bone. She jumps in place, shifting the straps. Now it's sliding down. Shit. Jump again. She's a turtle carrying its shell. Jane Eyre, staggering across the heath. A Penobscot under the weight of a canoe. Of course her load is heavy; these bags contain everything she possesses in the world.

What do you carry with you? What do you leave behind?

Gazing ahead at the dark blue sky striated with clouds, Molly reaches up and touches the charms around her neck. Raven. Bear. Fish.

The turtle on her hip.

She doesn't need much.

And even if she loses the charms, she thinks, they'll always be a part of her. The things that matter stay with you, seep into your skin. People get tattoos to have a permanent reminder of things they love or believe or fear, but though she'll never regret the turtle, she has no need to ink her flesh again to remember the past.

She had not known the markings would be etched so deep.

Approaching Vivian's house, Molly looks at her phone. It's later than she thought it would be — 8:54.

The fluorescent overhead bulb on the porch gives off a dim pink light. The rest of the house is dark. Molly heaves her bags onto the porch, rubs her shoulders for a minute, then walks around to the back, the bay side, peering up at the windows for any sign of life. And there it is: on the second floor of the far right side, two windows glow. Vivian's bedroom.

Molly isn't sure what to do. She doesn't want to scare Vivian, and now that she's here she realizes that even ringing the doorbell would startle her at this hour.

So she decides to call. Gazing up at Vivian's window, she dials her number.

"Hello? Who is it?" Vivian answers after four rings in a strained, too-loud voice, as if communicating with someone far out at sea.

336

"Hi, Vivian, it's Molly."

"Molly? Is that you?"

"Yes," she says, her voice cracking. She takes a deep breath. Steady, stay calm. "I'm sorry to bother you."

Vivian comes into view in the window, pulling a burgundy robe over her nightgown. "What's the matter? Are you all right?"

"Yes, I —"

"Goodness, do you know what hour it is?" Vivian says, fussing with the cord.

"I'm so sorry to call this late. I just — I didn't know what else to do."

There's silence on the other end as Vivian absorbs this. "Where are you?" she says finally, perching on the arm of a chair.

"I'm downstairs. Outside, I mean. I was afraid it would alarm you if I rang the bell."

"You're where?"

"Here. I'm here. At your house."

"Here? Now?" Vivian stands up.

"I'm sorry." And then Molly can't help it, she starts to cry. It's cold on the grass and her shoulders ache and Vivian is freaked out and the Island Explorer is done for the night and the garage is dark and creepy and there's nowhere else in the world she can think of to go.

"Don't cry, dear. Don't cry. I'll be right down."

"Okay." Molly heaves in a breath. *Pull yourself together!*

"I'm hanging up now."

"Okay." Through her tears, Molly watches Vivian replace the receiver on the hook, wrap her robe tighter and tie it, pat the silver hair at the nape of her neck. As Vivian leaves the bedroom Molly runs back to the front porch. She shakes her head to clear it, pulls her bags into a neat heap, wipes her eyes and nose with a corner of her T-shirt.

A moment later Vivian opens the door. She looks with alarm from Molly (who realizes that, despite wiping her eyes, she must have mascara smeared all over her face) to the bulky duffel bags to the overstuffed backpack. "For goodness' sake, come in!" she says, holding the door wide. "Come in this minute and tell me what happened."

Despite Molly's protests, Vivian insists on making tea. She takes down a cabbage-rose teapot and cups — a wedding gift from Mrs. Murphy that's been in a box for decades — along with some recently recovered spoons from Mrs. Nielsen's silver service. They wait in the kitchen for the water to boil, and then Molly pours water in the teapot and carries the tea service to the living room on a tray, with some cheese and crackers Vivian has

338

found in the pantry.

Vivian turns on two lamps and settles Molly in a red wingback. Then she goes over to the closet and takes out a quilt.

"The wedding ring!" Molly says.

Vivian holds the quilt by two corners and shakes it out, then carries it over and drapes it across Molly's lap. It is stained and ripped in places, thinned from use. Many of the small rectangles of fabric sewn by hand into interlocking circles have dissolved altogether, the ghostly remains of stitches holding snippets of colored cloth. "If I can't bear to give this stuff away, I might as well use it."

As Vivian tucks the quilt around her legs, Molly says, "Sorry for barging in like this."

Vivian flaps her hand. "Don't be silly. I could use the excitement. Gets my heart rate up."

"I'm not sure that's a good thing."

The news about Maisie sits in Molly's stomach like a stone. She doesn't want to spring it on Vivian just yet — too many surprises at once.

After Vivian has poured tea in two cups, handed one to Molly, taken one for herself, added and stirred in two lumps of sugar, and arranged the cheese and crackers on the plate, she settles into the other chair and folds her hands on her lap. "All right," she says. "Now tell me."

So Molly talks. She tells Vivian about living in the trailer on Indian Island, the car crash that killed her father, her mother's struggle with drugs. She shows her Shelly the turtle. She tells her about the dozen foster homes and the nose ring and the argument with Dina and finding out on the Internet that her mother's in jail.

The tea grows tepid, then cold, in their cups.

And then, because she is determined to be completely honest, Molly takes a deep breath and says, "There's something I should've told you a long time ago. The community service requirement wasn't for school — it was because I stole a book from the Spruce Harbor library."

Vivian pulls her burgundy fleece robe tighter around her. "I see."

"It was a stupid thing to do."

"What book was it?"

"*Jane Eyre.*"

"Why did you steal it?"

Molly thinks back to that moment: pulling each copy of the novel off the shelf, turning them over in her hands, returning the hardcover and the newer paperback, tucking the other one under her shirt. "Well, it's my favorite book. And there were three copies. I thought nobody would miss the crappiest one." She shrugs. "I just — wanted to own it."

Vivian taps her bottom lip with her thumb. "Terry knew?"

Molly shrugs. She doesn't want to get Terry in trouble. "Jack vouched for me, and you know how she feels about Jack."

"That I do."

The night is still, quiet except for their voices. The drapes are shut against the dark. "I'm sorry I came into your house this way. Under false pretenses," Molly says.

"Ah, well," Vivian says. "I suppose we all come under false pretenses one way or another, don't we? It was best not to tell me. I probably wouldn't have let you in." Clasping her hands together, she says, "If you're going to steal a book, though, you should at least take the nicest one. Otherwise what's the point?"

Molly is so nervous she barely smiles.

But Vivian does. "Stealing *Jane Eyre*!" She laughs. "They should've given you a gold star. Bumped you up a grade."

"You're not disappointed in me?"

Vivian lifts her shoulders. "Eh."

"Really?" Relief washes over her.

"You've certainly paid your dues, in any

341

case, putting in all these hours with me."

"It hasn't felt like punishment." Once upon a time — fairly recently, in fact — Molly would've gagged over these words, both because they're blatantly sycophantic and cringingly sentimental. But not today. For one thing, she means them. For another, she's so focused on the next part of the story that she can barely think of anything else. She plunges ahead. "Listen, Vivian," she says. "There's something else I need to tell you."

"Oh Lord." Vivian takes a sip of cold tea and sets her cup down. "What have you done now?"

Molly takes a deep breath. "It's not about me. It's about Maisie."

Vivian gazes at her steadily, her hazel eyes clear and unblinking.

"I went online. I just wanted to see if I could find anything, and it was surprisingly easy; I found records from Ellis Island —"

"The *Agnes Pauline*?"

"Yeah, exactly. I found your parents' names on the roster — and from there I got the death notices of your father and brothers. But not hers, not Maisie's. And then I had the idea to try to find the Schatzmans. Well, there happened to be a family reunion blog . . . and . . . anyway, it said that they adopted a baby, Margaret, in 1929."

Vivian is perfectly still. "Margaret."

Molly nods.

"Maisie."

"It has to be, right?"

"But — he told me she didn't make it."

"I know."

Vivian seems to gather herself up, to grow taller in her chair. "He lied to me." For a moment she looks off in the middle distance, somewhere above the bookcase. Then she says, "And they adopted her?"

"Apparently so. I don't know anything else about them, though I'm sure there are ways to find out. But she lived a long time. In upstate New York. She only died six months ago. There's a photo . . . She seemed really happy — children and grandchildren and all that." God, I'm an idiot, Molly thinks. Why did I say that?

"How do you know she died?"

"There's an obituary. I'll show you. And — do you want to see the photo?" Without waiting for an answer, Molly gets up and retrieves her laptop from her backpack. She turns it on and brings it over to where Vivian is sitting. She opens the family reunion photos and the obituary, saved on her desktop, and places the laptop in Vivian's lap.

Vivian peers at the picture on the screen. "That's her." Looking up at Molly, she says, "I can tell by the eyes. They're exactly the same."

"She looks like you," Molly says, and they both stare silently for a moment at the beaming elderly woman with sharp blue eyes, surrounded by her family.

Vivian reaches out and touches the screen. "Look at how white her hair is. It used to be blond. Ringlets." She twirls her index finger next to her own silver head. "All these years . . . she was alive," she murmurs. "Maisie was alive. All these years, there were two of them."

MINNEAPOLIS, MINNESOTA, 1939

It is late September of my nineteenth year and two new friends, Lillian Bart and Emily Reece, want me to go with them to see a new picture that's playing at the Orpheum Theatre in Minneapolis, *The Wizard of Oz.* It's so long it has an intermission, and we've made plans to stay the night. Lillian's fiancé lives there, and she goes almost every weekend, staying in a hotel for women. It's a safe, clean place, she assures us, that doesn't cost much money, and she has booked three single rooms. I've only been to the Twin Cities on day trips with the Nielsens — for a special birthday dinner, a shopping expedition, one afternoon at the art museum — but never with friends, and never overnight.

I'm not sure I want to go. For one thing, I haven't known these girls for long — they're both in my night class at St. Olaf. They live together in an apartment near the college.

When they talk about drinks parties, I'm not even sure what they mean. Parties where you have only drinks? The only party the Nielsens host is an annual open-house buffet lunch on New Year's Day for their vendors.

Lillian, with her friendly expression and golden blond hair, is easier to like than the arch and circumspect Emily, who has a funny half smile and severe dark bangs and is always making jokes I don't get. Their racy humor, raucous laughter, and breezy, unearned intimacy with me make me a little nervous.

For another thing, a big shipment of fall fashions is coming into the store today or tomorrow, and I don't want to return to find all of it in the wrong places. Mr. Nielsen has arthritis, and though he still comes in early every morning, he usually leaves around two to take an afternoon nap. Mrs. Nielsen is in and out; much of her time these days is taken up with bridge club and volunteering at the church.

But she encourages me to go with Lillian and Emily, saying, "A girl your age should get out now and then. There's more to life than the store and your studies, Vivian. Sometimes I worry you forget that."

When I graduated from high school, Mr.

Nielsen bought me a car, a white Buick convertible, which I mainly drive to the store and St. Olaf in the evenings, and Mr. Nielsen says it'll be good for the car to run it a little. "I'll pay for parking," he says.

As we drive out of town, the sky is the saccharine blue of a baby blanket, filled with puffy cottonball clouds. It's clear before we're ten miles down the road that Emily and Lillian's plans are more ambitious than they've let on. Yes, we'll go to *The Wizard of Oz,* but not the evening show that was the excuse for staying over. There's a matinee at three o'clock that will leave plenty of time to return to our rooms and dress to go out.

"Wait a minute," I say. "What do you mean, go out?"

Lillian, sitting beside me in the passenger seat, gives my knee a squeeze. "Come on, you didn't think we'd drive all this way just to go to a silly picture show, did you?"

From the backseat, where she's thumbing through *Silver Screen* magazine, Emily says, "So serious, Viv. You need to lighten up. Hey, d'you girls know that Judy Garland was born in Grand Rapids? Named Frances Ethel Gumm. Guess that wasn't Hollywood enough."

Lillian smiles over at me. "You've never been to a nightclub, have you?"

I don't answer, but of course she's right.

She tilts the rearview mirror away from me and starts to apply lipstick. "That's what I thought. We are going to have some real fun for a change." Then she smiles, her glossy pink lips framing small white teeth. "Starting with cocktails."

The women's hotel on a Minneapolis side street is just as Lillian described it, with a clean but sparsely furnished lobby and a bored clerk who barely looks up when he hands us our keys. Standing at the elevator with our bags, we plan to meet for the picture show in fifteen minutes. "Don't be late," Emily admonishes. "We have to get popcorn. There's always a line."

After dropping my bag in the closet of my narrow room on the fourth floor, I sit on the bed and bounce a few times. The mattress is thin, with creaky springs. But I feel a thrill of pleasure. My trips with the Nielsens are controlled, unambitious outings — a silent car ride, a specific destination, a sleepy ride home in the dark, Mr. Nielsen sitting erect in the front seat, Mrs. Nielsen beside him keeping a watchful eye on the center line.

Emily is standing alone in the lobby when I come downstairs. When I ask where Lillian is, she gives me a wink. "She's not feeling so well. She'll meet us after."

As we make our way to the theater, five blocks away, it occurs to me that Lillian never had any intention of going to the picture with us.

The Wizard of Oz is magical and strange. Black-and-white farmland gives way to a Technicolor dreamscape, as vivid and unpredictable as Dorothy Gale's real life is ordinary and familiar. When she returns to Kansas — her heartfelt wish granted — the world is black and white again. "It's good to be home," she says. Back on the farm, her life stretches ahead to the flat horizon line, already populated with the only characters she'll ever know.

When Emily and I leave the theater, it is early evening. I was so absorbed in the movie that real life feels slightly unreal; I have the uncanny sense of having stepped out of the screen and onto the street. The evening light is soft and pink, the air as mild as bathwater.

Emily yawns. "Well, that was long."

I don't want to ask, but manners compel me. "What did you think?"

She shrugs. "Those flying monkeys were creepy. But other than that, I don't know, I thought it was kind of boring."

We walk along in silence, past darkened

department store windows. "What about you?" she says after a few minutes. "Did you like it?"

I loved the movie so much that I don't trust myself to respond without sounding foolish. "Yes," I say, unable to translate into speech the emotions swirling through me.

Back in my room, I change into my other outfit, a chiffon skirt and floral blouse with butterfly sleeves. I brush my hair over my head and toss it back, then shape it with my fingers and spray it with lacquer. Standing on my toes, I look at my reflection in a small mirror above the bed. In the late afternoon light I look scrubbed and serious. Every freckle on my nose is visible. Taking out a small zippered bag, I spread butter-soft moisturizer on my face, then foundation. A smear of rouge, a pat of powder. I slide a brown pencil along my upper eyelids and feather my lashes, apply Terra Coral lipstick, then blot my lips, apply it again, and tuck the gold vial in my purse. I scrutinize myself in the mirror. I'm still me, but I feel braver somehow.

Down in the lobby, Lillian is holding hands with a guy I recognize as her fiancé, Richard, from the photograph she keeps in her purse. He's shorter than I expected, shorter than Lillian. Acne scars pock his cheeks. Lillian's wearing a sleeveless emerald shift dress, hemmed just above the knee (which is three inches shorter than anyone wears in Hemingford), and black kitten heels.

Richard yanks her close, whispers in her ear, and her eyes go wide. She covers her mouth and giggles, then sees me. "Vivie!" she says, tearing herself away. "Look at you! I don't think I've ever seen you with makeup. You clean up nice."

"You too," I say, though actually I've never seen her without.

"How was the movie?"

"It was good. Where were you?"

She glances at Richard. "I got waylaid." They both start to giggle again.

"That's one way to put it," he says.

"You must be Richard," I say.

"How'd you guess?" He claps me on the shoulder to show he's kidding around. "You ready for some fun tonight, Vivie?"

"Well, I sure am!" Emily's voice comes from over my shoulder, and I smell jasmine and roses — *Joy,* I recognize from the perfume counter at Nielsen's. Turning to greet her, I'm startled by her low-cut white blouse and tight striped skirt, her teetering heels and crimson nail polish.

"Hello, Em." Richard grins. "The fellas

are sure going to be happy to see you."

I am suddenly self-conscious in my prim blouse and modest skirt, my sensible shoes and churchy earrings. I feel like exactly what I am: a small-town girl in the big city.

Richard has his arms around both girls now, pinching them on the waist, laughing as they squirm. I glance at the desk clerk, the same one who was here when we checked in. It's been a long day for him, I think. He's leafing through a newspaper and only looks up when there's a raucous burst of laughter. I can see the headline from here: "Germans and Soviets Parade in Poland."

"I'm getting thirsty, girls. Let's find a watering hole," Richard says.

My stomach is rumbling. "Should we get dinner first?"

"If you insist, Miss Vivie. Though bar nuts would do it for me. What about you girls?" he asks the other two.

"Now, Richard, this is Viv's first time in the city. She's not used to your decadent ways. Let's get some food," Lillian says. "Besides, it might be risky for us lightweights to start drinking on an empty stomach."

"Risky how?" He pulls her closer and Lillian smirks, then pushes him away, making

352

her point. "All right, all right," he says, making a show of his acquiescence. "At the Grand Hotel there's a piano bar that serves chow. I seem to remember a pretty good T-bone. And I *know* they got a nice martini."

We make our way out onto the street, now humming with people. It's a perfect evening; the air is warm, the trees along the avenue are swathed in deep green leaves. Flowers spill out of planters, slightly overgrown and a bit wild, here at the furthest edge of summer. As we stroll along my spirits lift. Mingling in this wide swath of strangers shifts my attention from myself, that tedious subject, to the world around me. I might as well be in a foreign country for all its similarities to my sober real life, with its predictable routines and rhythms — a day in the store, supper at six, a quiet evening of studying or quilting or bridge. Richard, with his carnival-barker slickness, seems to have given up on even trying to include me. But I don't mind. It is marvelous to be young on a big-city street.

As we approach the heavy glass-and-brass front door of the Grand Hotel, a liveried doorman opens it wide. Richard sails in with Lil and Em, as he calls them, on his arms, and I scurry behind in their wake.

The doorman tips his cap as I thank him. "Bar's on the left just through the foyer," he says, making it clear he knows we're not hotel guests. I've never been in a space this majestic — except maybe the Chicago train station all those years ago — and it's all I can do not to gape at the starburst chandelier glittering over our heads, the glossy mahogany table with an oversized ceramic urn filled with exotic flowers in the center of the room.

The people in the foyer are equally striking. A woman wearing a flat black hat with a net that covers half her face stands at the reception desk with a pile of red leather suitcases, pulling off one long black satin glove and then the other. A white-haired matron carries a fluffy white dog with black button eyes. A man in a morning coat talks on the telephone at the front desk; an older gentleman wearing a monocle, sitting alone on a green love seat, holds a small brown book open in front of his nose. These people look bored, amused, impatient, self-satisfied — but most of all, they look rich. Now I am glad not to be wearing the gaudy, provocative clothing that seems to be drawing stares and whispers to Lil and Em.

Ahead of me, the three of them saunter across the lobby, shrieking with laughter, one of Richard's arms around Lil's shoulder and the other cinching Em's waist. "Hey, Vivie," Lil calls, glancing back as if suddenly remembering I'm here, "this way!" Richard pulls open the double doors to the bar, throws his hands into the air with a flourish, and ushers Lil and Em, giggling and whispering, inside. He follows, and the doors close slowly behind him.

I slow to a stop in front of the green couches. I'm in no hurry to go in there to be a fifth wheel, treated like I'm hopelessly out of it, old-fashioned and humorless, by the freewheeling Richard. Maybe, I think, I should just walk around for a while and then go back to the rooming house. Since the matinee nothing has felt quite real anyway; it's been enough of a day for me — much more, certainly, than I'm used to.

I perch on one of the couches, watching people come and go. At the door, now, is a woman in a purple satin dress with cascading brown hair, elegantly nonchalant, waving at the porter with a bejeweled hand as she glides into the foyer. Absorbed in watching her as she floats past me toward the concierge desk, I don't notice the tall, thin man with blond hair until he is standing in front of me.

His eyes are a piercing blue. "Excuse me,

miss," he says. I wonder if maybe he is going to say something about how I am so obviously out of place, or ask if I need help. "Do I know you from somewhere?"

I look at his golden-blond hair, short in the back but longer in front — nothing like the small-town boys I'm used to, with their hair shorn like sheep. He's wearing gray pants, a crisp white shirt, and a black tie and carrying a slim attaché case. His fingers are long and tapered.

"I don't think so."

"Something about you is . . . very familiar." He's staring at me so intently that it makes me blush.

"I —" I stammer. "I really don't know."

And then, with a smile playing around his lips, he says, "Forgive me if I'm wrong. But are you — were you — did you come here on a train from New York about ten years ago?"

What? My heart jumps. How does he know that?

"Are you — Niamh?" he asks.

And then I know. "Oh my God — Dutchy, it's you."

Minneapolis, Minnesota, 1939

Dutchy drops the attaché case as I stand up, and sweeps me into a hug. I feel the ropy hardness of his arms, the warmth of his slightly concave chest, as he holds me tight, tighter than anyone has ever held me. A long embrace in the middle of this fancy lobby is probably inappropriate; people are staring. But for once in my life I don't care.

He pushes me away to look at my face, touches my cheek, and pulls me close again. Through his chambray shirt I feel his heart racing as fast as mine.

"When you blushed, I knew. You looked just the same." He runs his hand down my hair, stroking it like a pelt. "Your hair . . . it's darker. I can't tell you how many times I've looked for you in a crowd, or thought I saw you from the back."

"You told me you'd find me," I say. "Remember? It was the last thing you said."

"I wanted to — I tried. But I didn't know

where to look. And then so much happened . . ." He shakes his head in disbelief. "Is it really you, Niamh?"

"Well, yes — but I'm not Niamh anymore," I tell him. "I'm Vivian."

"I'm not Dutchy, either — or Hans, for that matter. I'm Luke."

We both start laughing — at the absurdity of our shared experience, the relief of recognition. We cling to each other like survivors of a shipwreck, astonished that neither of us drowned.

The many questions I want to ask render me mute. Before I can even formulate words, Dutchy — Luke — says, "This is crazy, but I have to leave. I have a gig."

"A 'gig'?"

"I play piano in the bar here. It's not a terrible job, if nobody gets too drunk."

"I was just on my way in there," I tell him. "My friends are waiting for me. They're probably drunk as we speak."

He picks up his case. "I wish we could just blow out of here," he says. "Go somewhere and talk."

I do too — but I don't want him to risk his job for me. "I'll stay till you're done. We can talk later."

"It'll kill me to wait that long."

When I enter the bar with him, Lil and

358

Em look up, curiosity on their faces. The room is dark and smoky, with plush purple carpeting patterned with flowers and purple leather banquettes filled with people.

"That's the way to do it, girl!" Richard says. "You sure didn't waste any time."

I sink into a chair at their table, order a gin fizz at the waiter's suggestion, and concentrate on Dutchy's fingers, which I can see from where I'm sitting, deftly skimming the piano keys. Ducking his head and closing his eyes, he sings in a clear, low voice. He plays Glenn Miller and Artie Shaw and Glen Gray, music that everybody knows — songs like "Little Brown Jug" and "Heaven Can Wait," rearranged to draw out different meanings — and some old standards for the gray-haired men on bar stools. Every now and then he pulls sheet music from his case, but mostly he seems to play from memory or by ear. A small cluster of older ladies clutching pocketbooks, their hair carefully coiffed, probably on a shopping expedition from some province or suburb, smile and coo when he tinkles the opening of "Moonlight Serenade."

Conversation washes over me, slips around me, snagging now and then when I'm expected to answer a question or laugh at a joke. I'm not paying attention. How can I?

Dutchy is talking to me through the piano, and, as in a dream, I understand his meaning. I have been so alone on this journey, cut off from my past. However hard I try, I will always feel alien and strange. And now I've stumbled on a fellow outsider, one who speaks my language without saying a word.

The more people drink, the more requests they make, and the fuller Dutchy's tip jar grows. Richard's head is buried in Lil's neck, and Em is practically sitting in the lap of a gray hair who wandered over from the bar. "Over the Rainbow!" she calls out, several gin fizzes to the wind. "You know that one? From that movie?"

Dutchy nods, smiles, spreads his fingers across the keys. By the way he plays the chords I can tell he's been asked to sing it before.

He has half an hour left on the clock when Richard makes a show of looking at his watch. "Holy shit, excuse my French," he says. "It's late and I got church tomorrow."

Everyone laughs.

"I'm ready to turn in, too," Lil says.

Em smirks. "Turn into what?"

"Let's blow this joint. I gotta get that thing I left in your room," Richard says to Lil, standing up.

"What thing?" she asks.

"You know. The *thing*," he says, winking at Em.

"He's gotta get the thing, Lil," Em says drunkenly. "The *thing*!"

"I didn't know men were allowed in the rooms," I say.

Richard rubs his thumb and forefinger together. "A little grease for the wheel keeps the car running, if you get my gist."

"The desk clerk is easy to bribe," Lil translates. "Just so you know, in case you want to spend some quality time with dreamboat over there." She and Em collapse in giggles.

We make a plan to meet in the lobby of the women's hotel tomorrow at noon, and the four of them stand to leave. And then there's a change of plans: Richard knows a bar that's open until two and they go off in search of it, the two girls tottering on their heels and swaying against the men, who seem all too happy to support them.

Just after midnight, the street outside the hotel is lit up but empty, like a stage set before the actors appear. It doesn't matter that I barely know the man Dutchy has become, know nothing about his family, his adolescence. I don't care about how it might look to take him back to my room. I just want to spend more time with him.

"Are you sure?" he asks.

"More than sure."

He slips some bills in my hand. "Here, for the clerk. From the tip jar."

It's cool enough that Dutchy puts his jacket around my shoulders. His hand in mine as we walk feels like the most natural thing in the world. Through the low buildings, chips of stars glitter in a velvet sky.

At the front desk, the clerk — an older man, now, with a tweed cap tipped over his face — says, "What can I do for you?"

Oddly, I am not at all nervous. "My cousin lives in town. All right to take him up for a visit?"

The clerk looks through the glass door at Dutchy, standing on the sidewalk. "Cousin, huh?"

I slide two dollar bills across the desk. "I appreciate it."

With his fingertips the clerk pulls the money toward him.

I wave at Dutchy and he opens the door, salutes the clerk, and follows me into the elevator.

In the strange, shadowed lighting of my small room Dutchy takes off his belt and dress shirt and hangs them over the only chair. He stretches out on the bed in his undershirt and trousers, his back against the wall, and I lean against him, feeling his body curve around mine. His warm breath is on my neck, his arm on my waist. I wonder for a moment if he'll kiss me. I want him to.

"How can this be?" he murmurs. "It isn't possible. And yet I've dreamed of it. Have you?"

I don't know what to say. I never dared to imagine that I'd see him again. In my experience, when you lose somebody you care about, they stay gone.

"What's the best thing that happened to you in the past ten years?" I ask.

"Seeing you again."

Smiling, I push back against his chest. "Besides that."

"Meeting you the first time."

We both laugh. "Besides that."

"Hmm, besides that," he muses, his lips on my shoulder. "Is there anything besides that?" He pulls me close, his hand cupping my hip bone. And though I've never done anything like this before — have barely ever been alone with a man, certainly not a man in his undershirt — I'm not nervous. When he kisses me, my whole body hums.

A few minutes later, he says, "I guess the

best thing was finding out that I was good at something — at playing the piano. I was such a shell of a person. I had no confidence. Playing the piano gave me a place in the world. And . . . it was something I could do when I was angry or upset, or even happy. It was a way to express my feelings when I didn't even know what they were." He laughs a little. "Sounds ridiculous, doesn't it?"

"No."

"What about you? What's your best thing?"

I don't know why I asked him this question, since I don't have an answer myself. I slide up so I am sitting at the head of the narrow bed with my feet tucked under me. As Dutchy rearranges himself with his back against the wall on the other end, words tumble from my mouth. I tell him about my loneliness and hunger at the Byrnes', the abject misery of the Grotes'. I tell him about how grateful I am to the Nielsens, and also how tamped down I sometimes feel with them.

Dutchy tells me what happened to him after he left the Grange Hall. Life with the farmer and his wife was as bad as he'd feared. They made him sleep on hay bales in the barn and beat him if he complained.

His ribs were fractured in a haying accident and they never called a doctor. He lived with them for three months, finally running away when the farmer woke him with a beating one morning because a raccoon got into the chicken coop. In pain, half starved, with a tapeworm and an eye infection, he collapsed on the road to town and was taken to the infirmary by a kindly widow.

But the farmer convinced the authorities that Dutchy was a juvenile delinquent who needed a firm hand, and Dutchy was returned to him. He ran away twice more — the second time in a blizzard, when it was a miracle he didn't freeze to death. Running into a neighbor's clothesline saved his life. The neighbor found him in his barn the following morning and made a deal with the farmer to trade Dutchy for a pig.

"A pig?" I say.

"I'm sure he thought it a worthy trade. That pig was massive."

This farmer, a widower named Karl Maynard whose son and daughter were grown, gave him chores to do, but also sent him to school. And when Dutchy showed an interest in the dusty upright piano the widower's wife used to play, he got it tuned and found a teacher to come to the farm to give him lessons.

When he was eighteen, Dutchy moved to Minneapolis, where he took any work he could find playing piano in bands and bars. "Maynard wanted me to take over the farm, but I knew I wasn't cut out for it," he says. "Honestly, I was grateful to have a skill I could use. And to live on my own. It's a relief to be an adult."

I hadn't thought about it like this, but he's right — it is a relief.

He reaches over and touches my necklace. "You still have it. That gives me faith."

"Faith in what?"

"God, I suppose. No, I don't know. Survival."

As light begins to seep through the darkness outside the window, around 5:00 A.M., he tells me that he's playing the organ in the Episcopal Church on Banner Street at the eight o'clock service.

"Do you want to stay till then?" I ask.

"Do you want me to?"

"What do you think?"

He stretches out beside the wall and pulls me toward him, curving his body around mine again, his arm tucked under my waist. As I lie there, matching my breathing to his, I can tell the moment when he lapses into sleep. I inhale the musk of his aftershave, a whiff of hair oil. I reach for his hand and grasp his long fingers and lace them through mine, thinking about the fateful steps that led me to him. If I hadn't come on this trip. If I'd had something to eat. If Richard had taken us to a different bar. . . . There are so many ways to play this game. Still, I can't help but think that everything I've been through has led to this. If I hadn't been chosen by the Byrnes, I wouldn't have ended up with the Grotes and met Miss Larsen. If Miss Larsen hadn't brought me to Mrs. Murphy, I never would've met the Nielsens. And if I weren't living with the Nielsens and attending college with Lil and Em, I would never have come to Minneapolis for the night — and probably never would have seen Dutchy again.

My entire life has felt like chance. Random moments of loss and connection. This is the first one that feels, instead, like fate.

"So?" Lil demands. "What happened?"

We're on our way back to Hemingford, with Em stretched out and groaning on the backseat, wearing dark glasses. Her face has a greenish tint.

I am determined not to give anything away. "Nothing happened. What happened with you?"

"Don't change the subject, missy," Lil

says. "How'd you know that guy, anyway?"

I've already thought about an answer. "He's come into the store a few times."

Lil is skeptical. "What would he be doing in Hemingford?"

"He sells pianos."

"Humph," she says, clearly unconvinced. "Well, you two seemed to hit it off."

I shrug. "He's nice enough."

"How much money do piano players make, anyway?" Em says from the back.

I want to tell her to shut up. Instead I take a deep breath and say, breezily, "Who knows? It's not like I'm going to marry him or anything."

Ten months later, after recounting this exchange to two dozen wedding guests in the basement of Grace Lutheran Church, Lil raises her glass in a toast. "To Vivian and Luke Maynard," she says. "May they always make beautiful music together."

HEMINGFORD, MINNESOTA, 1940–1943

In front of other people I call him Luke, but he'll always be Dutchy to me. He calls me Viv — it sounds a bit like Niamh, he says.

We decide that we'll live in Hemingford so I can run the store. We'll rent a small bungalow on a side street several blocks from the Nielsens, four rooms downstairs and one up. As it happens — with, perhaps, a little help from Mr. Nielsen, who may have mentioned something to the superintendent at a Rotary meeting — the Hemingford School is looking for a music teacher. Dutchy also keeps his weekend gig at the Grand in Minneapolis, and I go in with him on Friday and Saturday nights to have dinner and hear him play. On Sundays, now, he plays the organ at Grace Lutheran, replacing the lead-footed organist who was persuaded it was time to retire.

When I told Mrs. Nielsen that Dutchy had

asked me to marry him, she frowned. "I thought you said you wanted nothing to do with marriage," she said. "You're only twenty. What about your degree?"

"What about it?" I said. "It's a ring on my finger, not a pair of handcuffs."

"Most men want their wives to stay home."

When I related this conversation to Dutchy, he laughed. "Of course you'll get your degree. Those tax laws are complicated!"

Dutchy and I are about as opposite as two people can be. I am practical and circumspect; he is impulsive and direct. I'm accustomed to getting up before the sun rises; he pulls me back to bed. He has no head at all for math, so in addition to keeping the books at the store, I balance our accounts at home and pay our taxes. Before I met him, I could count on one hand the times I'd had a drink; he likes a cocktail every night, says it relaxes him and will relax me, too. He is handy with a hammer and nail from his experience on the farms, but he often leaves projects half finished — storm windows stacked in a corner while snow rages outside, a leaky faucet disemboweled, its parts all over the floor.

"I can't believe I found you," he tells me

over and over, and I can't believe it either. It's as if a piece of my past has come to life, and with it all the feelings I fought to keep down — my grief at losing so much, at having no one to tell, at keeping so much hidden. Dutchy was there. He knows who I was. I don't have to pretend.

We lie in bed longer than I am used to on Saturday mornings — the store doesn't open until ten, and there's nowhere Dutchy has to be. I make coffee in the kitchen and bring two steaming mugs back to bed, and we spend hours together in the soft early light. I am delirious with longing and the fulfillment of that longing, the desire to touch his warm skin, trace the sinew and muscle just under the surface, pulsing with life. I nestle in his arms, in the nooks of his knees, his body bowed around mine, his breath on my neck, fingers tracing my outline. I have never felt like this — slow-witted and languorous, dreamy, absent-minded, forgetful, focused only on each moment as it comes.

When Dutchy lived on the streets, he never felt as alone, he tells me, as he did growing up in Minnesota. In New York the boys were always playing practical jokes on each other and pooling their food and clothes. He misses the press of people, the

371

noise and chaos, black Model Ts rattling along the cobblestones, the treacly smell of street vendors' peanuts roasting in sugar.

"What about you — do you ever wish you could go back?" he asks.

I shake my head. "Our life was so hard. I don't have many happy memories of that place."

He pulls me close, runs his fingers along the soft white underbelly of my forearm. "Were your parents ever happy, do you think?"

"Maybe. I don't know."

Pushing the hair back from my face and tracing the line of my jaw with his finger, he says, "With you I'd be happy anywhere."

Though it's just the kind of thing he says, I believe that it's true. And I know, with the newfound clarity of being in a relationship myself, that my own parents were never happy together, and probably never would have been, whatever the circumstance.

On a mild afternoon in early December I am at the store going over inventory orders with Margaret, the sharp-eyed accounts manager. Packing receipts and forms are all over the floor; I'm trying to decide whether to order more ladies' trousers than last year, and looking at the popular styles in the catalog as well as *Vogue* and *Harper's Bazaar.* The radio is on low; swing music is playing, and then Margaret holds her hand up and says, "Wait. Did you hear that?" She hurries over to the radio and adjusts the dial.

"Repeat: this is a special report. President Roosevelt said in a statement today that the Japanese have attacked Pearl Harbor, Hawaii, from the air. The attack of the Japanese has also been made on all naval and military 'activities' on the island of Oahu. Casualty numbers are unknown."

And like that, everything changes.

A few weeks later, Lil comes into the store to see me, her eyes red-rimmed, tears staining her cheeks. "Richard shipped out yesterday, and I don't even know where he's going. They just gave him a numbered mailing address that doesn't tell me anything." Sobbing into a crumpled white handkerchief, she says, "I thought this stupid war was supposed to be over by now. Why does *my* fiancé have to go?" When I hug her, she clings to my shoulder.

Wherever you look are posters encouraging sacrifice and support for the war effort. Many items are rationed — meat, cheese, butter, lard, coffee, sugar, silk, nylon, shoes; our entire way of business changes as we work with those flimsy blue booklets. We learn to make change for ration stamps, giving red point tokens as change for red stamps (for meat and butter) and blue point tokens for blue stamps (processed foods). The tokens are made of compressed wood fiber, the size of dimes.

In the store we collect ladies' lightly used stockings for use in parachutes and ropes, and tin and steel for scrap and metal drives. "Boogie Woogie Bugle Boy" is constantly on the radio. I shift our purchasing to reflect the mood, ordering gift cards and blue onionskin airmail letter forms by the gross, dozens of American flags in all sizes, beef jerky, warm socks, decks of playing cards to go in care packages to ship overseas. Our stock boys shovel driveways and deliver groceries and packages.

Boys from my graduating class are signing up and shipping out, and every week there's a farewell potluck dinner in a church basement or the lobby of the Roxy or in someone's home. Judy Smith's boyfriend, Douglas, is one of the first. The day he turns eighteen he goes down to the recuiter's office and presents himself for service. Hotheaded Tom Price is next. When I run into him on the street before he leaves, he tells me that there's no downside — the war's an open door to travel and adventure, with a good bunch of guys to mess around with and a salary. We don't talk about the danger — but what I imagine is a cartoon version, bullets flying and each boy a superhero, running, invincible, through a spray of gunfire.

Fully a quarter of the boys from my class volunteer. And when the draft begins, more and more pack up to leave. I feel sorry for the boys with flat feet or severe asthma or partial deafness who I see in the store after their buddies are gone, aimlessly wandering the aisles. They seem lost in their ordinary civilian clothes.

But Dutchy doesn't join the bandwagon. "Let them come for me," he says. I don't want to believe he'll get called up — after all, Dutchy is a teacher; he's needed in the classroom. But soon enough it becomes clear that it's only a matter of time.

The day Dutchy leaves for Fort Snelling in Hennepin County for basic training, I take the claddagh off the chain around my neck and wrap it in a piece of felt. Tucking it in his breast pocket, I tell him, "Now a part of me will be with you."

"I'll guard it with my life," he says.

The letters we exchange are filled with hope and longing and a vague sense of the importance of the mission of the American troops. And the milestones of his training: Dutchy passes his physical and scores high on the mechanical aptitude test. Based on these results he's inducted into the navy to help replace those lost at Pearl Harbor. Soon enough, he's on a train to San Diego for technical training.

And when, six weeks after he leaves, I write to tell him that I'm pregnant, Dutchy says that he is over the moon. "The thought of my child growing inside you will keep me going through the roughest days," he writes. "Just knowing that finally I have a family waiting for me makes me more determined than ever to do my duty and find my way home."

I am tired all the time and sick to my stomach. I'd like to stay in bed, but I know it's better to stay busy. Mrs. Nielsen suggests that I move back in with them. She says they'll take care of me and feed me; they're worried that I'm getting too thin. But I prefer to be on my own. I'm twenty-two years old now, and I've gotten used to living like an adult.

As the weeks pass I am busier than ever, working long days in the store and volunteering in the evenings, running the metal drives and organizing shipments for the Red

Cross. But behind everything I do is a low hum of fear. *Where is he now, what is he doing?*

In the letters I write to Dutchy I try not to dwell on my sickness, the constant queasy feeling that the doctor tells me means the baby is thriving inside me. I tell him instead about the quilt I'm making for the baby, how I cut the pattern out of newspaper and then fine sandpaper, which sticks to the material. I chose a pattern with a woven look at the corners that resembles the weaving of a basket, five strips of fabric around the border. It's cheerful — yellow and blue and peach and pink calico, with off-white triangles in the middle of each square. The women in Mrs. Murphy's quilting group — of which I am the youngest member and honorary daughter; they've cheered my every milestone — are taking extra care with it, hand sewing in precise small stitches a pattern on top of the design.

Dutchy completes his technical training and aircraft carrier flight deck training, and after he's been in San Diego for a month, he learns that soon he'll be shipping out. Given his training and the desperate situation with the Japanese, he figures he'll be heading to the Central Pacific to assist Allied forces in that region, but nobody knows for sure.

Surprise, skill, and power — this, the navy tells its sailors, is what it will take to win the war.

The Central Pacific. Burma. China. These are only names on a globe. I take one of the world maps we sell in the store, rolled tightly and stored in a vertical container, and spread it on the counter. My finger skims the cities of Yangon, near the coast, and Mandalay, the darker mountainous region farther north. I was prepared for Europe, even its far reaches, Russia or Siberia — but the Central Pacific? It's so far away — on the other side of the world — that I have a hard time imagining it. I go to the library and stack books on a table: geographical studies, histories of the Far East, travelers' journals. I learn that Burma is the largest country in Southeast Asia, that it borders India and China and Siam. It's in the monsoon region; annual rainfall in the coastal areas is about two hundred inches, and the average temperature of those areas is close to ninety degrees. A third of its perimeter is coastline. The writer George Orwell published a novel, *Burmese Days,* and several essays about life there. What I get from reading them is that Burma is about as far from Minnesota as it's possible to be.

Over the next few weeks, as one day grinds into the next, life is quiet and tense. I listen to the radio, scour the *Tribune,* wait anxiously for the mail drop, and devour Dutchy's letters when they come, scanning quickly for news — is he okay? Eating well, healthy? — and parsing every word for tone and nuance, as if his sentences are a code I can crack. I hold each blue-tinted, tissue-thin letter to my nose and inhale. He, too, held this paper. I run my finger over the words. He formed each one.

Dutchy and his shipmates are waiting for orders. Last-minute flight-deck drills in the dark, the preparations of sea bags, every corner filled and every piece in place, from rations to ammunition. It's hot in San Diego, but they're warned that where they're going will be worse, almost unbearable. "I'll never get used to the heat," he writes. "I miss the cool evenings, walking along the street holding your hand. I even miss the damn snow. Never thought I'd say that." But most of all, he says, he misses me. My red hair in the sun. The freckles on my nose. My hazel eyes. The child growing in my stomach. "You must be getting big," he says. "I can only imagine the sight."

Now they're on the aircraft carrier in Virginia. This is the last note he'll send before they embark; he's giving it to a chaplain who came on board to see them off. "The flight deck is 862 feet long," he writes. "We wear seven different colors, to designate our jobs. As a maintenance technician, my deck jersey, float coat, and helmet are an ugly green, the color of overcooked peas." I picture him standing on that floating runway, his lovely blond hair hidden under a drab helmet.

Over the next three months I receive several dozen letters, weeks after he writes them, sometimes two in the same day, depending on where they were mailed from. Dutchy tells me about the tedium of life on board — how his best friend from their basic training days, another Minnesotan named Jim Daly, has taught him to play poker, and they spend long hours below-decks with a revolving cast of servicemen in an endless ongoing game. He talks about his work, how important it is to follow protocol and how heavy and uncomfortable his helmet is, how he's beginning to get used to the roar of the plane engines as they take off and land. He talks about being seasick, and the heat. He doesn't mention combat or planes being shot down. I don't know if he isn't allowed to or if he doesn't want to frighten me.

"I love you," he writes again and again. "I can't bear to live without you. I'm counting the minutes until I see you."

The words he uses are the idioms of popular songs and poems in the newspaper. And mine to him are no less clichéd. I puzzle over the onionskin, trying to spill my heart onto the page. But I can only come up with the same words, in the same order, and hope the depth of feeling beneath them gives them weight and substance. *I love you. I miss you. Be careful. Be safe.*

HEMINGFORD, MINNESOTA, 1943

It is ten o'clock on a Wednesday morning and I've been in the store for an hour, first going over accounts in the back room and now walking down each aisle, as I do every day, to make sure that the shelves are tidy and the sale displays are set up correctly. I'm in the back aisle, rebuilding a small pyramid of Jergens face cream that has toppled into a stack of Ivory soap, when I hear Mr. Nielsen say, "Can I help you?" in a strange stiff voice.

Then he says, sharply, "Viola."

I don't stop what I'm doing, though my heart races in my chest. Mr. Nielsen rarely calls his wife by her name. I continue building the pyramid of Jergens jars, five on the bottom, then four, three, two, one on top. I stack the leftover jars on the shelf behind the display. I replace the Ivory soap that was knocked off the pile. When I'm done, I stand in the aisle, waiting. I hear whispering. After a moment, Mrs. Nielsen calls, "Vivian? Are you here?"

A Western Union man is standing at the cash register in his blue uniform and black-brimmed cap. The telegram is short. "The Secretary of War regrets to inform you that Luke Maynard was killed in action on February 16, 1943. Further details will be forwarded to you as they become available."

I don't hear what the Western Union man says. Mrs. Nielsen has started to cry. I touch my stomach — the baby. Our baby.

In the coming months, I will get more information. Dutchy and three others were killed when a plane crashed onto the fleet carrier. There was nothing anyone could do; the plane came apart on top of him. "I hope you will find comfort in the fact that Luke died instantly. He never felt a thing," his shipmate Jim Daly writes. Later I receive a box of his personal effects — his wristwatch, letters I wrote to him, some clothes. The claddagh cross. I open the box and touch each item, then close it and put it away. It will be years before I wear the necklace again.

Dutchy hadn't wanted to tell anyone on base that his wife was pregnant. He was superstitious, he said; he didn't want to jinx it. I'm glad of that, glad that Jim Daly's letter of condolence is one to a wife, not a mother.

The next few weeks I get up early in the morning, before it's light, and go to work. I reorganize entire sections of merchandise. I have a big new sign made for the entrance and hire a design student to work on our windows. Despite my size, I drive to Minneapolis and walk around the large department stores, taking notes about how they create their window displays, trends in colors and styles that haven't filtered up to us yet. I order inner tubes, sunglasses, and beach towels for summer.

Lil and Em take me to the cinema, to a play, out to dinner. Mrs. Murphy invites me regularly for tea. And one night I am woken by a searing pain and know it's time to go to the hospital. I call Mrs. Nielsen, as we've planned, and pack my small bag, and she picks me up and drives me there. I am in labor for seven hours, the agony so great in the last stretch that I wonder if it's possible to split in half. I start to cry from the pain, and all the tears I haven't shed for Dutchy come flooding out. I am overcome with grief, with loss, with the stark misery of being alone.

I learned long ago that loss is not only probable but inevitable. I know what it means to lose everything, to let go of one life and find another. And now I feel, with a strange, deep certainty, that it must be my lot in life to be taught that lesson over and over again.

Lying in that hospital bed I feel all of it: the terrible weight of sorrow, the crumbling of my dreams. I sob uncontrollably for all that I've lost — the love of my life, my family, a future I'd dared to envision. And in that moment I make a decision. I can't go through this again. I can't give myself to someone so completely only to lose them. I don't want, ever again, to experience the loss of someone I love beyond reason.

"There, there," Mrs. Nielsen says, her voice rising in alarm. "If you keep on like this you'll" — she says "go dry," but what I hear is "die."

"I want to die," I tell her. "I have nothing left."

"You have this baby," she says. "You'll go on for this baby."

I turn away. I push, and after a time the baby comes.

The little girl is as light as a hen in my arms. Her hair is wispy and blond. Her eyes are as bright as underwater stones. Dizzy with fatigue, I hold her close and shut my eyes.

I have told no one, not even Mrs. Nielsen, what I am about to do. I whisper a name in my baby's ear: May. Maisie. Like me, she is the reincarnation of a dead girl.

And then I do it. I give her away.

Spruce Harbor, Maine, 2011

"Oh, Vivian. You gave her away," Molly says, leaning forward in her chair.

The two of them have been sitting for hours in the wingbacks in the living room. The antique lamp between them casts a planetary glow. On the floor, a stack of blue onionskin airmail letters bound with string, a man's gold watch, a steel helmet, and a pair of military-issue socks spill out of a black steamer trunk stamped with the words U.S. NAVY.

Vivian smooths the blanket on her lap and shakes her head as if deep in thought.

"I'm so sorry." Molly fingers the never-used baby blanket, its basket-weave design still vivid, the stitches intricately pristine. So Vivian had a baby and gave her away . . . and then married Jim Daly, Dutchy's best friend. Was she in love with him, or was he merely consolation? Did she tell him about the baby?

Vivian leans over and shuts off the tape recorder. "That's really the end of my story."

Molly looks at her, puzzled. "But that's only the first twenty years."

Vivian shrugs lightly. "The rest has been relatively uneventful. I married Jim, and ended up here."

"But all those years . . ."

"Good years, for the most part. But not particularly dramatic."

"Did you . . ." Molly hesitates. "Were you in love with him?"

Vivian looks out the bay window. Molly follows her gaze to the Rorschach shapes of the apple trees, barely visible in the light from the house. "I can honestly say that I never regretted marrying him. But you know the rest, so I will tell you this. I did love him. But I did not love him like I loved Dutchy: beyond reason. Maybe you only get one of those in a lifetime, I don't know. But it was all right. It was enough."

It was all right. It was enough. Molly's heart clamps as if squeezed in a fist. The depth of emotion beneath those words! It's hard for her to fathom. Feeling an ache in her throat, she swallows hard. Vivian's resolute unsentimentality is a stance Molly understands only too well. So she just nods and asks, "So how did you and Jim end up together?"

Vivian purses her lips, thinking. "About a year after Dutchy died, Jim returned from the war and got in touch with me — he had a few small things of Dutchy's, a pack of cards and his harmonica, that the army hadn't already sent. And so it started, you know. It was a comfort to have someone to talk to, I think for both of us — another person who knew Dutchy."

"Did he know you'd had a baby?"

"No, I don't think so. We never talked about it. It seemed like too much to burden him with. The war had taken a toll on him; there were a lot of things he didn't want to talk about either.

"Jim was good with facts and figures. Very organized and disciplined, far more than Dutchy was. Honestly, I doubt the store would've done half as well if Dutchy had lived. Is that terrible to say? Well, even so. He didn't care a whit about the store, didn't want to run it. He was a musician, you know. No head for business. But Jim and I were good partners. Worked well together. I did the ordering and the inventory and he upgraded the accounting system, brought in new electric cash registers, streamlined the vendors — modernized it.

"I'll tell you something: marrying Jim was like stepping into water the exact same temperature as the air. I barely had to adjust to the change. He was a quiet, decent, hard-working man, a good man. We weren't one of those couples who finish each other's sentences; I'm not even sure I could've told you what was going on in his head most of the time. But we were respectful of each other. Kind to each other. When he got irritable, I steered clear, and when I was in what he called one of my 'black moods' — sometimes I'd go days without saying more than a few words — he left me alone. The only problem between us was that he wanted a child, and I couldn't give him that. I just couldn't do it. I told him how I felt from the beginning, but I think he hoped I'd change my mind."

Vivian rises from her chair and goes to the tall bay windows. Molly is struck by how frail she is, how narrow her silhouette. Vivian unfastens the silk loops from their hooks at each side of the casing, letting the heavy paisley curtains fall across the glass.

"I wonder if . . ." Molly ventures cautiously. "Have you ever wondered what became of your daughter?"

"I think about it sometimes."

"You might be able to find her. She would be" — Molly calculates in her head — "in her late sixties, right? She could very well

390

be alive."

Adjusting the drape of the curtains, Vivian says, "It's too late for that."

"But — why?" The question feels like a dare. Molly holds her breath, her heart thumping, aware that she's being presumptuous, if not downright rude. But this may be her only chance to ask.

"I made a decision. I have to live with it."

"You were in a desperate situation."

Vivian is still in shadow, standing by the heavy drapes. "That's not quite true. I could have kept the baby. Mrs. Nielsen would've helped. The truth is, I was a coward. I was selfish and afraid."

"Your husband had just died. I can understand that."

"Really? I don't know if I can. And now — knowing that Maisie was alive all these years . . ."

"Oh, Vivian," Molly says.

Vivian shakes her head. She looks at the clock on the mantel. "Goodness, look at the time — it's after midnight! You must be exhausted. Let's find you a bed."

Spruce Harbor, Maine, 2011

Molly is in a canoe, paddling hard against the current. Her shoulders ache as she digs into the water on one side and then the other. Her feet are soaking; the canoe is sinking, filling with water. Glancing down, she sees her ruined cell phone, the sodden backpack that holds her laptop. Her red duffel topples out of the boat. She watches it bob for a moment in the waves and then, slowly, descend below the surface. Water roars in her ears, the sound of it like a distant faucet. But why does it seem so far away?

She opens her eyes. Blinks. It's bright — so bright. The sound of water . . . She turns her head and there, through a casement window, is the bay. The tide is rushing in.

The house is quiet. Vivian must still be asleep.

In the kitchen, the clock says 8:00 A.M. Molly puts the kettle on for tea and rummages through the cupboards, finding steel-cut oats and dried cranberries, walnuts, and honey. Following the directions on the cylindrical container, she makes slow-cooked oats (so different from the sugary packets Dina buys), chopping and adding the berries and nuts, drizzling it with a little honey. She turns off the oatmeal, rinses the teapot they used the night before, and washes the cups and saucers. Then she sits in a rocker by the table and waits for Vivian.

It's a beautiful, postcard-from-Maine morning, as Jack calls days like this. The bay sparkles in the sun like trout scales. In the distance, near the harbor, Molly can see a fleet of tiny sailboats.

Her phone vibrates. A text from Jack. *What's up?* This is the first weekend in months that they haven't made plans. Her phone *brr*s again. *Can I c u later?*

Tons of homework, she types.

Study 2gether?

Maybe. Call u later.

When?

She changes the subject: *ME postcard day.*

Let's hike Flying Mtn. Fuck hw.

Flying Mountain is one of Molly's favorites — a steep five-hundred-foot ascent along a piney trail, a panoramic view of

Somes Sound, a meandering descent that ends at Valley Cove, a pebbled beach where you can linger on large flat rocks, gazing at the sea, before circling back to your car or bike on a fire road carpeted with pine needles.

Ok. She presses send and immediately regrets it. Shit.

Within seconds, her phone rings. *"Hola, chica,"* Jack says. "What time do I pick you up?"

"Umm, can I get back to you?"

"Let's do it now. Ralph and Dina are holy rolling, right? I miss you, girl. That stupid fight — what was it about, anyway? I forgot already."

Molly gets up from the rocker, goes over and stirs the oatmeal for no reason, puts her palm on the teakettle. Lukewarm. Listens for footsteps, but the house is quiet. "Hey," she says, "I don't know how to tell you this."

"Tell me what?" he says, and then, "Whoa, wait a minute, are you breaking up with me?"

"What? No. It's nothing like that. Dina threw me out."

"You're kidding."

"Nope."

"She threw you . . . When?"

394

"Last night."

"Last night? So . . ." Molly can practically hear the wheels turning. "Where are you now?"

Taking a deep breath, she says, "I'm at Vivian's."

Silence. Did he hang up?

Molly bites her lip. "Jack?"

"You went to Vivian's last night? You stayed at Vivian's?"

"Yes, I —"

"Why didn't you call me?" His voice is brisk and accusatory.

"I didn't want to burden you."

"You didn't want to *burden* me?"

"I just mean I've relied on you too much. And after that fight —"

"So you thought, 'I'll go burden that ninety-year-old lady instead. Much better than burdening my *boyfriend.*'"

"Honestly, I was out of my mind," Molly says. "I didn't know what I was doing."

"So you hiked over there, did you? Somebody give you a ride?"

"I took the Island Explorer."

"What time was it?"

"Around seven," she fudges.

"Around seven. And you just marched up to her front door and rang the bell? Or did you call first?"

All right, that's enough. "I don't like your tone," Molly says.

Jack sighs.

"Look," she says. "I know this is hard for you to believe, but Vivian and I are friends."

There's a pause, and then Jack says, "Uh-huh."

"We have a lot in common, actually."

He laughs a little. "Come on, Moll."

"You can ask her."

"Listen. You know how much I care about you. But let's get real. You're a seventeen-year-old foster kid who's on probation. You just got kicked out of another home. And now you've moved in with a rich old lady who lives in a mansion. A lot in common? And my mom —"

"I know. Your mom." Molly sighs loudly. How long is she going to be beholden to Terry, for God's sake?

"It's complicated for me," he says.

"Well . . ." Molly says. Here goes. "I don't think it's so complicated now. I told Vivian about stealing the book."

There's a pause. "Did you tell her that my mom knew?"

"Yeah. I told her you vouched for me. And that your mom trusted you."

"What'd she say?"

"She totally understood."

396

He doesn't say anything, but she senses a shift, a softening.

"Look, Jack — I'm sorry. I'm sorry for putting you in that position in the first place. That's why I didn't call you last night; I didn't want you to feel like you had to save my butt once again. It sucks for you, always doing me a favor, and it sucks for me, always feeling like I have to be grateful. I don't want to have that kind of relationship with you. It's not fair to expect you to take care of me. And I honestly think your mom and I might get along better if she doesn't think I'm trying to work all the angles."

"She doesn't think that."

"She does, Jack. And I don't blame her." Molly glances over at the tea service drying in the rack. "And I have to say one more thing. Vivian said she wanted to clean out her attic. But I think what she really wanted was to see what was in those boxes one last time. And remember those parts of her life. So I'm glad, actually, that I was able to help her find these things. I feel like I did something important."

She hears footsteps in the upstairs hall — Vivian must be on her way downstairs. "Hey, I've gotta go. I'm making breakfast." She flicks on the gas burner to warm the

397

oatmeal, pouring a little skim milk into it and stirring.

Jack sighs. "You're a major pain in the ass, did you know that?"

"I keep telling you that, but you don't want to believe me."

"I believe you now," he says.

A few days after Molly arrives at Vivian's, she texts Ralph to let him know where she is.

He texts back: *Call me.*

So she calls. "What's up?"

"You need to come back so we can deal with this."

"Nah, that's okay."

"You can't just run away," he says. "We'll all be in a pile of shit if you do."

"I didn't run away. You kicked me out."

"No, we didn't." He sighs. "There are protocols. Child Protective Services are going to be all over your ass. So will the police, if this gets out. You have to go through the system."

"I think I'm done with the system."

"You're seventeen. You're not done with the system till the system is done with you."

"So don't tell them."

"You mean lie?"

"No. Just . . . don't tell them."

He's silent for a moment. Then he says, "You doing okay?"

"Yup."

"That lady is okay with you being there?"

"Uh-huh."

He grunts. "I'm guessing she's not a certified foster care provider."

"Not . . . technically."

"Not technically." He laughs drily. "Shit. Well, maybe you're right. No need to do anything drastic. When're you eighteen, again?"

"Soon."

"So if it's not hurting us . . . and it's not hurting you . . ."

"That money comes in handy, huh?"

He's silent again, and for a moment Molly thinks he's hung up on her. Then he says, "Rich old lady. Big house. You've done pretty well for yourself. You probably don't want us to report you missing."

"So . . . I still live with you, then?"

"Technically," he says. "Okay with you?"

"Okay with me. Give Dina my best."

"I'll be sure to do that," he says.

Terry is not particularly happy to find Molly in the house on Monday morning. "What's this?" she says, her voice a sharp exclamation. Jack hasn't told her about Molly's new living arrangements; apparently he was hoping the situation would somehow magically resolve itself before his mother found out.

"I've invited Molly to stay," Vivian announces. "And she has graciously accepted."

"So she's not . . ." Terry starts, looking back and forth between them. "Why aren't you at the Thibodeaus'?" she asks Molly.

"It's a little complicated there right now," Molly says.

"What does that mean?"

"Things are — unsettled," Vivian says. "And I'm perfectly happy to let her bunk in a spare room for the moment."

"What about school?"

"Of course she'll go to school. Why wouldn't she?"

"This is very . . . charitable of you, Vivi, but I imagine the authority ties —"

"It's all worked out. She's staying with me," Vivian says firmly. "What else am I going to do with all these rooms? Open a bed-and-breakfast?"

Molly's room is on the second floor, facing the ocean, down a long hall at the opposite side of the house from Vivian's. In the window in Molly's bathroom, also on the ocean side, a light cotton curtain dances constantly in the breeze, sucked toward the screen and out again, billowing toward the sink, an amiable ghostly presence.

How long has it been since anyone slept in this room? Molly wonders. Years and years and years.

Her belongings, all that she brought with her from the Thibodeaus', fill a scant three shelves in the closet. Vivian insists that she take an antique rolltop desk from the parlor and set it up in the bedroom across the hall from hers so she can study for finals. No sense in confining yourself to one room when there are all these options, is there?

Options. She can sleep with the door open, wander around freely, come and go without someone watching her every move. She hadn't realized how much of a toll the years of judgment and criticism, implied and expressed, have taken on her. It's as if she's been walking on a wire, trying to keep her balance, and now, for the first time, she is on solid ground.

Spruce Harbor, Maine, 2011

"You're looking remarkably normal," Lori the social worker says when Molly shows up at the chemistry lab for their usual biweekly meeting. "First the nose ring disappears. Now you've lost the skunk stripe. What's next, an Abercrombie hoodie?"

"Ugh, I'd kill myself first."

Lori smiles her ferrety smile.

"Don't get too excited," Molly says. "You haven't seen my new tramp stamp."

"You didn't."

It's kind of fun to keep Lori guessing, so Molly just lifts her shoulders in a shrug. Maybe, maybe not.

Lori shakes her head. "Let's have a look at those papers."

Molly hands over the community service forms, dutifully filled out and dated, along with the spreadsheet with the record of her hours and the required signatures.

Scanning the forms, Lori says, "Impressive. Who did the spreadsheet?"

"Who do you think?"

"Huh." Lori juts out her bottom lip and scribbles something at the top of the form. "So did you finish?"

"Finish what?"

Lori gives her a quizzical smile. "Cleaning out the attic. Isn't that what you were supposed to be doing?"

Right. Cleaning out the attic.

The attic actually *is* cleaned out. Every single item has been removed from every single box and discussed. Some things have been brought downstairs, and some unsalvageable pieces thrown away. True, most of the stuff got put back in the boxes and is still in the attic. But now the linens are neatly folded; breakables are carefully wrapped. Molly got rid of boxes that were oddly sized or misshapen or in bad shape and replaced them with new thick cardboard boxes, uniformly rectangular. Everything is clearly labeled by place and date with a black Sharpie and neatly stacked in chronological sequence under the eaves. You can even walk around up there.

"Yeah, it's finished."

"You can get a lot done in fifty hours, huh?"

Molly nods. You have no idea, she thinks.

Lori opens the file on the table in front of her. "So look at this — a teacher put a note in here."

Suddenly alert, Molly sits forward. Oh shit — what now?

Lori lifts the paper slightly, reading it. "A Mr. Reed. Social studies. Says you did an assignment for his class . . . a 'portaging' project. What's that?"

"Just a paper," she says cautiously.

"Hmm . . . you interviewed a ninety-one-year-old widow . . . that's the lady you did your hours with, right?"

"She just told me some stuff. It wasn't that big a deal."

"Well, Mr. Reed thinks it is. Says you went above and beyond. He's nominating you for some kind of prize."

"What?"

"A national history prize. You didn't know about this?"

No, she didn't know about this. Mr. Reed hasn't even handed the paper back yet. She shakes her head.

"Well, now you do." Lori folds her arms and leans back on her stool. "That's pretty exciting, huh?"

Molly feels like her skin is glowing, like she's been slathered in some kind of warm honeylike substance. She feels a grin growing on her face and has to fight to stay cool. She makes an effort to shrug. "I probably won't get it or anything."

"You probably won't," Lori agrees. "But as they say at the Oscars, it's an honor to be nominated."

"Load of crap."

Lori smiles, and Molly can't help it, she smiles back.

"I'm proud of you, Molly. You're doing well."

"You're just glad I'm not in juvie. That would count as a fail for you, right?"

"Right. I'd lose my holiday bonus."

"You'd have to sell your Lexus."

"Exactly. So stay out of trouble, okay?"

"I'll try," Molly says. "No promises. You don't want your job to get too boring, do you?"

"No danger of that," Lori says.

The household hums along. Terry keeps to her routine, and Molly pitches in where she can — throwing in a load of laundry and hanging it on the line, making stir-fries and other veggie-heavy dinners for Vivian, who doesn't seem to mind the extra cost and the lack of living creatures on the menu.

After some adjustment, Jack has warmed to the idea of Molly living here. For one thing, he can visit her without Dina's disapproving glare. For another, it's a nice place to hang out. In the evenings they sit on the porch in Vivian's old wicker chairs as the sky turns pink and lavender and red, the colors seeping toward them across the bay, a magnificent living watercolor.

One day, to everyone's shock and amazement except Molly's, Vivian announces that she wants to get a computer. Jack calls the phone company to find out how to install Wi-Fi in the house, then sets about getting a modem and wireless router. After talking through the various options, Vivian — who as far as anyone knows has never so much as nudged awake an electronic keyboard — decides to order the same matte silver thirteen-inch laptop Molly has. She doesn't really know what she'll use it for, she says — just to look things up and maybe read the *New York Times*.

With Vivian hovering at her shoulder, Molly goes to the site and signs in on her own account: click, click, credit card number, address, click . . . okay, free shipping?

"How long will it take to arrive?"

"Let's see . . . five to ten business days. Or maybe a little longer."

"Could I get it sooner?"

"Sure. It just costs a little more."

"How much more?"

"Well, for twenty-three dollars it can be here in a day or two."

"I suppose at my age there's no point in waiting, is there?"

As soon as the laptop arrives, a sleek little rectangular spaceship with a glowing screen, Molly helps Vivian set it up. She bookmarks the *New York Times* and AARP (why not?) and sets up an e-mail account (DalyViv@gmail.com), though it's hard to imagine Vivian using it. She shows Vivian how to access the tutorial, which she dutifully follows, exclaiming to herself as she goes: "Ah, that's what that is. You just push that button — oh! I see. Touchpad . . . where's the touchpad? Silly me, of course."

Vivian is a fast study. And soon enough, with a few quick strokes, she discovers a whole community of train riders and their descendants. Nearly a hundred of the two hundred thousand children who rode the trains are still alive. There are books and newspaper articles, plays and events. There's a National Orphan Train Complex based in Concordia, Kansas, with a website that includes riders' testimonies and photographs and a link to FAQs. ("Frequently asked questions?" Vivian marvels. "By whom?") There's a group called the New

York Train Riders; the few remaining survivors and their many descendants meet annually in a convent in Little Falls, Minnesota. The Children's Aid Society and the New York Foundling Hospital have websites with links to resources and information about historical records and archives. And there is a whole subgenre of ancestor research — sons and daughters flying to New York clutching scrapbooks, tracking down letters of indenture, photographs, birth certificates.

With help from Molly, Vivian sets up an Amazon account and orders books. There are dozens of children's stories about the trains, but what she's interested in is the documents, the artifacts, the self-published train-rider stories, each one a testimony, a telling. Many of the stories, she finds, follow a similar trajectory: *This bad thing happened, and this — and I found myself on a train — and this bad thing happened, and this — but I grew up to become a respectable, law-abiding citizen; I fell in love, I had children and grandchildren; in short, I've had a happy life, a life that could only have been possible because I was orphaned or abandoned and sent to Kansas or Minnesota or Oklahoma on a train. I wouldn't trade it for the world.*

"So is it just human nature to believe that

things happen for a reason — to find some shred of meaning even in the worst experiences?" Molly asks when Vivian reads some of these stories aloud.

"It certainly helps," Vivian says. She is sitting in one wingback with a laptop, scrolling through stories from the Kansas archives, and Molly in the other, reading actual books from Vivian's library. She's already plowed through *Oliver Twist* and is deep into *David Copperfield* when Vivian squeaks.

Molly looks up, startled. She's never heard Vivian make that sound. "What is it?"

"I think . . ." Vivian murmurs, her face glowing bluish in the skim-milk tint from the screen as she moves two fingers down across the trackpad, "I think I may have just found Carmine. The boy from the train." She lifts the computer from her lap and hands it to Molly.

The page is titled *Carmine Luten — Minnesota — 1929.*

"They didn't change his name?"

"Apparently not," Vivian says. "Look — here's the woman who took him out of my arms that day." She points at the screen with a curved finger, urging Molly to scroll down. "An idyllic childhood, the piece says. They called him Carm."

409

Molly reads on: Carm, it appears, was lucky. He grew up in Park Rapids. Married his high school sweetheart, became a salesman like his father. She lingers over the photographs: one taken of him with his new parents, just as Vivian described them — his mother, slight and pretty, his father tall and thin, chubby Carmine with his dark curly hair and crossed eyes nestled between them. There's a picture of him on his wedding day, eyes fixed, wearing glasses, beaming beside a round-cheeked, chestnut-haired girl as they cut a many-tiered white cake — and then one of him bald and smiling, an arm around his plumper but still recognizable wife, with a caption noting their fiftieth wedding anniversary.

Carmine's story has been written by his son, who clearly did lots of research, even making the pilgrimage to New York to scour the records of the Children's Aid Society. The son discovered that Carmine's birth mother, a new arrival from Italy, died in childbirth, and his destitute father gave him up. Carmine, it says in a postscript, died peacefully at the age of seventy-four in Park Rapids.

"I like knowing that Carmine had a good life," Vivian says. "That makes me happy."

Molly goes to Facebook and types in the

name of Carmine's son, Carmine Luten Jr. There's only one. She clicks on the photo tab and hands the laptop back to Vivian. "I can set up an account for you, if you want. You could send his son a friend request or a Facebook message."

Vivian peers at the pictures of Carmine's son with his wife and grandchildren on a recent vacation — at Harry Potter's castle, on a roller coaster, standing next to Mickey Mouse. "Good Lord. I'm not ready for that. But . . ." She looks at Molly. "You're good at this, aren't you?"

"At what?"

"Finding people. You found your mother. And Maisie. And now this."

"Oh. Well, not really, I just type in some words —"

"I've been thinking about what you said the other day," she breaks in. "About looking for the child I gave away. I never told anybody this, but all those years I lived in Hemingford, anytime I saw a girl with blond hair around her age, my heart jumped. I was desperate to know what became of her. But I thought I had no right. Now I wonder . . . I wonder if maybe we should try to find her." She looks directly at Molly. Her face is unguarded, full of longing. "If I decide that I'm ready, will you help me?"

Spruce Harbor, Maine, 2011

The phone rings and rings in the cavernous house, several receivers in different rooms trilling in different keys.

"Terry?" Vivian's voice rises shrilly. "Terry, can you get that?"

Molly, sitting across from Vivian in the living room, puts her book down and starts to rise. "Sounds like it's in here."

"I'm looking for it, Vivi," Terry calls from another room. "Is a phone in there?"

"It might be," Vivian says, craning to look around. "I can't tell."

Vivian is sitting in her favorite chair, the faded red wingback closest to the window, laptop open, nursing a cup of tea. It's another teacher-enrichment day at school, and Molly is studying for finals. Though it's midmorning, they haven't yet opened the curtains; Vivian finds the glare on her screen too strong until about eleven.

Terry bustles in, half muttering to herself

and half to the room. "Jeez Louise, this is why I like landlines. I never should've let Jack talk us into cordless. I swear — oh, here it is." She pulls a receiver out from behind a pillow on the couch. "Hello?" She pauses, hand on her hip. "Yes, this is Mrs. Daly's residence. Can I ask who's calling?"

She nestles the receiver in her chest. "The adoption registry," she stage-whispers.

Vivian motions her over and takes the phone. She clears her throat. "This is Vivian Daly."

Molly and Terry lean in closer.

"Yes, I did. Uh-huh. Yes. Oh — really?" She covers the receiver with her hand. "Someone matching the details I submitted had already filled out a form." Molly can hear the voice of the woman on the other end of he line, a tinny melody. "What's that you say?" Vivian puts the phone to her ear again and cocks her head, listening to the answer. "Fourteen years ago," she tells Molly and Terry.

"Fourteen years ago!" Terry exclaims.

A mere ten days ago, after rooting around on the Internet for a little while, Molly located a cache of adoption registry services, narrowing her search to the one rated highest among users. The site, described as a system for matching people who want to establish contact with their "next-of-kin by birth," seemed reputable and aboveboard — nonprofit, no fee required. Molly e-mailed the link for the application form to herself at school, where she printed it off for Vivian to fill in, a scant two pages, with the names of the town, the hospital, the adoption agency. At the post office Molly made a photocopy of the birth certificate, which Vivian has kept in a small box under her bed for all these years, with the original name — May — she gave her daughter. Then she put the forms and the photocopy in a manila envelope addressed to the agency and mailed them off, fully expecting to hear nothing for weeks or months, or possibly ever.

"Do I have a pen?" Vivian mutters, looking around. "Do I have a pen?"

Molly hurries into the kitchen and rummages through the junk drawer, pulling out a handful of writing implements, then scribbling on the closest paper at hand, the *Mount Desert Islander,* to find one that actually has ink. She brings a blue ballpoint and the newspaper back to Vivian.

"Yes, yes. All right. Yes, that's fine," Vivian is saying. "Now how do you spell that? D-u-n-n . . ." Setting the newspaper on the round table next to her chair, she writes a

414

name, phone number, and e-mail address above the headline, laboring over the "@." "Thank you. Yes, thank you." Squinting at the receiver, she clicks the off button.

Terry goes to the tall windows and pulls back the drapes, fastening the loops on each side. The light that floods in is hard and bright.

"For heaven's sake, now I can't see a thing," Vivian scolds, shading her screen with her hand.

"Oh, sorry! Do you want me to close them?"

"It's all right." Vivian shuts her laptop. She peers at the newspaper as if the digits she printed on it are some kind of code.

"So what did you find out?" Molly asks.

"Her name is Sarah Dunnell." Vivian looks up. "She lives in Fargo, North Dakota."

"North Dakota? Are they sure you're related?"

"They say they're sure. They've checked and cross-checked birth records. She was born on the same day, in the same hospital." Vivian's voice quavers. "Her original name was May."

"Oh my God." Molly touches Vivian's knee. "It is her."

Vivian clasps her hands in her lap. "It's her."

"This is really exciting!"

"It's terrifying," Vivian says.

"So what happens next?"

"Well, a phone call, I suppose. Or an e-mail. I have her e-mail address." She holds up the newspaper.

Molly leans forward. "Which do you want to do?"

"I'm not sure."

"A call would be more immediate."

"It might startle her."

"She's been waiting for this for a long time."

"That's true." Vivian seems to hesitate. "I don't know. Everything is moving so fast."

"After seventy years." Molly smiles. "I have an idea. Let's google her first and see what we find."

Vivian makes an "abracadabra" motion with her hand over the silver laptop. "Fast."

Sarah Dunnell, it turns out, is a musician. She played violin with the Fargo Symphony Orchestra and taught at North Dakota State University until her retirement several years ago. She's a member of the Rotary Club and has been married twice — for many years to a lawyer, and now to a dentist who is on the symphony board. She has a son and a daughter who appear to be in their early forties, and at least three grandchildren.

In the dozen or so photos in Google images, mostly head shots of Sarah with her violin and Rotary award ceremony groupings, she is slim, like Vivian, with an alert, guarded expression. And blond hair.

"I suppose she dyes it," Vivian says.

"Don't we all," Molly says.

"I never did."

"We can't all have gorgeous silver hair like yours," Molly says.

Things happen quickly now. Vivian sends Sarah an e-mail. Sarah calls. Within days, she and her dentist husband have booked a flight to Maine for early June. They'll bring their eleven-year-old granddaughter, Becca, who grew up reading *Blueberries for Sal* and is, Sarah says, always up for an adventure.

Vivian reads some of the e-mails out loud to Molly.

I always wondered about you, Sarah writes. *I'd given up hope of ever finding out who you are and why you gave me away.*

It's exciting, this getting-ready business. A troupe of workers marches through the house, painting trim, fixing broken baluster shafts on the porch facing the bay, cleaning

417

the Oriental rugs, and patching the cracks in the wall that appear every spring when the ground thaws and the house resettles.

"It's time to open up all the rooms, don't you think?" Vivian says one morning over breakfast. "Let the air in." To keep the bedroom doors from slamming shut in the wind from the bay, they prop them open with old hand irons Molly found in one of the boxes in the attic. Having all those doors and windows open on the second floor creates a breeze that blows through the house. Everything seems lighter, somehow. Open to the elements.

Without asking Molly's assistance, Vivian orders some new clothes for herself from Talbots on her laptop with a credit card. "Vivian ordered clothes from Talbots. On her laptop. With a credit card. Can you believe those words just came out of my mouth?" Molly tells Jack.

"Before we know it, frogs will be falling from the sky," he says.

Other signs of the apocalypse proliferate. After a pop-up ad appears on her screen, Vivian announces that she plans to sign up for Netflix. She buys a digital camera on Amazon with one click. She asks Molly if she's ever seen the sneezing baby panda video on YouTube. She even joins Facebook.

"She sent her daughter a friend request," Molly tells Jack.

"Did she accept?"

"Right away."

They shake their heads.

Two sets of cotton sheets are taken from the linen closet and washed, then hung to dry on the long clothesline beside the house. When Molly plucks them off the line, the sheets are stiff and sweet-smelling. She helps Terry make the beds, stretching the clean white sheets over mattresses that have never been used.

When is the last time any of them felt this kind of anticipation? Even Terry has gotten into the spirit. "I wonder what kind of cereal I should get for Becca," Terry muses as they drape the Irish Wreath quilt on the girl's bed, across the hall from her grandparents' suite.

"Honey Nut Cheerios are always a safe bet," Molly says.

"I think she'd prefer pancakes. Do you think she'd like blueberry pancakes?"

"Who doesn't like blueberry pancakes?"

In the kitchen, while Molly cleans out cabinets and Jack tightens the latches on the screen door, they discuss what Sarah and her family might want to do on the island. Stroll around Bar Harbor, get ice cream at Ben & Bill's, eat steamed lobster at Thurston's, maybe try Nonna's, the new Southern Italian place in Spruce Harbor that got a rave in *Down East* . . .

"She's not here to do touristy things. She's here to meet her birth mother," Terry reminds them.

They look at each other and start laughing. "Oh yeah, that's right," Jack says.

Molly is following Sarah's son, Stephen, on Twitter. The day of the flight, Stephen writes, "Mom's off to meet her ninety-one-year-old birth mother. Go figure. A whole new life at the age of sixty-eight!"

A whole new life.

It's a Maine postcard day. All the rooms in the house are ready. A large pot of fish chowder, Terry's specialty, simmers on the stove (with a smaller pot of corn chowder, a nod to Molly, beside it). Corn bread cools on the counter. Molly has made a big salad and balsamic dressing.

Molly and Vivian have been roaming around all afternoon, pretending not to watch the clock. Jack called at 2:00 P.M. to say that the flight from Minnesota landed in Boston a few minutes late, but the puddle-jumper to Bar Harbor airport had taken off and was scheduled to land in half an hour, and he was on his way. He'd taken

Vivian's car, a navy blue Subaru wagon, to pick them up (after vacuuming it out and giving it a good wash with dishwashing liquid and a hose in his driveway).

Sitting in the rocker in the kitchen, looking out at the water, Molly feels oddly at peace. For the first time since she can remember, her life is beginning to make sense. What up until this moment has felt like a random, disconnected series of unhappy events she now views as necessary steps in a journey toward . . . *enlightenment* is perhaps too strong a word, but there are others, less lofty, like *self-acceptance* and *perspective.* She has never believed in fate; it would've been dispiriting to accept that her life so far unfolded as it did according to some preordained pattern. But now she wonders. If she hadn't been bounced from one foster home to the next, she wouldn't have ended up on this island — and met Jack, and through him, Vivian. She would never have heard Vivian's story, with all its resonance to her own.

When the car pulls into the driveway, Molly hears the crunch of gravel from the kitchen, at the opposite end of the house. She's been listening for it. "Vivian, they're here!" she calls.

"I hear," Vivian calls back.

421

Meeting in the foyer, Molly reaches for Vivian's hand. This is it, she thinks, the culmination of everything. But all she says is, "Ready?"

"Ready," Vivian says.

As soon as Jack shuts off the engine, a girl springs from the backseat, wearing a blue-striped dress and white sneakers. Becca — it must be. She has red hair. Long, wavy red hair and a smattering of freckles.

Vivian, gripping the porch rail with one hand, puts her other over her mouth. "Oh."

"Oh," Molly breathes behind her.

The girl waves. "Vivian, we're here!"

The blond woman getting out of the car — Sarah — looks toward them with an expression Molly's never seen before. Her eyes are wide open, searching, and when her gaze alights on Vivian's face, it is startling in its intensity, stripped of any pretense or convention. Yearning and wariness and hopefulness and love . . . does Molly really see all this on Sarah's face, or is she projecting? She looks at Jack, lifting the bags out of the trunk, and he nods and gives her a slow wink. *I get it. I feel it too.*

Molly touches Vivian's shoulder, frail and bony under her thin silk cardigan. She half turns, half smiles, her eyes brimming with tears. Her hand flutters to her clavicle, to the silver chain around her neck, the clad-dagh charm — those tiny hands clasping a crowned heart: love, loyalty, friendship — a never-ending path that leads away from home and circles back. What a journey Viv-ian and this necklace have taken, Molly thinks: from a cobblestoned village on the coast of Ireland to a tenement in New York to a train filled with children, steaming westward through farmland, to a lifetime in Minnesota. And now to this moment, nearly a hundred years after it all began, on the porch of an old house in Maine.

Vivian puts her foot on the first step and stumbles slightly, and each person moves toward her, as if in slow motion — Molly, just behind her, Becca, nearing the bottom step, Jack at the car, Sarah crossing the gravel, even Terry, coming around the side of the house.

"I'm all right!" Vivian says, grasping the rail.

Molly slips an arm around her waist. "Of course you are," she whispers. Her voice is steady, though her heart is so full it aches. "And I'm right here behind you."

Vivian smiles. She looks down at Becca, who is gazing up at her with large hazel eyes. "Now then. Where shall we begin?"

ACKNOWLEDGMENTS

The strands of this novel — Minnesota, Maine, and Ireland — have been woven together with the help of a number of people. Visiting my husband's mother, Carole Kline, at her home in Fargo, North Dakota, a number of years ago, I read a story about her father, Frank Robertson, that appeared in a volume called *Century of Stories: Jamestown, North Dakota, 1883– 1983* edited by James Smorada and Lois Forrest. The piece, "They Called It 'Orphan Train': And It Proved There Was a Home for Many Children on the Prairie," featured Frank and his four orphaned siblings who were placed in foster care in Jamestown and eventually all adopted by the same family. Though they were not, as it turned out, "orphan train" orphans, my curiosity was piqued. I was stunned to learn about the breadth and scope of the orphan train movement, which transported a reported

425

two hundred thousand children from the East Coast to the Midwest between 1854 and 1929.

In the course of my research, I spoke to Jill Smolowe, a writer and reporter for *People,* who thought there might be enough material on the surviving "train riders," as they call themselves, for a *People* magazine feature. Though the story never materialized, the folder of material and contacts Jill compiled proved tremendously useful. Most significant, Jill introduced me to Renee Wendinger, president of the Midwest Orphan Train Riders from New York organization, whose mother, Sophia Hillesheim, was a train rider. At the Orphan Train Riders of New York's forty-ninth reunion in 2009 in Little Falls, Minnesota, Renee introduced me to half a dozen train riders, all now in their nineties, including Pat Thiessen, a train rider from Ireland whose experience uncannily resembled the one I had sketched for my character. Throughout the writing of this novel Renee has patiently and generously offered her wise counsel in ways large and small, from correcting egregious errors to providing historical nuance and shading. Her book, *Extra! Extra! The Orphan Trains and Newsboys of New York,* has been an invaluable resource. The novel would not have been the same without her.

Other resources I relied on during my orphan train research were the Children's Aid Society; the New York Foundling (I attended their 140th homecoming in 2009 and met a number of train riders there); the New York Tenement Museum; the Ellis Island Immigration Museum; and the National Orphan Train Complex in Concordia, Kansas, a museum and research center with a vibrant online presence that includes many train rider stories. In the Irma and Paul Milstein Division of U.S. History, Local History and Genealogy at the New York Public Library, I found noncirculating lists of orphaned and indigent children from the Children's Aid Society and the New York Foundling, first-person testimonials from train riders and their families, handwritten records, notes from desperate mothers explaining why they had abandoned their children, reports on Irish immigrants, and many other documents that aren't available anywhere else. Books I found particularly helpful include *Orphan Train Rider: One Boy's True Story* by Andrea Warren; *Children of the Orphan Trains, 1854–1929* by Holly Littlefield; and *Rachel Calof's Story: Jewish Homesteader on the Northern Plains* edited by J. Sanford Rikoon (which I found at Bonanzaville, a pioneer prairie village and museum complex in West Fargo).

During my years as Writer-in-Residence at Fordham University, I was privileged to receive a Faculty Fellowship and a Fordham Research Grant, which enabled me to conduct research in Minnesota and Ireland. A fellowship from the Virginia Center for the Creative Arts gave me space and time to write. Irish native Brian Nolan took me on an insider's tour of County Galway. His stories about his childhood housekeeper Birdie Sheridan provided inspiration for Vivian's grandmother's life. In the village of Kinvara, Robyn Richardson ferried me from pubs to Phantom Street and handed me an important resource: *Kinvara: A Seaport Town on Galway Bay* by Caoilte Breatnach and Anne Korff. Among other books, *An Irish Country Childhood* by Marrie Walsh helped me with period and place details.

At the same time that I was writing this book, my mother, Tina Baker, began teaching a course on Mount Desert Island in Maine called "Native American Women in Literature and Myth." At the end of the course, she asked students to use the Indian concept of portaging to describe "their journeys along uncharted waters and what they chose to carry forward in portages to come," as she writes in the compilation of their narratives, *Voices Yearning to be Heard: Acadia Senior College Students Pay Tribute to the Missing Voices of History.* The concept of portaging, I realized, was the missing strand I needed to weave my book together. Additional titles shaped my perspective: *Women of the Dawn* by Bunny McBride, *In the Shadow of the Eagle: A Tribal Representative in Maine* by Donna Loring (a member of the Penobscot Indian Nation and a former state legislator), and *Wabanakis of Maine and the Maritimes* by the Wabanaki Program of the American Friends Services Committee. The websites of the Abbe Museum in Bar Harbor, Maine, and the Penobscot Indian Nation provided valuable material as well.

I relied on good friends and family for support, counsel, and advice: Cynthia Baker, William Baker, Catherine Baker-Pitts, Marina Budhos, Anne Burt, Deb Ellis, Alice Elliott Dark, Louise DeSalvo, Bonnie Friedman, Clara Baker Lester, Pamela Redmond Satran, and John Veague. My husband, David, read the manuscript with a keen eye and a generous heart. Penny Windle Kline briefed me on adoption protocols and provided crucial resources. Master Sergeant Jeffrey Bingham and his uncle

Bruce Bingham, a retired brigadier general in the U.S. Army, offered fact checking for the World War II sections of the novel. Bunny McBride, Donna Loring, Robyn Richardson, and Brian Nolan read sections relevant to their expertise. Hayden, Will, and Eli, my sons, gently corrected any errant teen-speak. My agent, Beth Vesel, was in her remarkable way both mentor and friend. And my editor at Morrow, Katherine Nintzel — in addition to her usual good sense and intelligent advice — suggested a structural change at the eleventh hour that transformed the narrative.

This book would not exist without the train riders themselves. Having been privileged to meet six of them (all between the ages of ninety and one hundred) and read hundreds of their first-person narratives, I am filled with admiration for their courage, fortitude, and perspective on this strange and little-known episode in our nation's history.

P.S.
INSIGHTS, INTERVIEWS
& MORE . . .

■ ■ ■ ■
ABOUT THE BOOK
■ ■ ■ ■

CHRISTINA BAKER KLINE
TALKS WITH
ROXANA ROBINSON

Roxana Robinson is the author of *Cost* — named by the *Washington Post* as one of the five best fiction books of 2008 — as well as three earlier novels, three short story collections, and the biography *Georgia O'Keeffe: A Life.* Four of these publications were *New York Times* Notable Books. Robinson's work has appeared in *The New Yorker, The Atlantic, Harper's, Best American Short Stories,* the *New York Times,* and elsewhere. She was named a Literary Lion by the New York Public Library and has received fellowships from the National Endowment for the Arts, the MacDowell Colony, and the John Simon Guggenheim Foundation. Her novel *Sparta* is forthcoming.

RR: ***Could you talk about how this book started? What gave you the idea for it?***
CBK: About a decade ago, while visiting my

in-laws in North Dakota, I came across a nonfiction book printed by the Fort Seward Historical Society called *Century of Stories: Jamestown and Stutsman County, 1883–1983*. In it was an article titled "They called it 'Orphan Train' — and it proved there was a home for many children on the prairie." My husband's grandfather Frank Robertson and his siblings featured prominently in the story. This was news to me — I'd never heard of the orphan trains. In the course of researching this family lore, I found out that although orphan trains did, in fact, stop in Jamestown, North Dakota, and orphans from those trains were adopted there, the Robertson clan came from Missouri. But my interest was piqued, and I knew I wanted to learn more about this little-known period in American history.

RR: *What was it that was most compelling to you about the idea of an orphan train?*

CBK: I think I was drawn to the orphan train story in part because two of my own grandparents were orphans who spoke little about their early lives. As a novelist, I've always been fascinated with how people tell the stories of their lives and what those stories reveal — intentionally or not — about who they are. I'm intrigued by the spaces between words, the silences that conceal long-kept secrets, the elisions that belie surface appearance.

My own background is partly Irish, and so I decided that I wanted to write about an Irish girl who has kept silent about the circumstances that led her to the orphan train. I wanted to write about how traumatic events beyond our control can shape and define our lives. "People who cross the threshold between the known world and that place where the impossible does happen discover the problem of how to convey that experience," Kathryn Harrison writes. Over the course of this novel, my central character, Vivian, moves from shame about her past to acceptance, eventually coming to terms with what she's been through. In the process, she learns about the regenerative power of reclaiming — and telling — her own life story.

Like my four previous novels, *Orphan Train* wrestles with questions of cultural identity and family history. But I knew right away that this was a bigger story and would require extensive research. The vast canvas appealed to me immensely. I was eager to broaden my scope.

RR: *Did you go to the Midwest to see any of the sites you describe here?*

CBK: I've been going to Minnesota and North Dakota for decades. I know Minneapolis fairly well and feel a great affinity for the region. My husband's family has a lake home near Park Rapids, Minnesota, and I've spent a lot of time there. Several of the small towns I describe in this novel are invented, as is Spruce Harbor, Maine, the setting for the present-day story. (Spruce Harbor is also the setting for another of my novels, *The Way Life Should Be*.) Planting an imaginary town in a real landscape gives me freedom as a writer to invent as I go.

RR: *What sort of research did you do for the book, and did you interview people who were connected to the train? What was that like?*

CBK: After finding articles online from the *New York Times* and other newspapers, I read hundreds of first-person testimonials from train riders, orphan-train reunion groups, and historical archives. That research led me to the New York Public Library, where I found a trove of original contemporaneous materials. I devoured nonfiction histories, children's novels, and picture books, and conducted research at the New York Tenement Museum and Ellis Island. I also traveled to County Galway in Ireland to research my character's Irish background.

In the course of writing this book I attended train riders' reunions in New York and Minnesota, and interviewed train riders and their descendants. There aren't many train riders left; those who remain are all over ninety years old. I was struck by how eager they were to tell their stories, to each other and to me. In talking to them and reading their oral histories, I found that they tended not to dwell on the considerable hardships they'd faced; instead, they focused on how grateful they were for their children, grandchildren, and communities — for lives that wouldn't have been possible if they hadn't been on those trains. I realized that in fiction I could do something that is difficult to do in real life: I could dwell on the stark details of the experience without needing to create a narrative of redemption.

RR: *What was the most surprising thing that came out of the research? What was it that you hadn't expected?*

CBK: For decades, many train riders believed that the train they rode on was the only one. They didn't know that they were part of a massive seventy-five-year social experiment. It wasn't until their own children and grandchildren got involved and started asking questions (there are more than two million descendants, according to some estimates) that they met other train riders and began sharing their stories.

RR: *You have two teenage girls as main characters, and though they are widely separated by time and circumstances, they share some things. Could you talk about that?*

CBK: When you write novels, you go on instinct much of the time. As I began writing about Molly, a seventeen-year-old Penobscot Indian foster child, believe it or not, I didn't immediately notice parallels to Vivian, a wealthy ninety-one-year-old widow. But as I wrote my way into the narrative I could see that in addition to some biographical parallels — both characters have dead fathers and institutionalized mothers, both were passed from home to home and encountered prejudice because of cultural stereotypes, both held on to talismanic keepsakes from family members — they are psychologically similar. For both of them, change has been a defining principle; from a young age, they both had to learn to adapt, to inhabit new identities. They've spent much of their lives minimizing risk, avoiding complicated entanglements, and keeping silent about the past. It's not until Vivian — in answer to Molly's pointed questions — begins to face the truth about what happened long ago that both of them have the courage to make changes in their lives.

RR: *Can you talk about your own feelings of connection to Maine, a place you use often in your work?*

CBK: Though both of my parents are Southern, we moved to Maine when I was six years old and never looked back. I'm not naïve enough to consider myself a Mainer — though two of my younger sisters might be able to, having been born in-state (Mainers tend to be inconsistent on this subject) — but I did spend my formative years in Bangor, a mid-Maine town of thirty-five thousand on the Penobscot River. About a decade ago my parents retired to Bass Harbor, a tiny coastal village on Mount Desert Island. My three sisters have houses within two miles of my parents' home, and one lives there with her family year-round. I am lucky enough to spend summers and other vacations on the island; my three boys consider it their homeland. For me, it's as simple as this: Maine is a part of who I am.

RR: *Can you talk about the presence of time in this book, the way you use it to define and expand?*

CBK: The present-day story in *Orphan Train* unfolds over several months and the historical section spans twenty-three years, from 1929 to 1943. It took some time to figure out how to balance the sections so that they complemented and enhanced each other.

Too often, when I'm reading novels with separate storylines, I find that I prefer one over the other and am impatient to return to the one I like. I tried to avoid this with *Orphan Train* by weaving the stories together so that they contained echoes of, and references to, each other — for example, Vivian's grandmother gives her a Claddagh necklace in one section, and then pages later Molly comments on the necklace in the present-day story. But I didn't want the references to be too literal or overt. It was complicated! I also wanted the historical section to end abruptly with a surprising revelation (which I won't give away here), and for the present-day story to pick up where it left off, laying bare the mechanics of the storytelling: that Vivian is telling Molly her story in the present day. Sometimes I gave myself a headache trying to figure out how it all fit together. More than once, my editor, thank goodness, came in and saved the day.

A SHORT HISTORY OF THE REAL ORPHAN TRAINS

ORPHAN TRAIN is a specifically American story of mobility and rootlessness, highlighting a little-known but historically significant

Elizabeth Street in New York City, where Niamh lived, in the early twentieth century.

Photograph courtesy of the Library of Congress Prints & Photographs Online Catalog, Lewis Wickes Hines Collection of the National Child Labor Committee.

A bootblack like Dutchy, near City Hall Park, New York City, 1924.

Photograph courtesy of the Library of Congress Prints & Photographs Online Catalog, Lewis Wickes Hines Collection of the National Child Labor Committee.

moment in our country's past. Between 1854 and 1929, so-called orphan trains transported more than two hundred thousand orphaned, abandoned, and homeless children — many of whom, like the character in this book, were first-generation Irish Catholic immigrants — from the coastal cities of the eastern United States to the Midwest for "adoption," which often turned out to be indentured servitude. Charles Loring Brace, who founded the program, believed that hard work, education, and firm but compassionate childrearing — not to mention midwestern Christian family values — were the only way to save these children from a life of depravity and poverty. Until the 1930s, there was no social safety net; it is estimated that more than ten thousand children were living on the streets of New York City at any given time.

Many of the children had experienced great trauma in their short lives and they had no idea where there were going. The train would pull into a station and the local

A group of early-twentieth-century orphan-train riders with their chaperones.

Photograph courtesy of the Children's Aid Society Archive, New York City.

Homes Wanted

FOR CHILDREN.

A Company of Orphan Children of different ages will arrive at

Oakland, Jowa, Friday, Dec. 9, '04.

The Distribution will take place at the Opera House at 10:30 a.m. and 1:30 p.m.

The object of the coming of these children is to find homes in your midst, especially among farmers, where they may enjoy a happy and wholesome family life, where kind care, good example and moral training will fit them for a life of self-support and usefulness. They come under the auspices of the New York Children's Aid Society, by whom they have been tested and found to be well-meaning and willing boys and girls.

The conditions are that these children shall be properly clothed, treated as members of the family, given proper school advantages and remain in the family until they are eighteen years of age. At the expiration of the time specified it is hoped that arrangements can be made whereby they may be able to remain in the family indefinitely. The Society retains the right to remove a child at any time for just cause and agrees to remove any found unsatisfactory after being notified.

Applications may be made to any one of the following well known citizens who have agreed to act as local committee to aid the agent in securing homes.

Committee: S. S. Rust, E. M. Smart, A. C. Vieth, E. C. Read, W. B. Batler, Dr. R. G. Smith, N. W. Wentz.

Remember the time and place. All are invited.
Come out and hear the address.

Office: 105 East 22d St., New York City.

H. D. CLARK, Iowa Agent,
Dodge Center, Minn.

Notices like this one were posted in the days and weeks before a train arrived in town.

Photograph courtesy of the Children's Aid Society Archive, New York City.

townspeople would assemble to inspect them — often literally scrutinizing teeth, eyes, and limbs to determine whether a child was sturdy enough for field work, or

448

intelligent and mild-tempered enough to cook and clean. Babies and healthy older boys were typically chosen first; older girls were chosen last. After a brief trial period, the children became indentured to their host families. If a child wasn't chosen, he or she would get back on the train to try again at the next tow.

Some children were warmly welcomed by new families and towns. Others were beaten, mistreated, taunted, or ignored. They lost any sense of their cultural identities and backgrounds; siblings were often separated, and contact between them was discouraged. City children were expected to perform hard farm labor for which they were neither emotionally nor physically prepared. Many

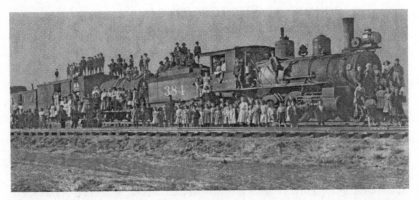

A rare photograph of an entire trainful of children on its way to Kansas.

Photograph courtesy of the Children's Aid Society Archive, New York City.

A young girl like Niamh/Dorothy, sewing to earn money.

Photograph courtesy of the Library of Congress Prints & Photographs Online Catalog, Lewis Wickes Hines Collection of the National Child Labor Committee.

of them were first-generation immigrants from Italy, Poland, and Ireland and were teased for their strange accents; some barely spoke English. Jealousy and competition in the new families created rifts, and many children ended up feeling that they didn't belong anywhere. Some drifted from home to home to find someone who wanted them. Many ran away. The Children's Aid Society did attempt to keep track of these children, but the reality of great distances and spotty record keeping made this difficult.

Many train riders never spoke about their early lives. But as the years passed, some

Train rider Pat Thiessen in 1920, dressed up for her first Easter with her new family in Minnesota.

Photograph courtesy of the Thiessen family.

train riders and their descendants began to demand that they be allowed access to records that until that time had been closed to them. One train rider I spoke with, ninety-four-year-old Pat Thiessen, told me that when, in her fifties, she finally got her birth certificate with her parents' names on it, she shouted with joy. "I was so happy to know about myself, just a little," she said. "It [still] feels incomplete. I keep wondering: What were my grandparents like? What did they have in my family that I could've enjoyed? Who would I be? I think of all of these things, you know. I had a good home; I don't mean that. But I always felt they were not my people. And they weren't."

READING GROUP GUIDE

1. On the surface, Vivian's and Molly's lives couldn't be more different, but in what ways are their stories similar?

2. In the prologue, Vivian mentions that her "true love" died when she was twenty-three, but she doesn't mention the other big secret in the book. Why not?

3. Why hasn't Vivian ever shared her story with anyone? Why does she tell it now?

4. What role does Vivian's grandmother play in her life? How does the reader's perception of her shift as the story unfolds?

5. Why does Vivian seem unable to get rid of the boxes in her attic?

6. In *Women of the Dawn,* a nonfiction book about the lives of four Wabanaki Indians

that is excerpted in the epigraph, Bunny McBride writes: "In portaging from one river to another, Wabanakis had to carry their canoes and all other possessions. Everyone knew the value of traveling light and understood that it required leaving some things behind. Nothing encumbered movement more than fear, which was often the most difficult burden to surrender." How does the concept of portaging reverberate throughout this novel? What fears hamper Vivian's progress? Molly's?

7. Vivian's name changes several times over the course of the novel — from Niamh Power to Dorothy Nielsen to Vivian Daly. How are these changes significant for her? How does each name represent a different phase of her life?

8. What significance, if any, does Molly Ayer's name have?

9. How did Vivian's first-person account of her youth and the present-day story from Molly's third-person-limited perspective work together? Did you prefer one story to the other? Did the juxtaposition reveal

things that might not have emerged in a traditional narrative?

10. In what ways, large or small, does Molly have an impact on Vivian's life? How does Vivian have an impact on Molly's?

11. What does Vivian mean when she says, "I believe in ghosts"?

12. When Vivian finally shares the truth about the birth of her daughter and her decision to put May up for adoption, she tells Molly that she was "selfish" and "afraid." But Molly defends her and affirms Vivian's choice. How did you perceive Vivian's decision? Were you surprised she sent her child to be adopted after her own experiences with the Children's Aid Society?

13. When the children are presented to audiences of potential caretakers, the Children's Aid Society explains that adoptive families are responsible for the child's religious upbringing. What role does religion play in this novel? How do Molly and Vivian each view God?

14. When Vivian and Dutchy are reunited,

Vivian remarks, "However hard I try, I will always feel alien and strange. And now I've stumbled on a fellow outsider, one who speaks my language without saying a word." How is this also true for her friendship with Molly?

15. When Vivian goes to live with the Byrnes, Fanny offers her food and advises, "You got to learn to take what people are willing to give." In what ways is this good advice for both Vivian and Molly? And in contrast, what are some instances when their independence helped them?

16. Molly is enthusiastic about Vivian's reunion with her daughter but makes no further efforts to see her own mother. Why is she unwilling (or unable) to effect a reunion in her own family? Do you think she will someday?

17. Vivian's claddagh cross is mentioned often throughout the story. What is its significance? How does its meaning change or deepen over the course of Vivian's life?

ABOUT THE AUTHOR

Christina Baker Kline is a novelist, non-fiction writer, and editor. In addition to *Orphan Train,* her novels include *Bird in Hand, The Way Life Should Be, Desire Lines,* and *Sweet Water.*

Kline also commissioned and edited two widely praised collections of original essays on the first year of parenthood and raising young children, *Child of Mine* and *Room to Grow.* She coauthored a book on feminist mothers and daughters, *The Conversation Begins,* with her mother, Christina L. Baker, and she coedited *About Face: Women Write About What They See When They Look in the Mirror* with Anne Burt.

Kline grew up in Maine, England, and Tennessee, and has spent a lot of time in Minnesota and North Dakota, where her husband grew up. She is a graduate of Yale, Cambridge, and the University of Virginia, where she was a Hoyns Fellow in Fiction Writing. She has taught creative writing and literature at Fordham and Yale, among other places, and is a recent recipient of a Geraldine R. Dodge Foundation fellowship. She lives in Montclair, New Jersey, with her family.